Lorraine Connection

Dominique Manotti is a professor of nineteenth-century economic history in Paris. She is the author of a number of novels including *Rough Trade* (winner of the French Crime Writers Association Award) and *Dead Horsemeat*, both published in English by Arcadia Books. *Dead Horsemeat* was shortlisted for the 2006 Duncan Lawrie International Dagger Award.

Ros Schwartz dropped out of university and ran away to Paris in the early seventies. Since 1981 she has translated a wide range of fiction and non-fiction from the French, including novels by Aziz Chouaki, Fatou Diome, Jacqueline Harpman, Sébastien Japrisot, Yasmina Khadra and Dominique Manotti, as well as political scientists Thérèse Delpech and Olivier Roy. She regularly publishes articles and gives workshops and talks on the art of translation.

Amanda Hopkinson is Director of the British Centre for Literary Translation at the University of East Anglia. She is a literary translator from Spanish, French and Portuguese, most recently of *Malvinas Requiem* by the Argentine writer, Rodolfo Fogwill and *Dead Horsemeat* by French novelist Dominique Manotti. She also writes books on Latin American photography, including recent monographs on the Mexican Manuel Alvarez Bravo and the Amerindian Peruvian photographer Martin Chambi.

DOMINIQUE MANOTTI

Lorraine Connection

Translated by Amanda Hopkinson and Ros Schwartz

ARCADIA BOOKS

Arcadia Books Ltd
15–16 Nassau Street
London W1W 7AB

www.arcadiabooks.co.uk

First published in the United Kingdom by Arcadia Books 2008
Originally published by Éditions Payot & Rivages as *Lorraine Connection* 2006
Copyright © Dominique Manotti 2006

This English translation from the French
Copyright © Ros Schwartz and Amanda Hopkinson 2008

A catalogue record for this book is available from the British Library

ISBN 978-1-905147-60-1

Typeset in Minion by Discript Limited, London WC2N 4BN
Printed in Finland by WS Bookwell

This book is supported by the French Ministry for Foreign Affairs, as part of the Burgess programme headed for the French Embassy in London by the Institut Français du Royaume-Uni.
ii institut français

Arcadia Books supports English PEN, the fellowship of writers who work together to promote literature and its understanding. English PEN upholds writers' freedoms in Britain and around the world, challenging political and cultural limits on free expression. To find out more, visit www.englishpen.org or contact English PEN, 6–8 Amwell Street, London EC1R 1UQ

Arcadia Books distributors are as follows:

in the UK and elsewhere in Europe:
Turnaround Publishers Services
Unit 3, Olympia Trading Estate
Coburg Road
London N22 6TZ

in the US and Canada:
Independent Publishers Group
814 N. Franklin Street
Chicago, IL 60610

in Australia:
Tower Books
PO Box 213
Brookvale, NSW 2100

in New Zealand:
Addenda
PO Box 78224
Grey Lynn
Auckland

in South Africa:
Quartet Sales and Marketing
PO Box 1218
Northcliffe
Johannesburg 2115

Arcadia Books is the *Sunday Times* Small Publisher of the Year

Warning

This is a novel. Everything is true and everything is false.

PART ONE

A room enclosed by four grey sheet-metal walls, bisected by a conveyor belt carrying two rows of television screens and their cathode ray tubes, under the glare of neon lights from which a stray electric wire dangles. Two rows of four women sit facing each other on either side of the conveyor. Autumn is around the corner and it is very chilly: when they took up their positions this morning it was still dark outside. All the women know each other and feel almost close in this confined space where they work as a team on collective output and bonuses, but no one feels like talking, since the prospect of long nights and short days dampens their spirits.

The women, also looking grey in their short overalls, lean forward, their eyes constantly moving from the aggressive oblong-shaped bases of the cathode tubes filing past them to the tilting polished-steel mirrors overhead. The same crushing images of the same tubes are reflected from a different angle, as if magnified. Holding tiny soldering irons, they add a few final spots of solder then, on leaving the production line, the finished cathode ray tubes are conveyed to the next workshop on the other side of the sheet-metal wall, where they will be packaged, stored, and ultimately despatched elsewhere, generally to Poland, where they will be given plastic casings and become television sets.

The girls can hear only muffled sounds from the factory floor, but the noise from the conveyor belt bounces off the sheet-metal walls and dictates the rhythm of their days. *Clack*, the conveyor starts up, *hiss*, two seconds, the tubes start moving, *clack*, stop. Each girl leans forward, the soldering irons sputter, one, two, three, four blobs, and in ten seconds they straighten up. Rolande, at the end of the line, gives the tubes a quick once-over to check the accuracy of the soldering. *Clack, sssh*, the belt moves forward, minds blank, their hands and eyes work automatically. *Clack*, one, two, three, four, glance, *clack, sssh*… Aisha's face between two tubes, wan, twenty years old, *should be in better health. Clack*, one, *I was in better shape at twenty*, two, *pregnant, ditched*, three, *alcoholic mother, violent*, four, *who was already sponging off me*, glance, *clack, sssh. Aisha, her eyes vacant, violent father. Clack*, one, *my son, ruffling his hair,* two, *caressing his face, affection,* three, *the factory no way, never,* four, *study, study, study,* glance, *clack, sssh. Aisha, work, can't stand it any more, clack,* one, *since the accident,* two, *the accident, the blood,* three, *blood everywhere,* four, *throat slit,* glance, *clack, sssh. Aisha covered in blood. Clack,* one, *she's afraid,* two, *me too,* three, *all of us, afraid,* four, *the sheet-metal walls exude fear, clack, sssh. Aisha, her father yelling, clack,* one, blinding flash, from floor to ceiling. On the other side of the production line a tube explodes, the briefest scream, ear-splitting.

Émilienne keels over backwards, Rolande's palm automatically hits the emergency button, the production line comes to a halt, a wire is fizzling all the way up to the neon light, orangey-yellow sparks and a very strong smell of burning rubber or some other substance, sickening. Silence. Rolande clambers on to a chair and picks her way over the conveyor between two cathode tubes. Émilienne is lying on the floor on her back, white, rigid, eyes closed, lips blue. Six months pregnant. Her belly protrudes through her half-unbuttoned overalls. An alarm goes off somewhere on the other side of the partition. In the total silence of the cramped room, Rolande speaks quietly, in a precise monotone: 'Aisha, run to the offices, grab a phone and call an ambulance, the fire brigade. Go, hurry.' Aisha rushes off. Rolande kneels down, Émilienne's hair is spread on the worn-out vinyl tiles. The floor's filthy, when was it last cleaned? She feels ashamed, removes her overalls and places them under the head of the injured, possibly dead, woman. Émilienne doesn't appear to be breathing. She leans over her, attempts mouth-to-mouth, senses a breath. She gently unbuttons the neck of Émilienne's blouse and frees her legs from under the overturned chair. A scorch mark on the seat. The girls are all on their feet, staring expressionlessly, their mouths closed, leaning against the sheet-metal walls, as far away as possible from Émilienne. *What was I thinking about earlier? Fear? This is its natural home.* Réjane, who sits next to Émilienne on the production line, murmurs in a quavering voice, her hands trembling:

'Maybe we should give her heart massage.'
'Do you know how?'
'No.'
'Me neither.'

One women slaps Émilienne's face and dabs at it with a wet cloth, the other massages her hands, weeping.

Antoine Maréchal, bespectacled and in blue overalls, is juggling schedules and attendance sheets in the personnel office. He is the foreman of the assembly-finishing-packaging section, and each day is a monumental challenge to maintain output with absenteeism ranging between ten and twenty per cent. Closer to twenty per cent on this autumn day. What dross, all bloody Arabs or women. They don't know the meaning of work. The Human Resources Manager in person comes into the office, thirty-something, in a tailored suit, expensive shoes of Italian leather, an incompetent, cocksure young upstart, still wet behind the ears. Maréchal, in his fifties, a lumbering figure in his overalls and safety boots, shudders with repressed hatred.

'Mr Maréchal, how convenient, just the person I wanted to see. The latest figures show an absenteeism rate of thirteen per cent in your section over the last month.'

'I know. I'm dealing with it.'

'It's the highest rate in the factory. If you don't do something about it, you'll be jeopardising the survival of the entire company.'

Maréchal removes his glasses, snaps down the sides and puts them in his overalls pocket, next to the red ballpoint pen and the blue ballpoint pen, and rests both hands on the desk, which creaks.

'Listen, Mr Human Resources Manager, you're new here. I've been here since the day this factory opened, and not a month has gone by without the management threatening closure. Anyone would think they'd only opened it so they could close it down. So that kind of talk won't go very far with me. I don't give a damn if your place closes down. I've got my house, it's not long till I retire, I'll pocket my bonus and go off gathering mushrooms.' The pager clipped to Maréchal's belt starts beeping. 'Excuse me, I'm wanted on the factory floor.'

He leaves the Head of HR casting around for a reply and goes next door into the main factory building. The clanging, clattering, scraping and the din of engines. Confused sounds, he thinks. Memories of the powerful, constant roar of the blast furnace, the roar of fire. Nostalgia? Not really. *It cost my father his life.*

He was confused too. The main factory building, divided into numerous enclosed areas which you have to cross or skirt around to reach the long, central corridor, cluttered with a discarded Fenwick engine, empty pallets and dustbins. In front of him, a gaping doorway leading to a narrow room entirely taken up by a machine which, at the time of its installation, was to revolution- ise the chemical treatment of microprocessors. A purpose-built room, specially insulated against dust and temperature variations to prevent the machine from overheating and breaking down for lack of ventilation. Idle for a year and a half. *Some clever buggers must have dismantled it and nicked some of the parts, can't blame them.* A rush of anger. *And it's my section that's jeopardising the future of the factory. Wanker.*

Aisha's running down the main corridor towards him. Trouble of one kind or another. Without stopping, she yells at him:

'An accident, a short circuit, Émilienne's dead! I'm going to call an ambulance.'

Maréchal catches himself thinking *if she's dead, it's too late,* and hastens his step, while Aisha runs on in the direction of the offices. He goes into the finishing workshop and the first person he sees, in the opposite doorway, is Nourredine, the packaging foreman. A good worker, fair enough, but a real troublemaker, always protesting, wanting to put forward his own ideas. What the hell's he doing here? The place stinks. He immediately spots the scorch marks caused by the short circuit running from floor to ceiling. He looks down and sees Émilienne's body lying at his feet, and, kneeling beside her, Rolande and Réjane, who is shak- ing, sobbing and wailing:

'She's been electrocuted, she's dead.'

Émilienne, unconscious, pale, her lips blue, her body racked with spasms accompanied by groans. *Right, she's not dead. Women always exaggerate. I need to take charge of the situation and show that bloody Arab.* A quick glance around the room. The girls are all there, pinned against the walls, white as ghosts. Rolande looks less shaken and anyway, she's the production-line supervisor, a good worker, she'll lead the others. He leans towards her:

'Everything's fine, the ambulance is on its way. Move away, you need to give your friend air. Until the ambulance arrives you must all go back to your places. Once the ambulance is here, we'll see what has to be done.'

Rolande is still holding Émilienne's head. Nobody's paying any attention to the foreman. Rolande's mesmerised by the puddle of water spreading between Émilienne's legs.

Maréchal bends down and takes her arm.

'Her waters have broken.' Her head is bowed, her voice husky. Maréchal doesn't understand what she's saying.

'Ms Lepetit, do set an example. Go back to your seat. We must calm everyone down, let the paramedics do their job, and then get back to work. It's nothing to worry about, you'll see.'

Rolande seems to be waking from a nightmare, *it's nothing to worry about, bastard, get back to work, swine, don't you dare touch me.* She suddenly stands up, thrusts his hand from her arm and gives him a resounding clout that sends him sprawling on his back amongst the girls' legs. Not one of them holds out a hand to help him to his feet. He gets up, crimson with rage. Nourredine has come into the room and he leaps over the conveyor, grabs the foreman's shoulders and marches him outside.

'Calm down! You've no idea what they've just been through. The short circuit was so powerful that next door we could see the flash through the partition. And the woman's scream...' he has difficulty finding the words '...was like something from beyond the grave.'

The fire brigade arrives at the double, led by Aisha. Nourredine continues to push Maréchal out of the way. Within seconds, Émilienne is hooked up to a drip, placed on a stretcher and carried away.

Aisha's lying in the dark, in a cubicle in the medical room. Her production line has been halted, electricians have been called out urgently from Pondange to carry out repairs. The foreman said that everything would be sorted in time for the second shift. Meanwhile, the girls on the opposite line, supervised by Rolande, have gone back to work. To work. Aisha faints.

Between these sheet-metal walls, white from the flash of electricity, resonating with the scream, Émilienne's body, a few feet away from Aisha, keeling over backwards, rigid, entangled in her chair. And the other accident, no more than a month ago, right in front of her, the headless body, standing there for ages before collapsing, blood spurting out of the neck, the warmth of the blood on her hands, her face. *I am cursed. Forget. Forget. Think about something else. I don't want to go home before clocking-off time. My father at home with all his questions. Why aren't you at the factory? I shan't tell him anything. Not a word. Nothing happened. I can't talk any more.*

Maréchal draws back the curtain around the cubicle and comes in, almost on tiptoe.

'How do you feel, Miss Saidani?' No reply. 'I realise what a shock this has been for you. The nurse told me you were feeling a lot better.'

Clumsy, bumbling Maréchal. Definitely not bright.

'What do you want?'

'OK. Ms Lepetit has gone upstairs to talk to management and as you're the only one from the other production line to have stayed, I wondered whether you'd kindly take her place. Just while she's upstairs. It shouldn't be for long.'

Aisha sits bolt upright. To face all that right now – the sheet-metal walls, the production line, the neon lights, the dangling wires, the handle of the soldering iron in the palm of her hand – is to face her own death. But whether she does it today, or tomorrow... *the girls will be around me, supportive, their eyes saw what I've seen. If I have to choose between the production line and going home to my father, I prefer the production line. Besides, I'm doing it for Rolande.*

'All right.'

'The nurse will give you a little pick-me-up.'

In the admin section, Rolande is trying to walk straight and slowly. *They're probably going to ask me about the accident. That's going to be difficult. Because right now, what I need more than anything is to forget, completely, for a few days, until I've got over my fear. Then talk about it... I must ask for a few days off for the girls.* Flashback to the girls' faces, ashen against the sheet metal. *The shock was too brutal. Get them to understand. Find the words... and I'll find out how Émilienne is. Miscarriage? Dead? Be prepared for the worst, and above all, don't break down in front of 'them'.*

She is immediately shown into the office of the Head of HR himself. It's the first time she's set eyes on him. A quick glance to size him up. Young, flashy. *Not my type.*

'Ms Lepetit, I have very little to say to you. After your inexcusable behaviour towards Mr Maréchal, your section foreman, you are being dismissed for serious misconduct, and this decision takes effect as of now. You may not return to your work station. You will be accompanied to the cloakroom to remove your personal belongings, and then to the exit. You will receive your final pay cheque tomorrow.'

Her insides turn to liquid, her mind goes blank, not a word, not a coherent thought, only images, violent feelings, the flash, the white light, the scream, the smell, the fear. *And then my son's smile, in his boarding school uniform, my mother, drunk, asleep on the kitchen floor, who's going to pay? Work, pain, broken body, hands numb, hard, yes, but better than no job. Tomorrow, on the streets, homeless?*

Half unconscious, she's shoved out into the corridor. She leans against the wall, her eyes closed, dizzy, feels like throwing up. When she opens her eyes, Ali Amrouche is standing in front of her. He's holding her hands, tapping them, a concerned expression on his face. Amrouche, the union rep, always hanging around management, that's him.

'Rolande, don't you feel well? Rolande, talk to me.'

He places a hand on her shoulder, a gesture he's never made, or dared make before. He has nothing but respect for Rolande, but she's distraught. She feels the warm contact of his hand on her shoulder, it does her good, less alone, and the words return, jumbled at first. She leans against him, lets herself go, then the words come tumbling out and she tells him about the accident, in great detail – her every movement, Émilienne's body, lifeless, rigid: 'I touched death, Ali.' The helplessness, not knowing what to do to save a life, and the violent contractions, the groans as if Émilienne were in immeasurable pain and a hope, the baby that died, almost as if that would bring the mother back to life. With the words come tears, what a relief. 'And they fired me, Ali, because I knocked Maréchal to the floor.' A hint of a smile. 'For that price, I should have killed him, the fat bastard.'

'I'm taking you home, Rolande, and I'll come back and talk to management, straight away. It isn't possible, it's a mistake. It has to be a mistake.'

'Thank you, but no. See me to the exit, that'll help. I'll go home by myself, it's only a couple of minutes away.'

In the Head of HR's office, Ali Amrouche tries to explain.

'You can't fire Ms Lepetit. The whole factory will be up in

arms. She's a courageous woman, everybody looks up to her. We all know that she has to support her son and her penniless mother single-handed. Everyone was shaken up by the accident this morning in her section.'

'She's not the one who had the accident, it was Émilienne Machaut who, let me take the opportunity to inform you, is safe and sound.'

'What about the baby?'

'Miscarriage. It happens. None of that in any way justifies Ms Lepetit's behaviour in physically attacking her foreman.' He straightens his upper body, pushes his shoulders back. 'I'm here to restore order and discipline in this factory, both of which are sadly lacking. I will not stand for this behaviour.'

The Head of HR shuffles a file around his desk, taps the telephone, folds his hands. 'Mr Amrouche, my predecessor told me you were a reasonable man, a man of compromise, able to make allowances. So I am keen for you to be the first to know this: in one week, the works council will meet and the question of the last nine months' unpaid bonuses will once again be on the agenda. If the company were to pay those bonuses today, plus the arrears, its financial stability would be jeopardised. The financial situation is still precarious, as you well know, and there's a risk the factory will have to close. So, management is going to suggest – and when I say suggest, you know what I mean – that all bonuses be cancelled for this year and paid from next January.' He spreads his hands and raises his eyebrows.

'We've examined the figures from every angle. There's no other solution. We are relying on people like you to get everyone to accept it.'

Amrouche stares at the Head of HR. What does this man know about it? Weariness. How to explain the poverty, suffering, fear, and then the eruption of consuming anger and hatred to this fine gentleman with his smart shoes about to be blown to pieces?

'Does Maréchal approve of Rolande Lepetit's dismissal?'

The Head of HR stands up and turns to face the window.

'The matter is closed.'

Seated alone at a table in the empty cafeteria, Amrouche is drinking a coffee and thinking things over. *The Head of HR, what a shit. 'My predecessor spoke to me about you'… and drops two bombshells, without even being aware of it. What do I do? 'You're a reasonable man'. So what? The bonuses can wait until the works council meeting, I'm not supposed to know about that. As for Rolande, by the end of the lunch break the whole factory will have heard. If the guys find out that I knew and that I didn't say or do anything, they won't forgive me. Rolande, a woman who's been through the mill like me, and who gets on with things. Never off sick, a hard worker, tough, proud, honest. Better than me. A man of compromise, huh!* A bitter taste of coffee on his tongue and at the corners of his mouth. *A man who compromises? True enough: because I'm a broken man.* Images of the nearby Pondange iron and steelworks where he worked for ten years flood back. He loved the heat, the noise, the physical exertion, the danger too, and the sense of comradeship that went with it. Not like here. And then the exhilarating struggle to save the works. They'd felt so powerful, all united. Followed by total failure. The works dismantled, obliterated from the valley. A working class dynamited, like the blast furnaces. Tears welled up in his eyes each time he walked along the swollen river banks, the concrete bases where the blast furnaces once stood now overgrown with grass. One thing was certain: they were the winners, *them*, the other side. *You have to live with it. Be shrewd, hold out. For now, get Rolande reinstated. At least do that much. Go and see Maréchal, a racist bastard, but a former steelworker and capable of understanding, not like that arsehole Head of HR. He'll get her reinstated even if she did knock him flat.*

But no sign of Maréchal anywhere in his section, or in the offices. *He ought to be here at this time of day. What shall I do? I'll go and talk to Nourredine, he works in the same section as Rolande, he knows her and values her work.* Nourredine is shocked when Amrouche informs him of Rolande's dismissal. Rolande, with her tall, familiar form and her clear, warm, attentive gaze. Always ready to offer a sympathetic gesture or word in passing. *She helped me get through my early days in the factory, when I was just a shy and miserable kid. It's thanks to her I've found my place here. We can't abandon her, after the horror of the accident, on top of everything.* He asks the others to take over his job while he goes and has it out with Maréchal, who is nowhere to be found. Back to packaging and a brief collective discussion. The horror of the accident still hangs over them – the white light, the scream, the juddering sheet-metal walls, Émilienne's lifeless body glimpsed in the crush.

And the outcome? The production line wasn't even brought to a complete standstill. Some of the girls are back at work without a thorough safety check being done. Rolande is fired and that bastard Maréchal's made himself scarce. It might even transpire it was his idea, to create a diversion so that everyone would be talking about Rolande's dismissal instead of the accident. There's electricity everywhere, in one form or another, at all the work stations. If we don't do something, we'll all get electrocuted. It's vital to see the girls in finishing at coffee break.

A twenty-minute break, just time to catch the girls as they head down the main corridor to the cafeteria and the men from packaging drag them out of the back exit to the waste ground behind the factory, where they all sit around on discarded pallets. A strange place, this hastily erected sheet-metal cube on wasteland in the bottom of a valley overgrown with weeds and scrub. It stands on the site where, less than a generation ago, the Lorraine blast furnaces roared, one of the world's most powerful iron and steel industries. Now, the forests covering the hills slowly regain domination both of the landscape and the imagination of the people who live there. It's very chilly. Nourredine's friend Étienne watches the girls. They're beautiful, all of them. *Why didn't you think of chatting them up sooner? Are you blind, or what?* Amrouche hangs around and goes to sit down with them.

Nourredine climbs on to a pallet, tall and slim in his grey work overalls, his ascetic face tense and ill at ease. He blurts out: 'Maréchal got Rolande fired.' Amrouche, uncomfortable, says nothing. A few moments of total silence. The girls are shivering with the cold and fear. Then Aisha stands up, her arms folded over her chest, her voice and lips trembling slightly.

At last she has found the words to describe the death of the Korean engineer, only a month ago. Everyone's heard about it, but she witnessed it, she was at her work station in section four, next to the rotor when it broke down. The engineer came, he pressed the button at the end of the line to stop the conveyor, removed the safety housing from the rotor and got right inside the machine to repair it. Aisha was standing behind him. Another Korean was passing by, he didn't understand why the conveyor had stopped, didn't ask the women workers, and in any case, he didn't speak French. Then, before anybody could stop him, he pressed the button to switch the power back on and start up the conveyor again. There was no circuit breaker on the rotor, and the engineer's head was sliced clean off.

'I saw the headless body straighten up. People tell me it's impossible, but I tell you I saw it, and the blood spurting out. I felt the blood on my face, my hands, and then the body crumpled at my feet. I keep seeing it, over and over again, that headless body jerking, every night. And when I wake up in the dark, I feel the warmth of the blood on my face. They wanted me to go back to work the next day, at the same station. They thought that was quite normal. They said it's just an accident, clear up the mess, clean up, carry on. I could never have sat next to the rotor again. It was Rolande who arranged for me to come and work in finishing, so I could keep my job. And now, Émilienne's been electrocuted, the baby's dead, and Rolande's been booted out.'

Silence. Everyone on this patch of waste ground behind the sheet-metal factory is staring at Aisha, smooth strands of jet black hair framing her chalky face and the rest tied back. Right now she's tense, fiery, the embodiment of the tragedy in their day-to-day lives.

Amrouche closes his eyes. He too has his recurring nightmare. He's twenty, he works on the gangway above the factory floor, the molten-steel ladle explodes thirty feet beneath him, thirty tonnes of molten steel swallow up some fifteen men, the wild yells, the smell of charred flesh, unbearable. *Stop, snap out of it.* Someone says:

'My wife works in admin. She heard that they're not going to pay us our bonuses in December.' All eyes turn to Amrouche, who clears his throat.

'I think that may be true. I believe they've decided not to pay the monthly bonuses that were agreed last February, which were supposed to be paid in a lump sum in December. No bonuses for this year. The first bonus will be paid next January.'

Why on earth did I say that? Now the shit will really hit the fan. Too late now. Perhaps I wanted to distract Maréchal, he's a former steelworker? Most of all I wanted to stop the unbearable agony Aisha's speech caused me, the rush of memories of molten steel engulfing the men, my horror of accidents, and death, because it is the human condition, and there's nothing I can do about it, and I'd rather forget. But the bonuses, suddenly being robbed of the equivalent of almost a month's pay in accumulated bonuses, which they're entitled to, which they've been counting on, which they've already decided how to spend, that's completely different, that's another matter entirely, I've moved on to new terrain, familiar, signposted, strangely reassuring. The entire group, shivering with cold on this autumn day, is gripped by fear, anger, bitterness and dejection: the bonuses must be paid immediately. To which Nourredine adds: 'Rolande must be reinstated immediately.' The group returns to the building to do the rounds of all the workshops. Within half an hour, the entire factory has ground to a halt.

A discreet lunch in a hotel in Luxembourg, close to the French border, a table for two in a small private dining room. Maurice Quignard drinks a *pastis* while he waits. Sixtyish, tall, broad-shouldered, flat stomach, he is still athletic-looking. His tanned, lined face has a brutal look. After a long career in the steel industry, he has set up a consultancy advising on business reconversion. He works with a number of EU organisations and is an unpaid advisor to the board of directors of Daewoo Pondange on behalf of the European Development Plan committee. In a way, Daewoo is his baby. Thanks to his political connections in Lorraine, he acted as go-between with the Koreans, negotiated the conditions for the company to set up there, and ensures there is a plentiful supply of manna in the form of EU and French subsidies. Again, unpaid. In the interests of the region and of France. The idea of Daewoo and Matra making a joint bid to take over Thomson was born during an informal dinner with the chairman of the Lorraine region at his home, two years ago already. And now, he's close to achieving his goal. He knows that after Daewoo's takeover of Thomson Multimedia, the new company will be a global concern and there'll be an influential role for him as human resources advisor. A glorious end to his career. Not to mention the financial rewards. So he follows Daewoo's activities on a day-to-day basis, thanks to the contacts he's developed at every level of the company.

At around ten a.m. today, Maréchal had come to his office in Pondange and briefed him about the internal situation. Worrying. Another accident, serious. What's worse is the sacking of a good worker, a well-liked woman, another unnecessary provocation by that idiotic Head of HR. During their conversation a phone call from the factory had informed them that a strike had broken out on the shop floor. *What did I tell you?* Maréchal wasn't too worried: it's a spontaneous and localised movement, not one of them has any sense of organisation, you know what those layabouts are like. *By tomorrow I'll have everything back in hand, but frankly, we really could have avoided this.* And Quignard was furious. He's summoned the CEO to give him a piece of his mind. He's late, which doesn't help. Quignard is on his third *pastis*.

Park, the Korean CEO, arrives, a smile on his smooth round face. His tortoiseshell glasses give him a permanent air of slight amazement. Quignard speeds things up and asks for the starter to be served at once – a selection of cured meats – accompanied by a good Burgundy. The minute they are alone, he attacks, tough, impatient.

'A factory where there have been no incidents for two years, not a single hour's strike, where the unions are kept out... How on earth did you manage to set the place on fire at the worst possible moment in terms of our affairs?'

'On fire... I'd say that was a bit of an exaggeration.' His voice is soft, cultured, his French impeccable, barely a hint of an accent. At the factory, he never speaks French, which he claims not to know, but English or Korean. 'At present, two workshops have downed tools, less than twenty people.' *Out of the question to tell this loudmouth who despises me that an entire shift has just gone on strike, since he doesn't appear to have heard. There's plenty of time.*

'My contacts tell me that emotions are running very high in the factory. You have to admit that there have been a number of accidents, the rate of production is high and the pay isn't good. As long as that only translates into absenteeism, there's no problem. But in my young days, people used to say: one spark can set the plain on fire. So no sparks. You must keep your Head of HR in order.'

'I understand.'

The smile wiped off his face, a bitter crease at the corners of his mouth. *That Head of HR, a man he recommended to me himself. The son of a local big shot. Important for integrating the business into the local fabric, he said. Totally useless.*

The waiter brings the next course – a copious stew – and a second bottle of Burgundy. Quignard continues, still on the attack.

'Not the slightest ripple while the Thomson bid is pending.'

'That's a matter of a few days. We'll hold out until then.'

'No. Maybe just for a few hours until the government delivers its decision, and the main job will be done, granted, but we still have to see how the public will react and await the opinion of the Privatisation Commission. We need at least a good month of peace and quiet. It's not asking for the moon.'

'I can't budge on pay. Our hands are tied by a major bank repayment due in one week's time. I can only cover it through an advance on the delivery of our stocks, scheduled for the day after tomorrow. Finances are so tight that I haven't even renewed the fire insurance policy which has expired.'

'I know. You're financially overstretched, particularly under present circumstances. It's a rash thing to do, and pointless.' Quignard suddenly frowns. 'Tell me, there's no risk of the factory grinding to a halt in the next two days at least, is there? If you don't honour that payment, it will be disastrous for our business at national level.'

'I'm aware of that.'

'Do more than be aware. Take precautions, immediately.'

At least a hundred workers are sitting around in the cafeteria, mostly men and most of them very young. No more than about twenty women. Small clusters have formed around the work teams arguing about the bonuses in raised voices, but there's little communication between the groups. In fact the different shifts barely know each other and tend to be faintly wary. For nearly all the workers it's their first stoppage. Now what do we do? Kader, the best-known shop steward is on sick leave, announces a staff rep. He is greeted by jeers. Amrouche skulks in a corner by the main entrance, keeping a low profile. Nourredine looks uncertainly about him, nobody's rushing forward. He clambers on to a table. Who the hell's he? The guy from packaging, a big mouth… Does he have a mandate? No, no mandate… He awkwardly describes Émilienne's electrocution, his mouth dry. They pay him scant attention and seem more concerned with Rolande's dismissal, a lot of them know her, a brave woman, for sure, but always sucking up. 'Why don't we talk about the bonuses?' yells a young man.

Nourredine calls Amrouche who scowls and refuses to climb on to the table. He announces, without comment, that the bonuses for the current year have been cancelled and that the first bonus will be paid next January. A chorus of angry muttering and the discussion spreads. Some refuse to believe it, an agreement is an agreement, there's no going back on it. Others claim it serves them right for being so stupid as to have given those Korean sharks credit. A delegation is formed, led by Nourredine and Amrouche, tasked with meeting management to obtain information, demand prompt payment of the arrears and insist on Rolande's reinstatement. They head off in the direction of the offices.

In the cafeteria, the clusters have re-formed. Some start playing cards. Étienne goes over to Aisha.

'I'm Nourredine's friend. I've been in packaging for two years. How come we've never met?'

'I've only been in finishing for a month.'

'Of course.' Flashback: the pale face, the rotor. 'Rolande took me on in finishing…' *Whatever you do, don't mention the mangled body. I've put my foot in it.*

Smile. 'It did me so much good to talk about it, it's the first time. And the first time too that I've ever spoken in front of so many people, at least ten people. I feel a lot better.' She thinks: he's different.

Relieved. 'Can I buy you a coffee?'

There's a queue in front of the coffee machines. Étienne picks up two scalding cups, puts them on a cardboard tray, takes Aisha's hand and leads her across the eerily silent, deserted factory floor dimly lit by dreary daylight and the orange glow of the safety lights. So different, a bit strange, profoundly silent. Aisha does not withdraw her hand. In the wide, airy spaces of the packaging section, Étienne switches on a row of neon lights. He continues past the machines, which are strangely still, without pausing at the piles of polystyrene or wood, decorative as they are, or at the conveyor belt rising up to the ceiling with its load of packaged tubes, connecting to the warehouse. He leads Aisha towards an old wooden desk in a corner of the workshop and sets down the coffees.

'This is where we have our snack at break times. The cafeteria is too far away, it wastes too much time. Take a look.' Proudly, he opens a drawer that contains a gas ring. In the next drawer is an electric coffee machine. The back panel of the desk slides back to reveal a little fridge and a television set. 'The TV's only for the night shift.' He laughs. 'As for the rest, we have an agreement with Maréchal: he stays out of the workshop during breaks.'

They drink in silence. Aisha runs her finger over the stained desktop. A bit of freedom all to themselves, at the heart of the factory. The women's workshop on the other side of the sheet-metal partition, a whole other life. The misfortune of being a woman.

'You haven't seen everything yet.' Étienne sits her on one of the stools. 'Here's my work station, but the truth is we're often on our feet, we move around a lot.' He opens the top drawer of the desk, wide, deep, flat, crammed with miscellaneous cutlery and corkscrews, wiggles out a little board wedged at the back and takes out a tobacco pouch and rolling papers. 'A quick joint.'

'I don't smoke.'

'It's not a cigarette, it doesn't do any harm.'

His hands work rapidly, a swift lick, cigarette lighter, he takes a first deep drag, smiles, passes her the joint. Her mind a muddle, Émilienne, Rolande, the strike, Étienne's hand in her hair, in her hand, her body trembling, she takes the joint, raises it to her lips, takes a long drag, nostrils pinched, eyes closed, as she's seen her brothers do, inhales the smoke, not very strong, not as strong as she thought, exhales through her nose, without coughing. An airy sensation of well-being.

'A real pro,' laughs Étienne.

He switches off the light and the workshop is plunged into a yellowish half-light. Aisha, in a spin, draws frantically on the joint. Randomly Émilienne's voice comes back to her, helpless with laughter in the cafeteria, telling them about 'her first time', lying flat on her stomach on a dustbin under an archway, rain bucketing down. Rolande had smiled at her, then taken her by the arm and steered her to another table to eat her snack. 'I didn't even see his face,' repeated Émilienne, between two outbursts of laughter. Followed by her father's voice, grating and halting, cursing when she refused to go back to the village even for holidays. *I know what can happen there.* Étienne moves slowly towards her and takes her by the arm, the waist, to help her up. Fear, no going back now: *After him, I'm not returning to my father's house.* He leads her behind a pile of packing cases. She sees a mat.

'It's Nourredine's prayer mat.'

He smiles, kneels down. She sits down, feeling as if she's float-ing. He loosens her hair, which spreads out over her shoulders. She thinks, 'This is going from one man to another,' and lies down, her eyes closed. A cocoon of darkness, silence, Étienne kisses her cheeks, her eyes, her lips. She tenses, he slides his hand down her neck, places it on her hip, runs it down her thigh, slips it under her skirt. She lies still, rigid, her heart pounding. His hand moves slowly up towards her belly where it stops, spread flat, hot, insistent. She waits: *It's going to happen.*

Then everything moves very fast. Étienne pulls down his trou-sers, uses both hands to yank Aisha's tights and knickers down to her ankles, lies on top of her, penetrates her after two or three attempts. *It hurts, I've known worse, it's all happening far away.* He begins to move up and down, she feels a sharp pain, she cries out, then feels very little. He gets still more aroused, breathing heavily, lets out one last groan and rolls off to lie beside her, his face in her hair, smells nice and clean, little kisses on her cheeks, very sweet. She feels a warm liquid running down her thighs, laughs at the thought of the stains she's going to make on Nourredine's prayer mat, her recklessness. Her life's beginning to change, and that has to be good.

The delegation returns to the cafeteria and immediately every-body crowds round. Nourredine clambers up on to the table without waiting.

'Bonuses will be discussed at the works council in a week's time. We'll get no information before then. They say no decisions have been taken. But the Head of HR didn't deny the rumour. In our view, they've decided to cancel them and they're simply putting off the moment when they're going to tell us. As far as Rolande's situation is concerned, the Head of HR will discuss it with the shop stewards only once we get back to work.'

A few protests, cries of 'thieves' and 'bastards'. A short woman with permed hair calls the management 'serial killers'. The big question: *Now what do we do?* At first there's no answer. 'A week-long strike, until the works council meeting? That's a long time. And besides, this isn't really a good time, stocks are plentiful…' Nourredine suggests waiting for the second shift, which will arrive in less than two hours, and deciding together whether to continue with the strike or not. A reasonable-sounding proposal, unanimously accepted.

The groups disperse. Some go back to their card games in the cafeteria, others go and play music in the staffroom. Amrouche vanishes, he's probably gone back to hang out in the admin section. Small groups of women stand around chatting by the coffee machine. A few mothers unobtrusively slip away to get on with the washing and two men go off to pick mushrooms. With the arrival of the cooler weather there should be hedgehog mushrooms.

Nourredine is sitting at a table with Hafed, a member of the health and safety committee who was on the delegation. He's a young technician: slim, elegant, and a know-all, highly valued for his technical skills. One of those men who can't be intimidated by threats of losing his job. He lives with the certainty, justified or not, of being a man who is indispensable and sought-after. The two men, two different worlds, have never spoken to each other, but today they're drinking coffee together with a shared feeling of impotence.

One of the women from admin cautiously enters the cafeteria, trying to make herself as inconspicuous as possible. She slides in beside Nourredine, leans towards him and says very quietly: 'The CEO called a removals firm to clear all the stocks of finished products. I heard the interpreter, he was calling from the office next to mine while your delegation was waiting to speak to management.'

The two men exchange glances, instinctively clasp each other's hands in a handshake. In it together, cut to the quick. Faced with contempt, they feel like shouting, hitting out, smashing something, showing they exist. And they can hear, very clearly, the threat behind the slap in the face: first the stocks, then the machines, then the closure of the factory, something management has been threatening constantly for the last two years. 'It's war,' mutters Nourredine, gutted. Hafed smiles. 'Keep calm, it hasn't come to that yet, but we do have to agree on how to respond.'

An impromptu general meeting. Hafed, speaking in a neutral voice, informs the assembled workers. The collective reaction is immediate: 'All this belongs to us as much as it does to them.' 'We won't allow the lorries to enter the factory.' No more hesitation, indecision, dispersed groups, everybody joins in the discussion. 'How do we go about it?' 'Block the entrance gates.' 'Occupy the porter's lodge, essential if we want to control the opening and closing of the gates.' 'That means occupying the factory?' Yes, say it out loud, we're occupying the factory. And we've got to move fast, there's no shortage of removals firms in Lorraine. 'We occupy until the second shift arrives,' Nourredine decides. 'Then we'll discuss the next move with them.' Unanimous agreement.

The cafeteria empties and a hundred or so workers including around ten women surround the porter's lodge at the factory gates. Between it and the front of the building is a somewhat neglected open area of about thirty metres covered in unmown grass, wiry enough to withstand the Lorraine climate. Behind the tinted mirror glass façade are the executives' offices. The senior and middle managers, Korean and French, must all be there, watching from behind the windows. They are invisible, but the awareness of their presence weighs down on the workers, they feel exposed. At least there's no sign of any lorries, which feels like a small victory. Maybe there won't *be* any lorries, it could all be a false rumour. They take what comfort they can from that. Carry out another recce. Two huge sliding gates are electronically operated from the porter's lodge. One gate leads to the staff car park to the right of the factory; the left-hand one is the lorry route to the warehouse and the loading bays. To the right again there's a pedestrian entrance. Between the two gates stands the porter's lodge, a flimsy building with two huge windows. Twenty people should be able to fit in there. For the time being there are only two security guards, staring out of the windows at the workers without moving.

They must go in. Amrouche has joined the workers, his expression inscrutable. The delegation reconvenes and enters the porter's lodge. Again it's Nourredine who's the spokesperson. 'We're occupying, we're taking control of the gates.' The security guards are two men the wrong side of fifty, beefy, pot-bellied and wearing navy-blue jackets marked 'Security'. They shrug. 'As you like, we're not Daewoo employees and our chief has instructed us not to get involved. He simply told us to maintain a presence in the porter's lodge, and he's sending two colleagues as backup to patrol the premises. You'll be able to identify them, they'll be wearing the same uniform as us.' Nourredine asks them to show him how to open and close the gates. It all seems simple. Outside, a feeble sun has finally broken through and the workers have resumed their conversations. They amble around in small groups, already at a loose end. A few women go inside the porter's lodge to warm up, others start drifting back to the cafeteria.

The first workers from the second shift begin to arrive, mostly by car. Nourredine opens the right-hand gate. They leave their vehicles in the car park then return in small groups, and informal discussions break out between the two shifts. No bonuses this year. No, it's not a matter of December payments being delayed, but of no bonuses at all. What about the February agreement? All bullshit. The women talk among themselves. With Christmas coming, no bonuses means no presents for the kids. Reactions veer between anger and disbelief, in an atmosphere of chaos.

Just then Nourredine, who's still watching the main gate, sees a convoy of three huge articulated removal lorries emblazoned with their company logo crawling towards the roundabout in front of the factory gates. He presses the switch to close the gate, which doesn't budge. A surge of adrenaline, sweat, turmoiled thoughts, the lorries' arrival timed to coincide with that of the second shift, gates blocked open from the inside offices. *If the lorries get in, there'll be fights, the police, and we're fucked.* He rushes outside yelling:

'The lorries, the lorries! The gate's stuck, block the entrance, block the entrance.'

The lorries move forward in a slow, relentless convoy. The first one turns on to the roundabout in a majestic curve. The shapes of three men can just be made out in the cab. Two hundred or so workers, only the men, with Hafed in the front line, his jaws clenched. The rest race for the gate, arms linked, and grip the gateposts. They stand several lines deep, united, together, hearts pounding.

Behind the human barricade, Nourredine and five other workers all had the same idea at the same time. *Pile up some empty pallets and set fire to them with lighters, that's all we've got. Shit! Let's hope they catch alight.* They catch alight.

The first lorry turns into the factory access road. It's now less than twenty metres away, nosing its way forward, its huge bonnet looming above their heads. The men close their eyes, speechless. *We're not afraid … Less than five metres, don't think about bodies being run over, the wheel that crushes, don't think. United. A solid wall, stand firm. And don't fall.* Less than two metres. An order comes from the back, passed forward from row to row: 'When you hear shouts of "Fire" scatter to the sides as fast as possible!' The bumpers touch the men in the front line, and the lorry continues to inch forward. Who can hold back ten tonnes?

A prolonged shout, coming from six voices in chorus: 'Fire!' The human chains break apart: 'Get the driver, quick!' Six men armed with lengths of wood furiously push forward a heap of burning pallets, scraping the ground and sending out a shower of sparks. They slide them towards the bonnet of the lorry now level with the gate.

'Let's burn the bastards in their cabs!' yells Nourredine, pouring with sweat, his hands burned, completely carried away.

Panic aboard the first lorry. The driver throws it into reverse, retreats a few metres, too fast, the trailer careers off the road, its wheels sink into the soft earth, it jackknifes. Armed with baseball bats, the other two men jump down from the cab to protect the lorry. Hafed and a dozen or so workers step in.

'Stop now, that's enough. We stay on the factory premises, on our own ground. We don't set fire to the lorry. We've won. They're leaving. We let them go.'

Behind their window, the security guards contemplate the scene without moving a muscle.

The mass of workers are clustered behind the blazing pallets. The wood is well-ventilated and dry, it gives off a lovely clear bright flame. They watch the heavy articulated lorries attempting to manoeuvre their way out. Laughter and jeers: 'Watch out, you'll burn out your engine!' The drivers are none too adroit and a few clods of earth, a few stones, are hurled at the windscreens. It's a way of letting off steam, nothing really nasty. Nourredine has torn off his grey overalls and thrown them into the fire. Then the lorries leave in slow convoy, the same way they came. As they disappear into the distance, hazy through the flames, silence falls and lasts for a few minutes after they vanish in the direction of Luxembourg. Each person pictures a section of bonnet, the edge of a bumper, the tip of a wing, a wheel, each person relives the feeling of serried bodies, battling fear, the heat of the fire, and the overwhelming joy at the routing of the juggernaut, savouring the shared feeling that *together we are strong, the world is ours*. Fists

DOMINIQUE MANOTTI

raised in the direction of the blind windows of the executives' offices.

If we hadn't been warned, the lorries would have got in easily, thinks Nourredine, dazed and elated.

Then Hafed grabs a chair from inside the porter's lodge and clambers on to it.

'Since they've declared war on us, we must get organised and fight back.'

Early on this sunny afternoon the news of the strike, the offensive action and the victory over the bosses has spread throughout the neighbourhood. The factory is like a magnet and people have come from all over – the unemployed, the retired, on foot, by bicycle and car, to catch up on the news, see how the youngsters are coping, relive their own memories. When all the surrounding valleys were involved in the steel industry, when the word 'strike' meant something, when they attacked police stations with bulldozers, when they went on a mass march on Paris, when intentions were far from peaceful... Memories that reduce what has just happened at Daewoo to a mere blip. People cluster outside the gates, on the central reservation all the way to the roundabout. Amrouche comes out to greet a few old acquaintances. Workers from the night shift chat to the veterans before going inside the factory. There are also a few skivers like Karim Bouziane, off sick for six months for a supposedly sprained back as a result of shifting furniture for the Korean CEO during working hours. He soaks up the atmosphere outside the gates for a while then enters the factory. Nourredine lets him through with bad grace. What reason could be given for stopping him?

Rolande arrives with a radiant smile, pushing a trolley laden with potatoes, onions, eggs and bread.

'I heard about the occupation when I was at the supermarket, so I went round and asked the local shopkeepers for donations. All this is for you so you can have a hot meal tonight. My way of saying thank you.'

Nourredine, touched, lets her in.

'Come in, Rolande. At least as long as we're in charge, you're welcome here.'

Then it's the turn of the dignitaries, in their dark saloon cars and dark suits. All ill at ease, very ill at ease, the mayor with his tricolour sash, the deputy, more discreet, and the regional health and safety inspector who keeps a low profile. They shake a few hands, force a few smiles, tap Amrouche on the shoulder then come and talk to Nourredine and his crew in front of the gates.

'The valley needs these jobs... Watch what you do... Mr Park, the CEO, is a reasonable man, we know him well... You should try negotiating...'

What do they know of life in the factory, these three? And this health and safety inspector, with his useless site visits, his reports that are always favourable, not a single infringement in two years, in the most dangerous factory in the whole region, what does he know about the man who had his head sliced off, about Émilienne, Rolande or Aisha? Nourredine feels self-conscious in his tight-fitting jacket and grubby jeans. He's seized by a kind of rage and fantasises about grabbing the health and safety inspector by the lining of his jacket, shaking him and banging his head against the gatepost, smashing his forehead, his nose, seeing blood pour down his smart navy-blue suit, then letting him go and watching him crumple in a heap on the ground.

'...If Daewoo were to close down as a result of this strike, which is a possibility, I warn you, it would be disastrous for the entire valley.'

'We worked hard to set up this factory here,' adds the mayor. 'I know what it cost the town.'

Nourredine can't think of anything to say to them.

The fourth man, who has kept in the background until now, goes up to Nourredine, smiling, and holds out his hand. Tall and sturdy, he has a direct, straightforward manner. And his handshake clearly states that he's not afraid of sullying himself by shaking hands with a worker. The manner, the gesture, the tone of voice – imperceptible signals of kinship: they're from the same world, that of the factory, not exactly the same, but similar.

'Maurice Quignard. I represent the European Development Plan committee.' *European subsidies, the great cash cow*, translates Nourredine. 'I spoke to your CEO on the telephone before coming. You know, he's not a bad guy. I think this business is all a big misunderstanding. From what he tells me, the immediate sale of stocks should make it possible to pay some bonuses...' Nourredine reels, finds it hard to breathe. *After all, it is possible we rushed into this without thinking…* 'We just need to find grounds on which to negotiate.'

'Negotiate, that's all we've wanted to do since this morning.'

'There'll be no negotiations while the managers are being held.' Nourredine is frankly taken aback.

'Nobody's being held. We're stopping people from coming in, not from leaving.'

'And the negotiations won't take place here, under pressure, but at the town hall.'

'I'm not the sole decision-maker.' He casts about. 'We'll have to discuss it. Speaking for myself, there's no problem.'

Quignard steps inside the gate as if by right. Nourredine, caught unawares, wavers. Too late, Quignard is already in the porter's lodge, one of the two security guards offers him a chair, holds out a telephone. He settles in, calls management, he's very much at home. When he comes out again:

'In a quarter of an hour, the managers will start coming out, in their cars, of course. The senior managers will meet you in two hours' time at the town hall. If that's agreeable to you, of course.'

Then Quignard walks off in the direction of the roundabout, where his chauffeur-driven car is waiting, a big black Mercedes. He exchanges a few words with the three state officials, it'll all work out fine, no reason why it shouldn't, nobody wants war. A little further on, he passes a grim-faced Maréchal who's come to find out the latest.

'Antoine, are you going inside the factory?'

'No. My shift finishes at two p.m. and until I have more information, I'm not on strike.'

'So you can come with me to my office. Negotiations should begin very soon, and Park will keep me informed by telephone. I'd like to have your opinion.'

'Got anything to drink?'

A smile. 'As usual, your favourite brandy.'

'There's nobody's waiting for me at home.'

On the waste ground behind the factory, Karim has set up his little business. He likes the place. Before him the valley's verdant slopes stretch down to Pondange. When he was little, it was a street filled with blast furnaces – fire, noise, smoke and dust, day and night. His father wore himself out working at one blast furnace after another, and Karim's destiny, as the eldest son, was all mapped out. At sixteen, a steelworker, alongside his father. Today, his father is slowly dying on a good pension, while he's thriving on small time wheeling and dealing. The air is pure and the valley is green, life's good, seen from the Daewoo waste ground. He makes kindling from the pallets, sets up a makeshift barbecue and, with the collusion of the cafeteria manager, is cooking the sausages he sells cheaply on improvised wire skewers.

Two burly, thuggish-looking strangers with close-cropped hair, aggressive thirty-year-olds, are walking slowly towards him, their hands behind their backs. *They look like cops, and none too friendly* thinks Karim, who hesitates, glancing around. *Nowhere to run.* Spots the navy-blue 'Security' jackets, the uniform of Daewoo's security guards. Relieved, Karim smiles at them and proffers two skewers. 'For you, no charge.' The two men nod, take the sausages and walk off without a word. Karim continues serving his customers, and for a little bit extra, he slips a gram of hash into the paper napkin containing the pair of sausages he hands to his regulars. A smoking corner has been set up in the stockroom, in the midst of the polystyrene packaging, well away from the security guards' path.

Rolande is in the cafeteria and has taken over the kitchen area. She sets to work with precise gestures, assembling crockery and cutlery. Cheerfully she peels, rinses, chops and stirs. Earth mother. To her it's half a game, half sublimated desire. Her way of being part of the collective action.

The first car loses no time in leaving the executives' car park on the right-hand side of the building. It heads for the gate between two lines of men and women workers who have come running from all corners of the factory to stand and jeer. They stare at the car's occupant, lean over the bonnet, thump and occasionally kick the bodywork, feeling a real thrill at being the ones to instil fear. It's all good-natured ebullience for the moment. Étienne, all psyched up, has a good laugh. Aisha, starting out in the front line, amazed at her daring, soon tires of the game, too many men up too close, she allows herself to be edged out of the crowd and goes into the porter's lodge where the two inscrutable security guards are making coffee. They offer her a cup.

A first then a second car leave without hindrance. At the wheel are French managers, near strangers. They probably work in accounts. Then a Peugeot 606 driven by a Korean appears. A lot of people in the factory dislike the Koreans. That's the way it is, no special reason. This guy's reputed to make the women who clean the factory clean his apartment for no pay, the bastard. Someone shouts: 'Search the car.' One way of prolonging the fun. Suggestion adopted immediately, and executed. While a group of workers obstruct the saloon, Nourredine moves over to the door and glances at the back seat. Empty.

'Would you open up the boot please, sir.'

The Korean, his face terrified behind his thin, steel-rimmed glasses, suddenly winds up the windows and locks the doors, and signals that he doesn't understand. He turns green, blinks very quickly, and breathes haltingly, opening and shutting his mouth soundlessly. A fish in a goldfish bowl, ridiculous.

What happened? Did he panic? Or is it a deliberate attempt to force his way through? The car jumps forward and knocks down three workers. The crowd roars, around twenty men grab the bodywork and shake the car which bounces on its springs, almost lifts off the ground. One of the felled workers gets up and, standing in front of the bonnet, takes charge of the operation. Clear a space to my left, to my right, together, one... two... the car rocks... and three... one last push turns it on to its left side and it falls back with a crunch of crushed metal. The Korean, thrown against the left-hand door, hides his face in his hands and doesn't move.

'What's he carrying that's making him so scared? Drugs? Weapons?'

The boot's locked and won't open. *Grab the key from inside the car?* Nourredine's against it, too complicated, and might end up in a fight. Karim stands beside him with a little half-smile, and nudges him with his elbow.

'How much will you pay me to open it?' There follows a howl of protest. 'Just kidding. We're entitled to, aren't we? Today's our big day.'

He takes a minute screwdriver from the inside pocket of his leather bomber jacket and inserts it into the lock, turning it gently with his fingers, listening for the slightest reaction. He locates the notch, twists, applies some pressure. The boot opens with a grating sound and there, thrown in haphazardly are a computer and three boxes full of files. The game's up. Nourredine, a man who's never touched a drop of alcohol, feels intoxicated. Shapes sway around him. *If you take one step, you'll drop.* They're moving the files out. A hush falls on the little crowd. *Haven't had a bite to eat since this morning.* His blood pressure rockets then falls. *Want to puke.* Quignard's frank, direct handshake: *Your boss, not a bad guy, huge misunderstanding… Bollocks, yes. And what about you, seeing everything through rose-tinted spectacles, you poor bastard.* He shakes his head vigorously, the dizziness over, feels only rage.

Someone gives him a leg up and he climbs on to the car. All those faces turned towards him: Nourredine, the semi-skilled Arab worker, and beneath his feet, the Korean manager, cringing in his car. A surge of pride. The car rocks. Big smile.

'Better not rock it too hard. Right, this is what's happening. The Koreans are moving the files out in secret, to make it easier to close the factory down behind our backs. Are we going to let them get away with it?'

A hundred and fifty voices: 'No way!'

'I propose we occupy the admin section and confine the managers to their offices…' The workers hold their breath. '…until our demand on the payment of our bonuses is met. There's one solution to all this, just one. The warehouses are full. They sell the stocks under our control, and use the money to pay the agreed bonuses before they do anything else.'

The assembled workers discuss the idea, it offers something concrete at last. Selling the stocks is a good idea, they're worth more than the total owed on bonuses. Maybe, but locking in the managers… 'We need to check we have the backup.' 'Management leaves us no choice. It's one provocation after another. Anyone would think they're trying to…' 'That's what worries me.'

'Look, we've got to act fast and decisively. We all go there together, we lock them in: one night will be enough, tomorrow morning, they'll cave in. Look at the Korean in his car.' Gives a little kick to the roof which clangs. They all see the terrified face again, the car rocking, the power of concerted action. 'They're afraid of us. Let's make the most of it. If we don't get their respect today, then tomorrow, they'll close down and we'll be left with nothing. We lock them in now. All those in favour?'

There follows no more than an instant's indecision. Étienne raises his hand along with the whole first shift from packaging. All the rest of the hands go up. Aisha finds it hard to believe, but she's voting to lock the managers in. While four men retrieve the computer and the boxes of files from the boot (*nothing that belongs to the company must leave the premises without our consent*), the delegation re-forms and places itself at the head of the procession. The small troop starts to advance in a relatively ordered manner. The car lies abandoned on its side, facing the gate, the boot gaping. The Korean still hasn't budged.

Park, his face sallow, is clamped to his phone.

'They're on their way, they plan to occupy the offices... There's going to be trouble.'

'What kind of a damned stupid thing have you gone and done? It's a disaster. Explain what's going on.'

'When I started here, I set up a system of bogus invoices so as to pay the Korean managers a relocation allowance...'

A roar from the other end of the phone. Quignard leaps to his feet, knocking over his chair. He bangs his fist down on his desk, making the brandy glasses jump and knocking over a vase of chrysanthemums, soaking the files sitting on the desk. Maréchal grabs the glasses, puts them out of danger, and rights the vase.

'Delete the lot, for fuck's sake, what are you waiting for?'

Tell him they tried to smuggle the computer out and that it's in the hands of the strikers? Better to die.

'The bookkeeper who deals with it isn't in today, we don't know where the files are, we can't delete all the accounts...' Park squeals like a frightened rabbit, and the line goes dead.

The management block, a cube of reflective glass with two steps up to the main entrance, a rather unimpressive glorified hangar, is only a few minutes' walk away, but it's enough to give them all time to think about what they're doing. *We're venturing on to their territory, invading their space, barricading our bosses made of flesh and blood, pushing them around, locking them in with us, talking to them as equals. We're disrupting the social order. At least for a while. So each step counts, we'll remember each step.* And they keep close together, in silent, closed ranks. The women bring up the rear, hanging back a little, anxious, hesitant – too many men, too close together. Some discreetly slip away, through the factory and across the waste ground.

Amrouche marches despite himself, borne along by those behind him. *This is it, now, the explosion, the anger, my years of dread, the other side is so much stronger, they've always won, they'll always win. Lambs to the slaughter.* He leans towards Hafed.

'We've got to stop all this, it's going to be a disaster.'

'I don't understand why the management scumbags haven't already all gone home. What are they playing at? We can't do a thing.'

Nourredine, pushed forward by his comrades, stands in front of the door: locked. Tries to slide it open: jammed. He doesn't have time to turn around before a surge from the back of the group, gathering momentum from row to row, lifts the men at the front off the ground and flings them against the glass door which gives way and shatters. A moment's pause as Amrouche stumbles before ending up spreadeagled on the blue carpet amid shards of glass. Nourredine, his nose fractured and his face cut and bleeding, finds himself alone face to face with the Korean CEO who's standing in the middle of the lobby, rigid and pale. A voice shouts: 'Let's drag them out of their hiding places and bring them down here.' The men rush forward, trampling Amrouche underfoot, and disperse through the offices, flinging open doors, pulling the occupants out of their seats, half carrying them down to the lobby which gradually fills with panic-stricken suits. Winded, Amrouche has got to his feet and pushes the CEO towards the boardroom. He knows this room well, so many useless, never-ending discussions, those arseholes who never listen, and now... Hafed, slightly groggy, joins him. They bring the executives in one by one: 'No, not all the workers, there isn't room. Only the shop stewards, but we'll keep the door open. Immediate payment of the bonuses, everyone knows why we're here. We won't allow anyone to leave until our demands are met, but let's all calm down, we're not hooligans.'

Nourredine is sitting on a chair in the lobby, leaning forward, trying to plug his bleeding nose with a roll of toilet paper. His eyes are closed, his hands covered in blood, his brain sluggish and his thoughts confused. Hafed crouches beside him.

'Amrouche and I will deal with the management in the boardroom. You must get up to the offices. Do you hear me?' Groan.

'It's important. Organise the occupation. Pickets on the doors, patrols in the factory and the offices. OK?' Nourredine silently nods. Give the guys something to do. Then he repeats: 'It's important,' and goes back inside the boardroom.

Quignard tilts his chair back into the upright position, sits down, eyes closed and makes himself breathe slowly, regularly, exhaling through his mouth, his large hands placed flat on the desk. Maréchal has picked up his glass and is taking little sips to disguise his urge to laugh while waiting for Quignard to regain his composure.

'So now what's he done, your pyromaniac firefighter?'

'This is a nightmare, Antoine. I left them less than an hour ago. They were setting up a meeting to start negotiations, only now the workers are invading the managers' offices.'

'It's already happened to other bosses, and it didn't kill them.'

'Maybe, but Park takes the opportunity to tell me that he's siphoning off money via a system of bogus invoices to pay his gang of useless Korean managers bonuses. And to make matters worse, the evidence is there for all to see in the company's accounts... If some bright spark decides to snoop around... The factory has to be evacuated.' Quignard reaches for the telephone. 'I'm calling the superintendent...'

Maréchal halts his hand in mid-air.

'Don't do that. You'll end up with a massive fight, and the cops won't have the resources to deal with it. It takes time to get the riot police out, and you have to be able to give good reasons.'

The two men drink in silence. Quignard broods.

'Pyromaniac firefighter you said. That's an idea, the fire brigade. A fire breaks out and everyone's evacuated.' Renewed silence. The two men drink. Quignard mutters to himself: 'Especially as there's no danger of those shit-stirrers from the insurance company poking their noses in.' Then Maréchal, who's finished his drink, gets up.

'Karim Bouziane has set up a barbecue on the waste ground behind the factory. With the strike on, he must have been doing a roaring trade throughout the afternoon. Right, I'll let you get on, I'm going home. Thanks for the brandy.'

A farewell wave and the door slams.

Think, fast. A brandy. Tomaso, the right man for the job?

Quignard thinks back to their first meeting. A business contact had taken him to the Oiseau Bleu in Nancy. A very special place, he'd been told. A restaurant, the best in Nancy. The boss, Tomaso, had come to greet him. Behind the tall elegant form Quignard had sensed a relentless hardness, a blue-tinged steeliness that had immediately appealed to him. After the succulent dinner, they went downstairs to the nightclub in the basement of the restaurant, known for its whores, the best Nancy had to offer. He had become a regular at the Oiseau Bleu where he spent a lot more time than he did at home, and a friend of Tomaso's, who'd opened up to him a little. He was an old warhorse in the process of adjusting to civilian life, still bearing the scars of the battles and injuries that Quignard had dreamed of as a youth during his brief stint in the OAS, fighting underground in the doomed bid to maintain French rule in Algeria. Nostalgia, nostalgia. Besides Tomaso was forty. He could almost be his son, the son he'd never had. So Quignard had ensured that his security firm was awarded certain contracts, including that of Daewoo Pondange, and was very glad he had. Whether dirty tricks against troublesome trade-unionists, the transfer of suitcases full of cash, a spot of financial espionage – Tomaso had never turned down an assignment. On the contrary, he operated with the utmost efficiency and discretion. Of course he was the right man for the job of starting a dustbin fire in a factory under occupation.

Around twenty workers have gathered in the doorway, trying to see inside. Amrouche's voice can be heard opening the meeting in solemn tones.

While Nourredine sits there dazed, his head in his hands, finding it hard to breathe, the rest of them disperse among the offices, taking possession of the premises with obvious pleasure. The fitted carpets, walls, clean, furniture, tidy, soft pastel colours, a well-ventilated space, reveals another world to that inside the factory. They want to play around, sit in the swivel chairs, put their feet on the desks, use the metal filing cabinets as instruments for a novel kind of drum kit, set all the internal phone lines ringing. They're at home, or rather, they're acting as though they're at home. Then, tired of messing around, they come across a bottle of whisky in a drawer, which they serve in coffee cups. They telephone friends overseas, and a few trifles – electronic diaries, mobile phones, coloured felt-tip pens, souvenirs for the kids, a Montblanc fountain pen – vanish into anonymous pockets. Two men help themselves to a state-of-the-art computer and all its gadgets through a window overlooking the factory floor.

In the boardroom, the discussion is drawn out in endless preliminaries, as the interpreter translates each intervention into Korean or French. Amrouche goes through a list of grievances that have accumulated since the factory opened. The group of spectators in the doorway slowly dwindles. The afternoon drags on and people are beginning to get bored. The security guards patrol the main corridor, to general indifference. A group is sitting in a circle in the Head of HR's office, passing spliffs around. Pity the secretaries have already gone home, they'd have made the evening more fun. 'What about our women, where are they?' 'They've chickened out, I bet you.' Sniggers, male camaraderie. Around the coffee machine, others have resumed their perpetual card games. There's a TV in the boss's office. It proves impossible to find the remote and the TV set is thrown on the floor. Nourredine has fallen asleep in his chair, his head on his knees.

Étienne has brought back the computer seized from the Korean executive's car. He finds a quiet office and plugs it in. He knows a thing or two about computers, he does. Here's his chance to see what they get up to in the offices. It amuses and interests him. He opens up the computer, no problem, and starts tapping away. In the folder labelled 'management purchases-sales suppliers' there are several files, identified by numbers. He opens one at random, and discovers lists of names: French names, foreign names, all unknown. He clicks on one of them. In an inset on the left of the screen, a close-up of a woman giving a man a blow job, repetitive, forceful, animated graphics. Étienne clicks on another file, another graphic, blow job again, but different angle and position. He flicks gleefully through folders and files, jumping from masturbation to sodomy, threesomes and other variations. Étienne's jubilant: those bureaucrats, got to hand it to them, they're well organised. The image of Aisha lying on the floor in the dark comes back to him, he smells the fragrance of shampoo in her mass of black hair, and then the overpowering smell of blood. A virgin, a special feeling, a good feeling. Massive hard-on. He jumps. Karim is leaning over his shoulder with the easy familiarity between a supplier and one of his regular customers, and slips a ready-rolled joint into the pocket of his overalls.

'Little present for you. I'm shutting up shop and going home.'

His gaze lights on the screen. The image shows a woman on all fours being mounted by a dog – a white Great Dane with black patches, and he's panting, tongue hanging out. It takes Étienne's breath away. You don't often see that around here in Pondange.

There's a pause in negotiations. The managers have asked to be allowed to consult each other and Amrouche and Hafed have left them alone in the boardroom. During the break in discussions they do the rounds of the offices and take stock of the occupation. Amrouche enters the room where Étienne and Karim are chortling and thumping each other, glued to the computer, shoulder to shoulder. In one corner of the screen, a man is fucking a woman doggie-style, medium-close shot of their arses moving. Amrouche, deeply shocked, mutters a few exorcisms and goes out, slamming the door behind him. The noise makes Karim jump. He emerges from his reverie and his business instincts kick in.

'Can you make me a quick copy of the images? You're good at mucking around with these machines, then you enlarge them, we make a nice little diskette that I can sell for a good price. I've got the customers, and we go fifty-fifty.'

'Brilliant. Wait, it won't take a minute.'

Étienne rummages in the cupboards, finds some diskettes, inserts one, starts copying. The operation takes three minutes, the time it takes to light the joint and have a few tokes with Karim who pockets the diskette and vanishes in the direction of the cafeteria.

Étienne carries on smoking and daydreaming. How much would he make on the deal? A thousand francs? More? He looks back at the screen. The images have disappeared and his gaze is drawn to the name of a file he recognises. Nourredine Hamidi. Nourredine, my friend in packaging? Beneath the name is a sort of bank statement, a series of dates scrolls past, figures listed as debits, credits, and at the bottom of the list, the total assets: a hundred thousand francs. He toggles from file to file, suddenly paying close attention. Other names appear, also with bank statements, mostly unknown, but here's one with the name of holier-than-thou Amrouche. Not bad, a hundred and fifty thousand francs. And a little further down, Rolande Lepetit, fifty thousand francs only, poor old Rolande, always unlucky. And Maréchal, another two hundred thousand francs. Seniority has been taken into account. Initial reaction: They've got a stake in the company, they've done better than me, even Rolande with her prissy air. Second reaction: Hold on a minute, if Nourredine's got a packet in Daewoo, why's he going on about bonuses? He doesn't give a shit about bonuses. Who's side is he on? And Rolande, made redundant? I'd be surprised. Have to get to the bottom of this.

Étienne finds Nourredine asleep on a chair in the lobby and shakes him.

'You didn't tell us you had a packet stashed away in Daewoo, you dark horse.'

Nourredine surfaces groggily.

'Will you stop pissing around.'

'Come with me, let me show you your bank statement. Right now, you've got more than a hundred thousand francs.'

'You're either drunk or stoned.' Nourredine gets to his feet heavily, shaking his throbbing head, and makes for the toilets.

Drunk or stoned. What kind of an answer is that? Shocked, Étienne runs up and down the corridors to round up the guys.

'Nourredine, Rolande, Maréchal, and a load of others are receiving millions from the bosses of Daewoo, come and see, I've found the list of payments on one of the computers...' They laugh, and nobody moves... 'There are porn movies too.'

'Why didn't you say so to start with?'

Just then, two women come running in from the cafeteria.

'Come quickly, a fire's broken out in the main corridor.'

The offices empty. Nourredine dithers then goes into the boardroom. Silence falls at the sight of his swollen face and blood-stained clothes.

'Hafed, you're in charge of security. Come on, you're needed here.' Hafed leaves the room and the two men disappear in the direction of the factory.

Étienne is disgusted. Nobody's interested in the things that matter. A fire's broken out, you've got to be kidding. Another dustbin fire. I've seen one or two a month since I've been here. Whereas finding out whether Nourredine's getting money from Daewoo, yes or no... Ah well, it's *their* problem. Find Aisha, she's bound to be in the cafeteria and suggest another visit to Nourredine's prayer mat. And then, he's going home, he is. Pissed off with all these arseholes.

Karim's tired too, and beginning to feel bored. Rolande is standing over the cooker in the cafeteria and there's a lovely smell of fried onions. *I'll have a bite to eat, and I'm off. Nothing more doing around here.*

Dense black smoke fills a section of the central corridor. People are running in all directions looking for fire extinguishers. Many are missing, others are empty. Hafed finds one, removes his shirt and ties it around the lower part of his face like a mask, puts his jacket back on next to his bare skin and dives into the black cloud. He gropes his way to the blazing bin and douses it with foam, then knocks it over and kicks away the smouldering rubbish. Then Nourredine arrives with an extinguisher found underneath all the stocks and finishes the job. The smoke slowly disperses through the door at the end. Breathless, the two men stand a few metres back. Nourredine gazes at the blackened sheet-metal wall, the floor strewn with rubbish and mounds of foam melting into puddles seeping towards the factory floor. Is he perhaps thinking of the offices with their fitted carpets and pastel decor? He slides down on to the floor and sits cross-legged with his back against the sheet metal, his breath still rasping.

'It's disgusting.'

'Don't complain. We had a narrow escape. The sprinklers in this place don't work and the extinguishers are either empty or not working. We bring it up at every health and safety meeting, and it makes no difference.'

Nourredine, who recalls larking around with a bunch of guys on the waste ground squirting each other with foam from the extinguishers, looks away. Hafed walks towards the dustbin now lying on its side, and indicates a dozen or so charred remains with his foot.

'Maybe someone added some embers to this dustbin.' A silence. 'I suddenly feel as if I'm sitting on a bomb.'

'Didn't the security guards say that they'd take care of security?'

'Yes, you're right. We'll go and have a word with them at the gate.'

Outside, the night is pitch black. The overturned car is still there, but at first glance it looks as though the Korean has managed to extricate himself. The porter's lodge is brightly lit from the inside, and the two security guards watch them approach with a little smile. Nourredine is immediately on his guard: something smells fishy.

'Aren't there supposed to be some of our people in here round the clock to control all the comings and goings?'

'Yes. But I suppose in the excitement everyone went off to occupy the offices.'

'We're really useless.'

'More to the point, we're new at this. You can't make things up as you go along. And those with the experience, who've done it all before and could help us, aren't here. We're doing our best.'

As soon as Nourredine pushes open the door, the older of the two security guards launches an attack:

'So, you've let the prisoners go already? Maybe it wasn't worth all the fuss, guys.'

'What are you talking about?'

'The CEO has just left the factory with the entire management team.' Nourredine feels himself deflating like a burst balloon, crumpling into himself. 'No more than ten minutes ago.' Sounds reach him muted and distant, Hafed and the two security guards shrink and retreat in silhouette. 'Amrouche opened the gates for them, and they left on foot, scarpering like rabbits.' The man laughs. 'We didn't lift a finger, guys. This is your affair, not ours.'

Nourredine sits down, his head aching more and more, his vision blurred. He's suffocating. The temptation is to drop the whole thing and go home. The women there: his mother and his sisters, his very young wife... Move to another job, the little chip stall in the market square...

'I don't get it, Hafed. Can you explain?'

'What do you expect me to do? I was with you when the fire broke out, remember? When you came to get me from the board-room, Amrouche was suggesting we let the junior executives depart. We'd just done the round of the offices, and there were only about twenty of us occupying. That seemed too few to hold so many managers. We were deciding to hold the five most senior managers. I don't know what happened after that.'

No, I can't drop it now, not after we forced the juggernauts back, the overturned car, the invasion of the offices, this strength, never felt it before, men among men, the friends who listen to me, the trust, I'm someone else, I talk, I act. Not now. He gets up, takes a couple of steps, grabs the day book. No mention of the managers' departure and the opening of the gates, nothing about the dustbin fire. Only one rather terse entry: *17.15, the security patrol notifies us of cannabis dealing on the waste ground behind the factory. Given the general insecurity caused by the personnel's occupation of the factory, and after having taken orders from our superiors, we feel it is wiser not to include the waste ground in our round.* He feels a surge of anger, and suddenly his energy comes rushing back.

'You're not doing your job. Where were the security guards during the fire alert? Where is there any mention of the fire? The only thing you're interested in is damaging the workers' reputation.'

He tears the page out of the day book and holds it between two fingers, at eye level.

'Hafed, have you got a lighter?'

He takes it and emphatically sets fire to the sheet of paper, then watches it go up in flames very quickly. A few charred remains fall to the floor. Then he gives the lighter back to Hafed, spits on the ground and leaves the porter's lodge.

Nourredine and Hafed head towards the cafeteria, where they presume everyone will have gathered. Nourredine walks on in silence, frowning, letting out the occasional groan or odd word. Hafed watches him out of the corner of his eye, concerned to see him seething.

In the brightly-lit cafeteria, small groups are sitting around tables shouting, heatedly debating and making a great deal of racket. The two patrol guards are standing in front of the coffee machine, rummaging in their pockets for change. Amrouche is sitting alone in a corner, drinking coffee. Nourredine strides across the room, making a beeline for him. He's cleaned the blood from his face and hands, but his nose is caked with dried blood. There are blue and green rings under his eyes and his clothes are covered with dark red and blackish stains. Some people didn't recognise him when he came in. He is greeted with silence. He stops beside Amrouche, climbs on to a table, turns his back on him and addresses the group gathered in front of him in a loud voice.

'You're a traitor, Ali. We held a weapon in our hands, and you disarmed us.' Amrouche throws away the empty cup. He looks tired but placid.

'We took the only sensible decision that's been taken all day. If you would just calm down...' Nourredine pretends not to hear him.

'There's one option left, since you stole our boss from us. There are the chemicals stored behind the factory. First we go and get them, then we can break the warehouse door down. We remove them and store them in the packaging section, under close guard, and if the bonuses aren't paid, we pour them into the river tomorrow at midday. Maybe tomorrow evening, but no later.'

Amrouche gets to his feet and plants himself in front of Nourredine, at the front of the tight group surrounding him.

'Nobody will do that in this factory. Over my dead body, do you hear? How many of us are there here, have you counted? Eighty at the most. How many should we be? Three hundred and sixty to three hundred and eighty. Where are the others? At home. Your strikers are already in a minority. We wanted Rolande to be given her job back, and now all the talk is of bonuses. We're not capable of occupying the factory properly. The workers are wandering about all over the place and getting up to all sorts of stupid things. Anyone can just walk right in, there's no proper security. When we heard that a fire had broken out, I decided to have the managers evacuated. Do you think you're capable of preventing a nutter from setting fire to the place? You know damn well you're not. Each time you run into difficulties, you become more violent and fewer and fewer people follow you. Your idea of pouring chemicals into the river is a terrorist tactic. Pour a barrel of acid into the river and we all go straight to jail, and for as long as they like. You also know as well as I do that no one – no one, do you hear? – in Pondange will lift a finger to defend us. Because we're Arabs, because this factory is seen as a mere annex of the unemployment office. There's no real work here, we're being kept off the streets, and we're paid out of taxes. You know very well what the people of Pondange say. What's more, to them *Arab* and *terrorist* are one and the same thing.' He turns to the audience in silence. 'To be slung into jail like terrorists, is that what you want?'

Nourredine goes pale and gasps for breath. He stutters: 'Terrorist, terrorist, I'm no terrorist.' Hafed puts his arm around his shoulders and makes him come down from the table and sit down, then he speaks.

'What's done is done. We can't undo it and we must stay united. As long as we're in occupation, we hold on to the stock and that's our bargaining tool. Tomorrow, we resume negotiations. Now, the most important thing is to get organised. Organised,' he repeats. 'All day, we've rushed around non-stop. Now it's time to stop and get organised. We need a team in the porter's lodge coordinating everything. A team in the offices, to restore some order, find out where the records are kept, sort out the documents we seized from the car. Tomorrow we'll examine them to find out why they wanted to smuggle them out. And two teams to patrol the building all night, to completely empty the factory, gather all the people hanging around here, in the cafeteria, and take care of security. Those who are not on the first watch stay here and sleep, and take over at three a.m. Tomorrow at seven a.m., general meeting here to decide on the next step.'

Hafed and Amrouche are standing side by side: 'Let's vote. Those against?' Only five hands are raised in opposition to Hafed's proposal. Proposal accepted.

Nourredine, who is so choked he can no longer speak, leaps to his feet and punches Amrouche in the stomach. Hafed steps in, touches his arm and steers him outside to the car park. They walk in silence. As he gets his breath back, Nourredine slowly becomes aware of the moonless night, the pungent smell of damp earth, trees and mushrooms, the abnormal silence filled with furtive sounds, birds most likely, or animals, on the river banks. A light wind has risen, blowing down from the plateau. A night filled with stories of another life. He starts to breathe again, slowly, painfully, feels his broken nose.

'I'm knackered, Hafed. I want to lie down and sleep here for a bit.'

'No way. We've decided to get everyone together and you're not going to set a bad example. If you've calmed down, we're going back in, you're going to have a wash, eat something and then sleep. I'll take the first guard duty. You'll take the second. Tomorrow, think about tomorrow. We'll win.'

Nourredine is sleeping on a table in the canteen covered by table-cloths with a pile of napkins under his head while Amrouche goes to supervise the restoration of order to the offices. In the porter's lodge Hafed is collecting reports from the various patrols and writing them up in the day book, when Étienne bursts in yelling:

'Fire behind the warehouse... It's spreading everywhere... Help...'

By car, bicycle, on foot, the entire valley has turned out to watch the factory blaze. The police and the fire brigade have erected a safety barrier and onlookers are gathering on the roundabout, having abandoned their cars wherever they happened to be. It is a spectacular sight. The warehouse, the entire left section of the fac-tory, is on fire. Brilliant yellow flames light up the dark wooded slopes of the valley. The fire roars majestically, punctuated by explosions of varying degrees of intensity, sometimes a whole series of them, and plumes of black smoke drift on the wind towards the bottom of the valley. Suddenly part of the roof caves in giving off a huge shower of sparks which momentarily illumi-nates the shaft and gaping mouth of a disused iron mine halfway up the hillside, a ghostly silhouette which is again soon engulfed in blackness. The crowd lets out a sigh of wonder and fear.

Among the front rows of spectators are the striking Daewoo workers. They are in trauma. Aisha has found Rolande and is sobbing in her arms in uncontrolled, wordless despair. All sorts of things must have happened in the course of the day, thinks Rolande, who does not attempt to console her but just tries to envelop her in a little human warmth, without being able to take her eyes off the blaze. *We are lost souls.* Close by, Nourredine and Hafed face the fire, its flames are reflected on their distraught faces as they clutch each other's hands, their knuckles white from the force of their grip. 'Our strength is going up in smoke,' mur-murs Hafed, his voice crushed. 'It's us burning in there, we've been murdered.'

Étienne, ashen, goes from group to group repeating tirelessly: 'I saw the guys who started the fire, I saw the guys who started the fire.' People are mesmerised by the spectacle, and no one pays any attention to him. Amrouche, sitting on a mound some dis-tance away, away from the crowd, his head in his hands, weeps silently.

Quignard has slipped an anorak and trousers over his pyjamas and borrowed his wife's car. Sitting on the bonnet, a woollen hat pulled down over his eyes, he watches the blaze, seemingly unperturbed. How did a dustbin fire, the pretext for evacuating the premises rapidly, turn into this inferno? Tomaso comes and sits down beside him, a tall figure in a military parka. He gazes at the fire without a word, his long, bony face obscured by the shadow of the hood, impassive and mute. Quignard is grateful to him for being there. A gust of wind, the fire intensifies, roaring. It still makes less noise than a steelworks, he thinks with a half-smile.

Étienne walks past the two men, seeking a bit of attention.

'I saw the guys who started the fire, you know.'

A crushing moment of silence, then Quignard, icily: 'If that's true, young man, I advise you to keep your mouth shut here and save your statement for the police.'

Disappointed, Étienne decides to go home. Tomaso gets up and disappears. Maréchal comes and leans against the car, next to Quignard.

'I'd never have believed things would move so fast.' A few minutes' silence. His face is turned towards the factory, furrowed, his skin looks yellow in the light from the blaze. A smile glints in his eye. It seems that after all fire has returned to his valley.

PART TWO

15 October

Standing in front of the bay window, his jacket unbuttoned and his hands in his trouser pockets, Pierre Benoît-Rey gazes out at the Eiffel Tower all illuminated, looking almost within reach, and the esplanade of the Palais de Chaillot beyond. Waiting. Tonight the government will announce the buyer for Thomson, France's biggest military-electronics concern, a publicly-owned company it has decided to privatise. There are two rival bids, only two, for this huge deal on which the restructuring and perhaps even the survival of the French arms industry depends: Alcatel and Matra. And Pierre Benoît-Rey is head of the small team, or rather the commando, tasked by Alcatel's management to put together the Thomson bid and see it through, reporting directly to the CEO.

The waiting drags on. Benoît-Rey rests his forehead against the window, against the night, as he used to do when he was a child. The damp cold soothes his brow. He seriously needs soothing. The body of a ten-kilometre sprinter, red lips and an angelic face framed with dark hair; a pronounced fondness for cocaine and alcohol; a sharp brain, always ticking, too clever, some say, and perhaps they could be right. They also say that everything he touches turns to gold. Tonight we'll see. In a few minutes, it'll be either the Tarpeian Rock or the Capitoline Hill. A slight churning in the pit of his stomach. He goes over every detail of the deal in his mind. Alcatel is divesting itself of its equipment-manufacturing arm to concentrate on electronics. Fewer jobs, more excellence. With the revenue from the sale, it buys Thomson and its military electronics. The company restructures its electronics capability, creates synergies, and restructures the entire sector, which would be impossible without the mega profits from the military section. From this French giant, we and our British allies, who have bought up our equipment-manufacturing arm – which means we don't lose it altogether – create a European electronics giant that will challenge the Americans on their own turf. A brilliant piece of architecture, an empire within reach, like the Eiffel Tower, an engineer's dream. And I'll be flying. Director of strategy for the future group, most likely.

Time drags its heels. The three ministries involved, Defence,

Industry and Finance, are one hundred per cent behind us. Our rival, Matra, a company that's a quarter of the size of the one it wants to take over, is forced to juggle to finance the operation and is teaming up with an unlikely Korean partner to do so. The boss of Matra is a puffed-up frog who thinks he's bigger than the ox. We have a cast-iron bid: how can it go wrong? Soon, power over a global group. In the arms sector, to boot. The prize industry, politics, superprofits, secret services. Another stomach contraction, almost painful. Playing for high stakes. For the future. And tonight...

The phone rings and Benoît-Rey swings around. In the meeting room serving as their HQ four men – his entire team – are killing time. They exchange the odd word from time to time and a glass tinkles against the whisky bottle. All eyes are glued to the telephone on a corner of the big table in the centre of the room.

'It's your call, Pierre.'

He picks it up, listens, nods and hangs up without a word. Sits down, suddenly drained.

'Our chairman. He's just had a call from the Prime Minister's office. It's Matra.'

A long silence. The men look at each other. This failure is all theirs. They accepted the mission, they gambled, they lost. Their first failure on such a scale. Rossellini, in charge of the financial side of the bid is an elegant and athletic forty-something, a graduate of France's top management school, the École Nationale d'Administration. He's doing a stint as an auditor in the Finance Ministry where he still has a discreet, efficient network of personal contacts. He acted as Alcatel's financial director in the bid, a position that will be vacant in a few months: a financial director of one of the biggest global industrial groups at barely forty, a destiny he believed he was meant for. Only now he's suddenly relegated to being just another departmental head, and has to stomach it. Then Alain Bentadj, a young engineer trained at the prestigious École Polytechnique, expert in new technologies: a spell at Thomson, highly valued by the military for his technical capabilities, his inventiveness and the clarity of his vision, dreaming of an international career, abruptly finding himself demoted. What can he do at Alcatel if Matra's the leading arms manufacturer? He came to Alcatel precisely because the Thomson takeover was on the cards. What's he supposed to do? Change jobs? Not easy after a failure on this scale. And anyway where can he go if Matra dominates the industry? They're hardly going to welcome him with open arms. Frédéric Marion is head of communications. He thought he'd made a good fist of it, with the ministerial offices in his pocket. He'd dreamed of setting up his own PR and communications agency on the back of all this, its future assured with the giant Alcatel account. Those dreams have all just gone up in smoke. Roger Valentin sits alone on the sofa, the last man. He's heavily built and older, watching the others and suppressing a smile. Former deputy director of the secret services, he's now Alcatel's head of security, making more money in the space of a few years than he ever made in the public sector, but lacking either further ambition or anxieties.

Rossellini breaks the silence.

'Are we entitled to know why?'

'No. No other information. The Prime Minister chose Matra. That's it. That's all there is to it.'

'Right. The next question is where's a good place for a holiday at this time of year? There's no snow in the mountains and the coast's horrible.'

'There's the islands.' Benoît-Rey picks up the phone with a half-smile. 'I'd planned a little victory celebration at Joseph's too. I'd better cancel.'

'OK, one last drink and we go home to our families. It'll be strange for them, after hardly seeing us for four months while we've been practically married to each other.'

'I'll miss you, darling.'

'Alain, are you sure the beautiful Madame Bentadj will have waited for you?'

'Don't rub salt into the wound. I have no desire to return home unexpectedly.'

'An evening at Mado's, blow jobs all round, getting fucked brainless.'

'Now that's a much better idea...'

Valentin is still sitting silently on the sofa. The phone rings again. They look at each other. Benoît-Rey says, 'Nothing worse can happen now,' and picks up the receiver.

'Yes, we're still here, chief. Yes, Valentin too.' He utters groans and monosyllables, staring around wide-eyed. 'Yes, we'll be there.' And he hangs up.

'So, has the Prime Minister changed his mind?'

Shrug. 'Our CEO's received several phone calls. First of all from Prestat.'

'Who?'

Half-smile. 'Very funny. The CEO of Thomson Multimedia. He swears that the entire company, from senior management down to the workers, is going to fight the choice of Matra tooth and nail. They are absolutely against it because Matra's flogging them off to Daewoo, a Korean company that can't be trusted at all, in his view.' A pause. 'He's talking about strikes, demonstrations.'

'Nobody gives a fuck about multimedia. Thomson is first and foremost arms, it's only arms. We didn't know what to do about the multimedia arm either, we couldn't have kept hold of it, we'd have ended up selling it to the Japanese or to another Korean firm.'

'Maybe, but we never said so publicly. Then our chairman had a long phone conversation with one of his contacts in the Finance Ministry. The minister doesn't agree with the PM's choice, but he'll go along with it, of course.'

'Of course.'

'Apparently, the senior civil servants at the ministry are firmly opposed to the choice of Matra. Opinion is divided among the senior officials in the other ministries.' He pauses for breath. 'In short, the minister is encouraging us not to consider tonight's decision as final.'

'He's taking the piss.'

'Possibly, but that's not the view of our chairman. He wants us in his office at six p.m. tomorrow to present a new action plan – with the emphasis on "new" – one that's appropriate for this second round.'

Rossellini explodes: 'Now, it's our chairman who's taking the piss.'

'What second round? You've got to be joking. Who's going to overturn the Prime Minister's decision? The President? They're as thick as thieves.'

'The chairman was talking about a vote in the National Assembly...' An eruption of general mirth... 'Rejection by the Privatisation Committee or the Commission in Brussels.'

'Now that makes more sense, although it's highly unlikely. The Privatisation Committee has always backed the government.'

'No. It rejected a bid in 1994.'

'But until now, the government has always gone by the book, and always waited for its approval before making its decision public.'

'By the book…'

Benoît-Rey sits up and suddenly seems to regain his fighting spirit.

'Gentlemen, we have no choice. The acquisition of Thomson is as vital for Alcatel as it is for us. So let's go for it and see the game out. We've nothing else left to lose. If the Privatisation Committee follows its usual practice, we have one or two months at most before it announces its verdict.' He takes off his jacket and rolls up his shirtsleeves. 'The night's still young. We have time.' He looks at his watch. 'There's nobody left in the kitchens so I'll phone the downstairs brasserie and have them bring up sandwiches and beers.'

Benoît-Rey begins to clear away the empty glasses and bottles then takes notepads and pens out of the drawers and places them randomly on the table. The machine is back in operation, with mobile features and expressive hands. When the sandwiches arrive, they resume their places around the table, more resigned than enthusiastic, after all rather pleased to be in their cocoon immersed in familiar trappings: the atmosphere, the stress. Valentin extricates himself from the sofa and chooses a Camembert sandwich. And Benoît-Rey continues:

'The chief wants something new. First of all, I'd like to make sure that everything's clear. We consider the acquisition of Thomson to be vital, because in our high-tech sector only the military markets give the necessary stability to safeguard a long-term future. So we need Thomson in order to restructure Alcatel. And if we don't restructure Alcatel, we'll stagnate and then be gobbled up by the first-comer. Our British friends, for example.' A pause as an obsessive refrain goes round and round in their heads: merger, takeover, buyer, change of personnel, career in tatters, having to carve out a new niche. Benoît-Rey continues: 'Our bid was the best, we had solid, extensive backing. Yet we lost. Where did we go wrong?'

Rossellini, his tie loosened and expression impassive, drinks beer and whisky, English-style and without eating, repeatedly brushing away the strand of fair hair which keeps falling over his left eye.

'We lost for political reasons, I think it's as simple as that. Several of Alcatel's big bosses made their careers under the Socialist government. You too, Valentin, and you left the security service when the current lot came to power because they didn't want you heading it up. Matra's boss is much closer to the Prime Minister and the President.' He pauses, then continues, on a bitter note: 'I think I was wrong to get involved in all this. The Socialists are out of the running for the time being, and I don't give a damn.'

Got to get things back on track, fast.

'If it was a political decision, how do you explain the support from the ministerial departments?'

'Is that support as widespread as you say? Our only source of information so far is our chairman, and it's in his interest to present things that way to keep us going.'

'Valentin, what do you think?'

Interesting, first time they've asked me for my opinion. These youngsters are really up shit creek. He puts down his barely-touched sandwich and takes a sip of beer. Another precautionary pause. *This will take a while.*

'I don't think our failure is primarily or exclusively political. The fact is, there was never any competition between Matra and Alcatel for Thomson's takeover. The decision was made before the bidding process began, and for reasons that probably have nothing to do with industrial logic or politics, even with a capital P.'

'What makes you say that?'

'Firstly the decision to sell Thomson by mutual agreement rather than by putting it up for tender. That has never been done for such a large company. So it was clear, right from the start, that it would be the Prime Minister's decision alone, and for reasons of his own.'

'Thomson is up to its ears in debt.'

'That's an excuse and that's not the end of it. Just after the bidding process opened, Gomez – Thomson's boss – was fired, to everyone's surprise, in a real battle for power.'

'He's also in bed with the Socialists.'

'He's a crafty character who's got influential friends in all camps and has survived two government cohabitations. But above all he's a bitter personal enemy of Matra's boss. The way had to be cleared. Matra's takeover of Thomson would be out of the question if Gomez remained at Thomson's helm. It would have been him calling us this evening instead of Prestat, and that would have been a major problem for the Prime Minister, whereas the new boss of the Thomson group, appointed by the government and in post for three or four months, has no choice but to keep his mouth shut. Gomez was fired eight months ago. At that point, the decision had already been taken in favour of Matra. Allow me to continue. Matra put in its takeover bid late, as everyone knows. We can surmise, without being too paranoid, that they had access to ours, thanks to a few friends in high places. Under normal, transparent conditions, being late would have been enough for their bid to be disqualified. Finally, Daewoo's senior management booked Fouquet's several days ago. They're throwing a fabulous party to celebrate their victory – which they were certain of well before the official announcement – as we speak.'

Rossellini speaks frostily, with a disdainful smile:

'Basically, your theory doesn't make much difference, Valentin.' He whistles the sibilants. 'Whether Matra was chosen before the bidding process opened or at the end, the fact is they were chosen because they're close to the Prime Minister.'

Going round and round in his head, the same old nagging doubt: *What am I doing here? Talking to a cop. A police view of History. That fat Valentin, coarse and probably incompetent. I'm a fish out of water here. I'd do better to try and cover my arse rather than get deeper into this mess, in bad company.*

'Yes, it makes a lot of difference. The Prime Minister keeps his decision secret for months on end, not sharing it with his ministers, and lets the governmental departments carry on as if the whole process were being conducted under normal conditions. The natural suspicion is that if this decision is secret, it's because the plans to restructure the industry are covering up some highly compromising flaws. If I manage to uncover those flaws, then I don't need to worry about deadlines or authorities, I have the power to get the Prime Minister to change his mind. It'll be up to him to worry about how to save face. Finding motives, gathering evidence… In other words, this will turn into nothing more than an ordinary police investigation.'

Benoît-Rey, tense, listens attentively, is almost calm.

'Why didn't we think of that sooner?'

'I spoke to the chairman about it quite early on. He didn't agree. He believed in the integrity of the process and the viability of his industrial proposal, and was confident of winning the bid. He was probably alluding to our conversation when he told you to come up with something new.'

'I find that assumption and the implied method of working rather exciting. And of course, you already have a few concrete leads…'

'There are two avenues to pursue, although one is more interesting than the other. The first and most obvious is the Taiwanese arms market which Thomson and Matra have been involved in for five or six years. We don't know much about what's behind these deals, other than that billions of commission handled by Thomson have vanished. There's talk of a sum of five billion. When that sort of money's involved, nobody plays by the rules. Matra and Thomson have both benefited and could have a common interest in eliminating all those not in the know in order to protect their secret. Alcatel is a newcomer. Its intrusion could increase the risk of a leak and will be perceived as dangerous by many insiders.'

A breather. Valentin sips his beer. A bubble surfaces in Bentadj's memory, a few snatches of conversation overheard in the corridors of the Defence Ministry.

'A captain in the Taiwanese army who was investigating the terms of a sale of frigates to Taiwan by France, was assassinated…'

'Correct. Unsolved murder.' Valentin allows the corpse of the Taiwanese captain to haunt the meeting room for a few moments, the blood, the death so far away, so close to the world of big business. He sighs. That case is a tough one. Too big, too heavily protected, too dangerous. Disappointment, relief among his audience. Even if I'm convinced it played a part in the Prime Minister's decision. I propose that we only use what we know for certain. Gomez, Thomson's boss, has stored up a few time bombs against Lagardère, Matra's boss. If we find the right way to ask him he'll sell us a few, and even if they're fabricated we can use them to destroy the life and reputation of Matra's boss. That's useful, has to be done, but it won't be enough.' Valentin tilts back in his chair and looks at them with a half-smile. Know-all. *I've got an excuse, they're so exasperating.* 'Second avenue. I suggest that the Prime Minister's key concern over the privatisation of Thomson isn't arms, but the multimedia subsidiary. Of course, you guys dream only of arms and find that hard to swallow. Let's go back to square one. The government's first decision was to sell off the military division, which is in excellent shape, together with the multimedia operation, already up to its ears in debt. Observers all believe this strategy is financially unsound. Everyone else forgets about it. A few days later, Daewoo enters the Matra frame. Hang on, we need to think about this. Daewoo's no stranger to anybody. It's one of the major Korean conglomerates, the most recent and the most fragile, linked to the Korean dictators who chiefly finance it. It has been in serious financial difficulties since the fall of its dictator friends in the mid-eighties, and was bailed out at the last minute by the Korean government once before, back in 1985. Today observers in Seoul are sceptical about its ability to survive the recession that's hitting the Korean economy. To spell it out, over there Daewoo's considered to be a bankruptcy waiting to happen. Kim, Daewoo's Korean CEO, is no stranger either. He had to leave the country for a while in 1985. In 1995, he was caught red-handed, bribing a public official and he's just been sentenced to two and a half years in jail. He's not banged up yet, but he's cutting the risk by no longer residing permanently in Korea. Unbelievable, isn't it, to go and seek out that particular Korean? But he's well known in Parisian circles. He landed in France some time around 1985 right when he was beginning to have serious problems at home. At first he made numerous contacts and political friends on both the left and the right; latterly they tended to be more on the right. Let's move on swiftly, I don't want to bore you. He sets up a company in Lorraine with around a hundred employees. In 1987 he and his family are granted French citizenship amid total secrecy. Worse still, it's treated as a sort of ad hoc defence secret. He doesn't speak French, doesn't live in France, fulfils none of the conditions for citizenship, but the Prime Minister of the day exerts a bit of gentle pressure and his file records that he has been granted citizenship for "exceptional services to France". What services?' He pauses, nobody moves. 'You can see clearly that here's what I would call a flaw.

'Two years ago, Kim opens a cathode tube factory in Lorraine. A small factory. Has he already been told about the privatisation of Thomson Multimedia? Is he preparing his bid? It's entirely possible. This factory will enable him to sign a deal with Thomson Multimedia in 1995. It's baiting a sprat to catch a mackerel, but then he'll be able to claim he was working with Thomson before the takeover. I'm convinced that he was foisted on to Matra, that it wasn't Matra that went after him, but Matra's boss, Lagardère, can't say no to the President, for all sorts of reasons.

'To cap it all, last May the Prime Minister makes Kim a Commander of the Legion of Honour. Commander, no less. No mention of his French nationality. Why? Is he ashamed of it? Not at all, any more than of his being sentenced to prison for corruption in his own country. That much goes without saying.' Valentin leans forward, suddenly belligerent, punctuating his words with his fist. 'I want to know what those "exceptional services" were, I want to know what Kim did, or who he paid to receive such recognition on a regular basis. If I can find out, I'll have ammunition for blackmail and the Matra-Daewoo bid collapses.'

Silence. Benoît-Rey clears his throat and Valentin smiles at him.

'Don't lose heart, my dear Pierre. Welcome to the delightful world of arms dealing. As the Marquise du Deffand said: It is only taking the first step that is difficult.'

16 October

The following morning, after a few hours while they pretended to get some rest, mulling over extracts from dossiers, salvaging what they can, and voicing quite a lot of resentment, Benoît-Rey and Rossellini meet in Valentin's office for a working breakfast. They sit in an austere room next to the boardroom at the top of the building, lit by a curious window, round like a camera lens, which perfectly frames the Eiffel Tower rising in majestic isolation against the Paris sky. Valentin always works facing the window; watching the variations in light on the intricate girders helps him think.

A copious traditional continental breakfast awaits them on a table in the corner of the room. Valentin dunks his croissants in a bowl of coffee, while Benoît-Rey and Rossellini keep to lemon tea, toast without butter and just a smear of jam. They're conscious of their weight, keen to maintain their athletic physique. Rossellini plays tennis every day at the Tennis Club de Paris, between one and two p.m., no matter how much pressure he's under from work. Having finished his croissants, Valentin turns to him and launches his attack:

'I know we have little in common, you and I. But you're the person I want to convince, Rossellini, you most of all, because you're a key player. Part of our affair, probably the most important part, will be played out in the Finance Ministry and the surrounding milieus, as is often the case in this country, and that is your territory.' Rossellini drinks his tea without a glance at Valentin. 'I know you're reluctant and I well understand why. You think the game's over, and that you urgently need to rethink your future career. Let's look at things from a different angle. Whether you worry about your future now or in two months' time doesn't make much difference. In any case, it'll take you ten years to climb back to the top. Ten years is a long time. On the other hand, if we win, I disappear, no one likes the security service and dirty tricks, you get all the credit for the success, and the future's yours. In a nutshell, you've got a lot to gain, and absolutely nothing to lose that hasn't already been lost.'

Rossellini pours himself another cup of tea and adds another slice of lemon with slow, deliberate movements. He takes a sip, leans back in his chair and looks at Valentin for the first time.

'I came to more or less the same conclusions last night. Go on.'

'I've got a few contacts among Lagardère's sworn enemies. I won't go into detail, and I'm going to get my hands on their files – dropped charges, current proceedings, various libel cases. Pierre and I are going to reactivate all that. I expect you to arrange for Lagardère to receive a visit from the tax inspectors...'

'I can do that if you give me some ammunition. But a tax inspection is a drop in the ocean given what's at stake.'

'I know that. We'll carry out a campaign of harassment. But that's not the main thing. I want you to launch a stock market investigation into Matra share prices. Look for signs of insider dealing. On the radio this morning they announced a twenty-five per cent rise in the share price on opening.'

A cop. No more than a cop. Hopelessly thick. I should have known. Shit. Rossellini is very terse.

'I fear you're barking up the wrong tree, Valentin. Lagardère certainly wouldn't compromise the whole deal – a mega indus-trial deal – by doing something so stupid. It's not Matra's style.'

'Lagardère no, but Kim, Daewoo's CEO, would. He's the one who booked Fouquet's several days in advance. Would he miss out on an opportunity like this to make a quick buck, almost risk free? With his crooked ways? The evidence suggests not.' He stresses the word "evidence". 'He speculated, and he probably used the new stream of funds to grease the palms of his backers while he was at it. The stock market regulator will find out, and we'll have the key to Kim's sleaze operation.'

Rossellini has closed his eyes and is massaging his eyelids and the bridge of his nose. After all, seen in this light, it might not be impossible. He sits up.

'Let's say that you've convinced me, and let's set things in motion without wasting any time. But don't overestimate my contacts.'

'We'll cross-check my contacts and yours. You'll see, you'll be surprised. And besides, you have no option, Rossellini, and nei-ther do we. Make sure you do a good job.'

The solitary housing estate rises up in the middle of the Lorraine plateau, just above Pondange and its valley. It dominates the vast stretch of land which is bald on one side and has verdant woodland on the other. Half-empty car parks are dotted around the estate, a construction dating back to the last heyday of the iron and steel industry. It is well-maintained, recently renovated and the majority of the residents are unemployed. This morning, there's a biting wind and the few men and women who are leav-ing for work, dropping the kids off to school on the way, hurry towards their cars.

Two men in their thirties, athletic looking, with short hair, square jaws and inscrutable expressions, wearing work boots, jeans and leather jackets, are hanging around the building. Étienne Neveu's wife, a well-built woman with flaxen hair, is late. At last she emerges from block C, chivvying along two little girls, half dragging, half carrying them towards a battered Clio. She piles them on to the back seat, turns on the ignition, yanks the car into gear and drives off. The two men walk up to the door of block C, glance around, nobody in the lobby, too early, too cold for the young loafers. They go in, take the lift, third floor, the door on the left. One of them rings the bell. Silence. He rings again. Reluctant footsteps, and a sleepy voice enquires:

'What is it?'

'Étienne Neveu?'

'Yes...'

The man takes out a card wallet and presents it open in front of the spy hole, the colours of the French flag. Police. Étienne opens the door. He's in his pyjamas, barefoot, his hair dishevelled. He lets the two men in and they close the door softly behind them.

'Police. You are Étienne Neveu, you work at Daewoo Pondange, you were present yesterday during the occupation of the factory and at the time of the fire, and that night you claimed in public that you saw the arsonists. Is that correct?'

'Yes, that's correct.' He ushers them in. 'Come in, sit down.'

'No, we're in rather a hurry. We want you to come with us to Pondange police station to make a statement.'

'Right away?'

'Right away. You understand that it is crucial for our investigation. We'll drive you there and bring you back home as soon as we've finished. You can expect it to take a couple of hours.'

Two hours... There goes his lie-in to recover from the excitement of the day before. It's no joke, a fire. Sleep first, then slob around in my pyjamas in front of the TV, no wife and no kids. With a beer. Maybe even get a bit pissed, and then another snooze, so as to be on form for dinner. *I should have kept my mouth shut yesterday, fat lot of good it's going to do me...*

'Get dressed, Mr Neveu, we're waiting.'

To go to the police station, you've got to look smart, you don't want to find yourself in a position of inferiority. You never know, they might take advantage, the bastards. So, a clean pair of black jeans, Italian leather moccasins, a nice beige sweater and the brown parka. Satisfied glance in the mirror, and a little idea begins to form. Pondange, Aisha, why not? He's beginning to feel more cheerful...

The three men go downstairs together without exchanging a word. They meet no one in the lift. In the car park, the trio makes its way towards a grey Peugeot 206 where a man is sitting behind the wheel reading the *Républicain Lorrain*. He folds away the paper as they come towards the car. Perfectly synchronised, one of the men takes Étienne by the elbow and steers him towards the right rear door which he holds open for him, while the other opens the rear left door, gets in and sits down. Étienne leans forward to climb into the car, the man behind gives him a violent shove, and Étienne topples head first on to the back seat. The guy sitting inside the car guides his fall and pushes a wad soaked in chloroform under his nose, pressing down hard on his injured neck. His partner finishes bundling Étienne into the car, wedges him firmly in, barely a couple of convulsive jerks and the body is inert. Then he also gets in, slamming the door shut. The driver switches on the ignition, the three men exchange glances, the car slowly pulls away and moves towards the second car park which overlooks the Pondange valley. They drive between the edge of the woodland and a white van parked there, completely blocking the residents' view. The two passengers throw their police ID cards on to the front seat, get out of the Peugeot, grab Étienne's legs, pull him out of the car, load him on to one of their backs and vanish quickly into the trees.

After a few minutes' wait, everything is quiet, a man slides behind the wheel of the van, the Peugeot starts up, leaves the car park and turns on to the road to Nancy. The van follows at a distance.

The two men jog down overgrown, downhill paths through the woods as if training, taking turns to carry Étienne's limp body. Halfway down the incline, one of them points to a gap on the right, and the other follows him. They come to a halt on a concrete slab overhanging a scree-covered slope dotted with rocks. Étienne is deposited face-down on the slab. The taller of the two men presses his foot on the back of his neck and unwinds his long white silk scarf which he slips under Étienne's chin and around his forehead with precise movements. He leans forward, tests his foothold, and yanks hard with both hands. The cervical vertebrae snap cleanly making a dry crackling sound like a dead branch. One man takes the arms, the other the feet, hup-two, and they toss the body over the edge. It bounces on the scree then lands head first in a bush, dislocated. The killer winds the long white scarf around his neck again, zips his jacket up to the chin, and starts to walk away.

'Aren't we going to hide it with branches?'

'No. The more visible the body is, the easier it will be for the officials to treat it as an accident. And besides, this is the sealed-up entrance to a former iron mine shaft, the locals don't like coming here, old memories, probably, except in spring to hunt for morels. By then...'

17 October

The Pondange police station is halfway up a hill, in an elegant nineteenth-century mansion built of local yellow limestone. It stands in a garden which was once protected by high railings, when life there was fraught with danger, when the iron and steel-workers used to attack it with bulldozers and the cops locked up inside owed their salvation solely to the arrival of the riot police. That was a long time ago. Now the railings have been removed and the beautiful, sleepy villa in the centre of this tiny provincial town is surrounded by lawns.

The superintendent has assembled his officers, four men, in his first-floor office which occupies what probably used to be the master bedroom. It is a vast corner room with high coffered ceilings of dark wood, oak floorboards, two windows flooding the room with light, and a bare black marble mantelpiece running along one wall. The furniture – a desk, three armchairs, an oval table and a few very ordinary chairs – barely fills the space.

The officers are sitting around the table, a few sheets of paper and a ballpoint pen in front of them, listening carefully and obediently to their superintendent who stays standing. He always remains on his feet, there's never a chair for him. He paces up and down the room, his tall frame – close on six foot three of pure muscle – nearly filling the room. He maintains his physique with regular workouts and judo, and his waistline shows little evidence of the frequent meals eaten with the local bigwigs. His elegant, classic grey suit (tailor-made in Paris) and his dark red shirt and grey-and-red tie make him look slimmer, and he gives off a subtle whiff of eau de toilette and matching aftershave. With his experience – twenty-five years in the police rising through the ranks with a dogged determination – many think he'll end up chief superintendent in Nancy. Adding to his charm and authority, he speaks with a southern accent which ten years in Lorraine have barely mellowed.

'Yesterday I met the public prosecutor and Bastien, the investigating magistrate in charge of this case. For the time being, we are handling the investigation.' He stops, draws himself up, looks his men up and down and tugs at the creases in his jacket sleeves. 'I hope you realise what an opportunity this is for all of us here.' He starts pacing again. 'But it won't stay that way for long. If we don't make significant headway fast, it'll be handed to the Nancy judiciary police.' Another pause, the threat hangs in the air over the officers who gaze at the blank sheets of paper on the table and fidget with their ballpoint pens. The superintendent turns his back to his men and plants himself in front of the window overlooking the bottom of the valley and the Daewoo factory, or what's left of it. 'The firefighters are convinced it's arson. So it's vital we get results – and fast, for the sake of the valley's economy. We can't have people thinking that in Lorraine factories are burned down with impunity. It wouldn't be good for business or for jobs.'

'Right.' He moves to the end of the table, his hands lightly resting on its surface. 'So as not to waste any time, the magistrates in charge and I have drawn up an initial framework for the investigation. We can forget about gathering evidence from the scene of the fire – that can be left to the fire brigade's experts. They'll do a better job than we will. Besides, we're convinced that those mounds of cinders are unlikely to yield much, and it would take too long. We have decided to start by profiling. It's all the rage at the moment. Let's start with the French method: who benefits from the crime? Not the Daewoo bosses who are currently involved in a huge deal of national importance, the privatisation of Thomson, and the last thing they want is to be in the news at the moment.' A pause. 'What's more, the factory's insurance expired a month ago, so no compensation...

'Not convinced?' A mutter from the officers but the superintendent carries on, oblivious.

'...nor the unions, who were in the middle of pay and bonus negotiations which the boss agreed to fund by selling the stock. No more stock, no bonuses. The crime benefits neither the bosses nor the unions, so we can eliminate them from the investigation, which narrows the field. Now, the American method: we've drawn up a profile of the typical arsonist. What's the profile of the arsonist? If the bosses and the unions have been ruled out, we're looking for an individual who was there during the strike, active, fired-up, a non-unionised maverick, probably a hothead. Most likely someone with a history of petty crime.' He straightens up. 'Any comments?'

There aren't. In any case, the question is purely rhetorical; the superintendent isn't in the habit of consulting his subordinates.

'So our work plan is all mapped out.' He goes over to a flip-chart, picks up a felt-tip and writes as he speaks. 'First, draw up a list of those on the premises during the afternoon and evening on the day of the fire and note their whereabouts at various times, however approximate. Two of you take care of that.' Glances around. Berjamin and Loriot. 'Talk to the security guards, then the workers. I want that list on my desk in forty-eight hours at the latest. It won't be as difficult as it sounds – according to our sources there weren't more than eighty people in the factory at the time of the fire. But I want an absolutely reliable list. Make sure you get it.'

The officers take notes.

'So as not to waste any time, while your colleagues are drawing up those lists, you Lambert, and you Michel, start questioning the key witnesses. The security guards first, they're impartial observers. The Nancy security company 3G, which employs them, has been very cooperative. It has supplied us with the security guards' duty rotas and contact details. Start with the guards on the second shift. They were called in as backup at around three p.m. They don't know anyone in the company so they won't be biased. They were patrolling the factory continuously from three p.m. until the fire broke out so they've got an overall view of events. Also question Ali Amrouche, a decent guy who was directly involved in the whole business, always trying to calm things down, and who should be useful in helping us to determine the next stage of the investigation.

'Once these preliminaries are completed, we'll routinely question all those identified by Berjamin and Loriot as being on the premises. And in taking witness statements, be on the alert for hearsay: who was overexcited, who's violent, who's a hooligan. And through hearsay the name of our arsonist will eventually emerge. See if I'm not right on this'. A glance at his subordinates. 'People aren't stupid. They know a lot, often you just have to listen.' *That's what you call experience,* muses the superintendent. He puts the top back on the felt-tip and places it on the ledge of the flipchart. 'To work, and good luck.'

Valentin's gaze dissects the man who walks into his office: tall, slim, getting on for fifty, wearing an elegant navy pinstripe suit, royal blue printed tie, Hermès most likely; ink-dark hair, a bit thin on top, carefully plastered down; a mobile, smiling face with a high forehead. The ex-cop has put on the uniform of his new profession, private investigator for the insurance industry. Valentin gets up to greet him, walks around the desk, his gaze piercing as always. Finesse rather than force, a form of prosperity, that's a good sign. But beneath the veneer of elegance is the cop, cynical, burned-out, tough. *Just what I need.* He shakes his hand, gestures him to sit in an armchair.

'Thank you for coming, Mr Montoya. Coffee?'

'Yes please. Strong, no sugar.'

Middle-aged female assistant, copper tray, china cups, Italian espresso. So far, so good. Montoya feels a mixture of curiosity and slight apprehension as to what will follow. *A former security service chief. Respect. But there are skeletons in my cupboard. He's the one who asked me to come here, let him spit it out.*

'I heard a lot about you when I still worked for the police...'

Simple code between ex-cops, or a bit more? What does he know?

'...I'm handling a case that requires intelligence, professionalism. Imagination too, a lot of imagination.' Big smile. 'And no scruples.'

Montoya drinks his coffee and puts down his cup. Here we go, smiles back.

'What makes you think I'm your man?'

'1990, Tangier, the Hakim family.'

A violent flash, white and blue, the old town, the sea, a very big sting, dangerous, no cover, organised with his best informers, the Hakim brothers. Contact is made out at sea, the US Drug Enforcement Administration turns up. Why? How? A fuck-up. The traffickers chuck the goods into the sea, the Hakim brothers eliminate the traffickers, and he ends up killing an American agent and sinking the DEA's boat. Then he and the Hakims make off with the only boat whose motor's still working and what can be salvaged of the cargo, leaving the rest of the DEA crew adrift in an old tub. A French police officer is not supposed to shoot an American agent to protect his informants. The killing is blamed on unidentified traffickers on the run, and the affair is hushed up to avoid a serious diplomatic incident with the Americans. But he's fired. Only a very few people know about his true role. *Don't underestimate Valentin. Does that give him a hold over me? Yes, without a doubt.* Not all those involved are dead. The Americans are aggressive. And he needs to keep a few aces up his sleeve. Have to start bidding to find out.

'I'm with you, and I'm listening.'

'It's not a very big case. Or to be precise, it's a secondary aspect of a very big case. Around two to four weeks' work, less action than in Tangier, no shooting. But I need you because you have experience and a reputation for working fast. A hundred to two hundred thousand francs, depending on results. Well?'

'The trouble with men like you, Valentin, is that when you decide you want someone, you don't really give them any choice, do you?'

'No, I don't. Reputations are precarious in the insurance world.'

'Supposing I were interested?'

'A Daewoo factory burned down a few days ago in Lorraine, at Pondange. I want you to find me a coherent explanation, backed up by evidence, fabricated or not...' A pause, a half-smile. 'I don't mind either way. I want you to explain to me how the bosses set the factory on fire and their reasons for doing so. My sources tell me that you work as a private investigator for insurance companies on a lot of claims of this kind.' Montoya nods. 'So you have the expertise and the contacts.'

'Go on, say it, a reputation for frame-ups and dirty tricks from my days in the drug squad. Is that it?'

'Exactly.'

'It will be a pleasure to work with you. I'm sure I'll learn a lot. So, I'm in.' Pause. 'I can't drag an insurance company into this. I'll need a cover, of course.'

'Of course. I'll arrange one.'

18 October

Karim walks cautiously along the path through the woods from Pondange up to the entrance to the disused iron mine. He listens out for the slightest sound, not wanting anyone to see him or follow him. Up there, under the scree blocking the entrance, he's dug out a well-camouflaged tunnel and uses the entrance to the galleries as a storeroom for his various little businesses. It's an isolated spot, as the local people keep well away from the former mines. He only comes here very early in the morning and has never bumped into anyone. Twenty metres from the scree, he stops. A dark mass in a green bramble bush, a few metres from the foot of the scree. Out of the ordinary spells danger. Standing stock still, barely breathing, he listens. Scraping, sliding, faint crackling, birds taking flight, birdsong, nothing unusual. He approaches slowly, moving as little as possible. From ten metres away, there's no mistaking it, it's a human body, wearing black jeans and a brown parka. Caught head first in the bramble bush, his neck probably broken. Glance up to the top of the slope. Thrown from up there, probably. If he'd fallen, he'd be closer to the rocks. Karim removes his shoes and takes a few steps forward in his socks. He crouches down and can clearly make out the profile. Étienne Neveu. Rooted to the spot, his heart thumping, adrenaline rush. Étienne, so close, his arm around his shoulders, the shared spliff, the porn images, the little business deals, a friend you could say. *Weep my heart, in your despair, your solitude.* And a new image: the night of the fire, Étienne wandering from group to group between the cars, as if oscillating between the darkness and the flames, distraught: 'I saw the guys who started the fire.' Nobody was listening to him, but you heard him and you thought, 'Good, that'll keep the cops off my back.' Now, Étienne's been killed. A fire, a murder, big names. *And you, the Arab, the kid, the small-time wheeler-dealer, you risk ten years' inside, minimum, or your hide.* Gotta play this carefully. He straightens up, pins and needles in his legs. Go back down to Pondange leaving as little trace as possible. Think fast. Suddenly: an image. Quignard in an anorak and woolly hat, sitting on the bonnet of his car, brightly lit up by showers of sparks, and Étienne in front of him, probably – no, certainly – saying, 'I saw the guys who started the fire.' Perhaps signing his death warrant. Tell the cops about the body, see how they react, I'll soon find out.

At the police station, Lieutenant Émile Lambert bustles about, conscious of his responsibilities. He interviews the first witness.

Robert Duffaut, born 10 August 1963 in Nantes.
Residing at 29 rue d'Auxonne, Nancy. Profession:
Security guard employed by 3G, based in Nancy since 3
March 1996.
The witness states he was sent to the Daewoo factory
by his security company, 3G in Nancy, to provide
backup for the company's permanent team of two
security guards, who are employed by the same company,
3G, and who were confronted with disturbances among
the personnel which they believed could turn dangerous
if security were not maintained.
    He states he arrived on the premises at 15.00 hours,
accompanied by his colleague. They immediately started
patrolling the premises, and continued to do so until
21.30 hours, when they returned to the porter's lodge
to make their report. They were both still there when
the fire alarm went off at 21.43 hours.
Q. Who raised the alarm?
A. A man came running in. He was shouting: 'The place
is on fire,' and pointing towards the warehouses. I
don't know this man's name.
Q. When you were doing your rounds, did you notice any
particular incidents or suspicious behaviour?
A. I would like to mention that around 15.15 hours, my
colleague and I walked past the waste ground behind
the factory, and there, a young North African-looking
individual had set up a barbecue and was selling
kebabs. This barbecue was about ten metres from the
place where the fire started a little later. We made
a few inquiries. This individual is called Karim
Bouziane.
Q. In your opinion, could this barbecue have had
something to do with the outbreak of the fire?
A. I think so. Furthermore, around 19.00 hours, a

minor dustbin fire was reported in the main corridor
between the factory and the warehouse. It was quickly
extinguished by members of the Health and Safety
committee before we arrived on the scene. When we
arrived a few minutes later, we noted that embers
had been thrown into the dustbin, intentionally or
otherwise, and were certainly the cause of the dustbin
fire. As far as we could ascertain, those embers came
from the barbecue.

I must also inform you that around 17.00 hours, we
patrolled the stockrooms and we noted that a group
of several individuals were smoking marijuana in the
vicinity of highly flammable packaging materials.
Q. Do you know who their dealer is?
A. We have no proof, but the name bandied around by
those smoking is once again that of Karim Bouziane.
Apparently he sold the dope along with his sausages.
Q. In your view, could Karim Bouziane have set fire to
the factory?
A. There's no concrete proof. I don't know if he did,
or why he would want to. But in any case, he had the
wherewithal.
Q. Among your colleagues, or the individuals present
during the day in question, did you hear any names
being mentioned as possible instigators of the fire?
A. I did not talk to any Daewoo personnel after the
fire. But the name being whispered among the workers
is that of Karim Bouziane.
Q. Is there anything else you would like to mention?
A. No. Nothing else comes to mind.

'Nice work, Lieutenant Lambert,' comments the superintendent. 'You see the effectiveness of this method. Karim Bouziane may be a serious lead. But let's not rush, let's be methodical. You carry on listening to what people have to tell you, but if they don't spontaneously mention Karim Bouziane, you ask them discreetly about him, his barbecue and his dope dealing.'

The door of the superintendent's office is flung open; a very young, podgy uniformed officer bursts into the room, a terrified look on his face. The superintendent protests.

'Dumont, you don't enter my office without knocking.' Then, concerned: 'What's going on?'

'An anonymous phone call, superintendent. A body near the entrance to the mine above Pondange.'

The superintendent's infuriated. *That's all we need. Just as the investigation into the fire is getting underway. But what else can we do?*

Visit the scene. Étienne Neveu's body is there, in full view, lying in the bushes at the bottom of the scree. His wife had reported him missing the previous evening. He didn't go far, mutters a cop. The anonymous phone call: probably a lone early-morning walker. Then the deputy public prosecutor arrives and they make an initial report. Height of the scree, position of the body, neck very likely broken, looks like a fall. At the top of the scree slope, directly above the body, discovery of a footpath that leads directly to the car park on the estate where Étienne Neveu lived.

During the afternoon, information begins to filter in. Étienne Neveu seems to have been the victim of a fatal fall having taken a shortcut through the woods down to Pondange from his home. Death seems to have occurred between twenty-four and forty-eight hours before the discovery of the body. It seems highly likely that it was an accident. But the officials remain cautious, and are waiting for the result of the autopsy before closing the case.

Karim walks into the offices of the lawyer, Lavaudant, a stone's throw from the Place Stanislas in Nancy. It is a magnificent high-ceilinged room, the walls covered with floor-to-ceiling book-shelves in a dark wood filled with books bound in red leather. The vast windows are masked by thick red velvet curtains. It's late, and Lavaudant doesn't like Karim turning up in his working life unannounced. Apparently it's an emergency, and the meeting will be brief. He watches him cross the room, supple, relaxed in his movements, he fills the space. Always the same intensity of desire, despite the passing years, the wife and two kids at home, his wealthy clientele. *I may be a big shot but I can't resist those round buttocks, the taste of his golden skin, the acid smell of the nape of his neck. My hands start to tremble when this ruffian comes near me. I'll pay for this, one day.* Karim stares at the hands the lawyer has placed flat in front of him on his desk. *Always the same, you're dying to bugger me, and when you have, you cry with shame. I've got you in a vice.* He smiles and sits down.

'I need you, Claude.'

'I'm listening.'

'The Daewoo fire...'

'A nasty business.'

'I've just realised that I fit the profile of the arsonist.'

'Did you start the fire?'

'Of course not. Why would I have done that? You know, arson's out of my league. Besides, I'd have come to see you sooner. No. For the cops I'm the easiest scapegoat. I was at Daewoo during the strike. I made a barbecue and sold kebabs all afternoon, not far from the spot where the fire started. With a bit of dope too. I'm Arab and a dealer. If the cops arrest me, nobody will be surprised and nobody will defend me.'

'What do you want me to do about it?'

'The cops have got to leave me out of this, and you have to tell them to before they bang me up.'

'Can you see me saying to the superintendent at Pondange, whom I don't happen to know: "Please note, superintendent, that Mr Karim Bouziane has nothing to do with the fire at the Daewoo factory"?'

'No, but I can see you having a word with your father-in-law Quignard and him passing it on to the superintendent. He'll be able to convince him. They see each other every day. You'll do it, Claude, because when a man falls into the cops' hands, you never know what he might end up telling them.'

It is already late, the Gare de Lyon is gradually emptying, the rush is over at Le Train Bleu restaurant above the station. It is a place where Rossellini and Kaltenbach, the assistant director of the Revenue Department, are in the habit of eating, around the corner from the Ministry, and quiet at this time of day. Granted, the food is bland and expensive, boil-in-a-bag, but neither of them is a foodie, the wine is adequate and the setting ornate and luxurious with late nineteenth-century-style frescos, sculptures, and stucco, and a monumental silver meat trolley. The entire decor provides a welcome change of scene and fires their imagination.

Rossellini sinks on to the leather banquette and gazes up at the ceiling. So it's true. Kaltenbach confirms that the senior ministry officials are all hostile to the choice of Matra. Rossellini trusts him. It's the first time he's felt relaxed since that nightmare evening, not least thanks to the wine. At this precise moment, he decides to throw himself body and soul into Valentin's game. And he attacks.

'Lagardère's crazy about horses...'

Kaltenbach, not really surprised, looks up from his plate of chocolate profiteroles. Lagardère, now we're getting there.

'I'm listening.' Smile. 'But me, horses...'

'Of course. Me neither. But the financial set-up involved...'

'Now you're talking.'

'Lagardère set up a holding company that siphons off 0.2 per cent of Matra's revenues.' Nod. 'Its purpose is to pay the salaries of the group's ten most senior managers. The surplus profit is shared between Lagardère and his son.'

'So far, nothing unusual for this type of family company.'

'Wait. For several years, Lagardère's stud farms have been incorporated into the structure of the holding company and Lagardère has used the surplus to make up the losses from his horses. A Matra shareholder filed a complaint four years ago for misuse of company property. The affair followed its course, as they say. In other words, it was more or less hushed up. But as luck would have it, this week it will result in Lagardère being indicted.'

'Clever move. Have you got any more like that up your sleeve? Waiter, two brandies.'

'Don't you think that the management of the stud farms should be investigated by the tax authorities? Supposing the losses have been hugely overestimated and that Lagardère used some creative accounting to avoid paying tax...'

'An interesting possibility. Do you have anything to back it up?'

From his inside jacket pocket Rossellini takes out a few folded sheets of paper which he slips to Kaltenbach, who skims them quickly and nods.

'I see the stables in question are at Chantilly. I happen to know some tax inspectors in Picardy, who, without exactly being distributionists, find it outrageous that Lagardère's tax return is similar to that of someone on the minimum wage. I can get them on to it. I can't guarantee results, the evidence is rather slim.'

'I'm not interested in the results, but in the tax inspection. And the sooner the better. We'll take care of the publicity.'

19 *October*

The alarm goes off and Ali Amrouche surfaces groggily. It's been like this every night since the fire, long hours of insomnia followed by collapse into a deep sleep as dawn breaks. He's been summoned to the police station, as a witness. To what? The end of the world? He gets up, his body stiff. He keeps the shutters closed because from his window he can see the charred remains of Daewoo's hangars, metal carcasses and ash heaps, and he can't bear it. He showers and shaves carefully. You need to watch out when you go to the cops. Always a worry. You can do what you like as far as the cops are concerned, you'll always be the Arab. He goes downstairs. On the ground floor is a large room bathed in light, furnished with three big armchairs, the TV and house plants. It looks out on to his garden, a square of lawn and a little vegetable patch, well maintained, even pampered. He loves this house, the only plot of land he's ever owned. He wants to die here. A bitter taste in his mouth. He'll have to work for a few more years before he can retire. I'd carved out a nice little job for myself, no pressure, everyone knew me. And then the fire, with probable unemployment to come. Will it mean selling the house in order to survive before finally ending up in an old people's home? Fear in his belly and rage in his heart. He moves into the kitchen, a quick coffee and a big cheese sandwich. The police station is a ten-minute walk away. In other circumstances it would be a pleasant stroll on a cool, bright day.

Ali Amrouche, born on 28 February 1944 in Tizi Ouzou, Algeria. Resident in France since 1964, nationality French. Address: 7 rue des Bois, Pondange.
Q. You are a staff representative at the Daewoo factory?
A. Yes, I am a staff representative.
Q. What part did you play in the events of 14 October?

Amrouche gets up, paces up and down, speaking vehemently, his words tumbling out fast. The lieutenant can't keep up and soon stops taking notes.

'Things turned bad. It started with the accident in the finishing section and Rolande Lepetit being fired by the Head of HR. A pathetic guy, the Head of HR, I tell you. Nobody was prepared to take that lying down. She was such a courageous woman, a good worker, bringing up her kid on her own, with a dependent mother to look after as well…'

The lieutenant tries to steer Amrouche back on track: 'Sit down. We're not here to discuss Rolande Lepetit's character…'

But Amrouche doesn't even hear him: 'I was the one who went to see Nourredine, who told him. Naturally, since I'm the staff rep, I can't let them get away with that. I wanted to talk to him about what we could do for Rolande. I trusted him, I thought he could help me get her reinstated.' Amrouche speaks faster, losing control, and the lieutenant gives up trying to slow him down. 'But he made things worse, he accused Maréchal. But Maréchal had nothing to do with it. Nourredine started urging violence, he suggested setting fire to the lorries and overturning the engineer's car. He was the one who wanted to lock the senior managers in, and led the group that broke down the door to the managers' offices. After that, I don't know, I was in a meeting, but he must have got into a fight, he ended up with a broken nose and was covered in blood. And I don't know whether or not he was involved in the dustbin fire, there were traces of soot on his clothes. Maybe he'd already tried to start a fire. When I saw him again in the cafeteria, things had become really serious. At that point he was proposing to pour chemicals into the river. I was against it and he called me a traitor. But I'm older than him, I used to work in the blast furnaces, and people respect me around here. He's a terrorist, that's what he is, and I told him so. Then he hit me and said: "Terrorist, I'll show you what a terrorist is. We're all going to go up in smoke." I don't know what would have happened if the other workers hadn't separated us. And then he left the cafeteria and I didn't see him again. I went back to the offices. And the fire started not long after. I think he started the fire.'

Amrouche stops talking. The lieutenant takes charge again.

'We're going to sum all that up calmly, point by point. Give me time to write down your replies, for the statement.'

Amrouche, utterly drained, continues his account in half sentences, and in a more neutral tone. The lieutenant conscientiously starts going through the motions:

```
Q. Do you know Karim Bouziane?
A. Yes.
Q. In your opinion, could he have been involved in
this attack?
A. No. He's a little schemer, not an arsonist.
Q. What name or names are being bandied around among
your colleagues as people who could have started the
fire?
A. The name that kept coming up from the beginning is
Nourredine. I think he's the terrorist who started the
fire, even if I don't have any evidence.
```

When Lambert makes his report, the superintendent is surprised and puzzled by Amrouche's vehemence.

'I told you not to be in too much of a hurry. We can't discount this testimony. Check up to see if this Nourredine has a record. Nourredine what, by the way?'

'Nourredine Hamidi.'

'Anything on file is of interest, from teenage fights to nicking things from the supermarket. Anything that went down on record, at one time or another. This afternoon, I'm going to Étienne Neveu's funeral. To gauge the mood and listen to what people are saying. We'll review the situation together tomorrow morning, before getting back to business.'

The afternoon sun is warm in the little cemetery sheltered from the winds, on the outskirts of the town, where there's almost a holiday atmosphere. A brief ceremony for Étienne Neveu. A simple blessing in a tiny chapel, not even a funeral: his wife wants to bury him in her village, up on the plateau, about fifty kilometres away, far from the town, the factories, the Arabs. The priest reads prayers in hushed tones to a compact group composed of the widow, her parents and her two children, all wearing black. Outside the chapel and a little apart, Quignard, in a grey coat, hat in hand, contemplates the mourners. Poor woman, poor kids. Recalls Etienne's jittery voice, *I saw the guys who started the fire, you know.*

He suddenly feels shattered, devoid of willpower. All night he had turned his ambitious plans over and over in his mind, the alliance between Europe and Asia in boom industry sectors. *With me as the architect. My grand design, my work, my contacts...* and it would all be compromised if an idiot happened to be in the wrong place at the wrong time. *I saw the guys who started the fire.* The full impact of the impending scandal. *Me, in the eye of the cyclone, powerful, removed from the action. But I'm probably too old.* The following morning, Tomaso was on the phone: 'Problem sorted.' Not a word more. He, careful not to ask any questions. Then one thing leading to another: the discovery of the body, an accident, no investigation. Disconcertingly obvious, simple. *I'll help his family.* The superintendent comes over to him. The two men greet each other. Quignard, in a low voice:

'Well, superintendent, can we expect a rapid conclusion to the investigation into the fire? It's so important for the valley...'

'Too soon to be able to tell.' A long silence. The superintendent lets his gaze rest on the group of Étienne's friends gathered in front of the chapel. Karim has just joined them. 'You know the factory well, what do you make of Karim Bouziane?'

'He's a bit of a delinquent, but nothing serious. He's someone who knows exactly where the power is and where his interests lie.'

'What about Nourredine Hamidi?'

Quignard turns his head and looks at the superintendent, who doesn't move a muscle.

'A different kettle of fish. Violent, an agitator. The day of the disturbances, 14 October, all day he kept adding fuel to the flames.' A smile. 'Until they spread,' he adds meaningfully.

'Ali Amrouche?'

'A trustworthy man, I'm going to recruit him for the emergency committee that my company's forming to manage the Daewoo personnel while they're temporarily laid off, and afterwards if need be.'

Karim watches the exchange between Quignard and the superintendent. Several times, while they're talking, the two men look at him. Smug. Quignard's expression didn't escape him. He hasn't wasted his afternoon. It's back to business as usual. He's there, slightly self-conscious, standing on the fringe of the tight-knit group made up of the entire packaging department, gathered around Nourredine, silent, emotional and ill at ease. Memories, the amazing desk, the TV, the dope, most of that was thanks to Étienne, a crazy nice guy, and dead. A really stupid accident. Maybe one spliff too many? Down there, behind the hostile family unit, dead and buried according to a rite that for most of them is essentially foreign. Dead like the factory that died in the fire. Life's falling apart.

The girls from finishing didn't know him so well, they've come mainly for the pleasure of meeting up with each other, which they don't often get the chance to do now. They whisper, such a young guy, and with a wife and two kids, that's sad, it really is. The woods in autumn, where accidents can easily happen. Rolande talks about dead leaves making the ground slippery. 'How's Émilienne doing?' 'Not very well, she can't get over the shock of losing the baby. They're talking about taking her to a psychiatrist, that's not good.' A silence. Since the fire, things haven't been good for anyone. 'What about Aisha?' 'Not here,' says Rolande. 'She stays stuck indoors all day. I think she's having a hard time with her father.' Silence.

Maréchal and Amrouche remain apart, behind a headstone.

'Quignard asked me to request that you go and see him in his office, at ten o'clock tomorrow morning.'

Wary, aggressive. 'What does he want from me?' Maréchal smiles.

'To offer you a job.'

Amrouche, shaken, speechless with uncontrolled emotion.

In the chapel, the priest has fallen silent. Quignard is the first to walk past the coffin and genuflect. Then he bows to the widow.

'My condolences.'

'Thank you for everything you've done for my family, Mr Quignard.'

He clasps her hand for a long time. 'I am only doing my duty.' Then he walks back to the car park at the entrance to the cemetery where his car and driver are waiting, and stays talking to Maréchal for a long time. He says goodbye to each of those who are leaving, Karim, Nourredine, Amrouche (*See you tomorrow? In my office?*). When Rolande walks past, Maréchal stops her and introduces her to Quignard.

'Ms Lepetit, I am now the authorised representative of Daewoo.

I have quashed the regrettable decision to dismiss you. You are of course reinstated. I wanted to inform you myself.'

Rolande, her face expressionless, seems indecisive, at a loss for words. She falters.

'That's good news.'

And she hurries off to join the girls who are making their way back to town on foot.

'She's a bit uptight, your protégée. A little "thank you" wouldn't kill her.'

20 October

At the police station, Lieutenant Lambert is handing over to Lieutenant Michel. Today the first witness to be interviewed, security guard Schnerb.

Gaston Schnerb, born on 5 June 1939 in Metz, residing at 26 rue de la Fraternité, Pondange, security guard employed by 3G for four years and assigned to the porter's lodge at Daewoo since the company opened.
Q. Where were you during the day of the disturbances at Daewoo?
A. My colleague and I came on duty at midday. We were supposed to finish at 20.00, but at the request of our superiors we remained until the premises were evacuated at approximately 22.00. On our arrival, we were informed that the workers had downed tools, so we telephoned our superiors who gave us very strict instructions: stop the patrols; avoid provoking trouble; keep a note of everything in the daybook. We followed these instructions to the letter. Two other security guards sent as backup by 3G arrived at Daewoo at 15.05 and covered the patrol duty. So we didn't budge from the porter's lodge until the premises were evacuated at around 22.00.
Q. The porter's lodge was occupied during the disturbances. What exactly happened?
A. At 13.12 some employees turned up at the security

control centre. They were led by Nourredine Hamidi,
who entered and informed us that he was taking charge
of opening and shutting the gates. We allowed him to
do so, following our instructions. At 13.50 three
lorries arrived to pick up some goods. Nourredine
Hamidi wanted to prevent them from entering the
factory, but he was unable to operate and so close the
automatic gates. We did not intervene. The lorries
were slowed down by the workers from the second shift
trying to enter the factory at the same time. Then
Nourredine Hamidi took it into his head to set fire
to the empty pallets stacked near the porter's lodge
and push them under the engine of the leading lorry to
blow it up. He was in a state of extreme agitation,
shouting: 'I'm going to burn the whole place down.'
Faced with the prospect of a degenerating situation,
the drivers decided to turn back.
Q. Are there usually empty pallets stacked up near the
porter's lodge?
A. No. I didn't see who stacked them there. It was
probably done before we came on duty.
Q. Then what happened?
A. At 16.30 the executives began to leave the factory,
by car, as usual. But Nourredine Hamidi hadn't calmed
down. As the third car drove up, he stood right in
front of the bonnet to prevent it from moving forward,
and he and some of his workmates overturned it. Then
he clambered on to the car yelling: 'We're going to
lock the bosses in.' He marched at the head of the
group and even from a distance we could see people
smashing in the main door of the office building and
storming inside. Then we found ourselves alone again
in the porter's lodge.
Following this, some executives pulled up at the
gate wanting to leave. We opened the gate for them
and they departed. They told us that there were only
five people left in the offices, including the CEO.
Not long after that, at 18.46, there was a fire alert
regarding a dustbin fire inside the factory. We stayed
put. During the fire alert, Ali Amrouche escorted

the CEO and the remaining four managers to the gate,
telling them to get away as quickly as possible. He
looked terrified but he didn't tell us why, or of whom
he was afraid.

At 19.15 Nourredine Hamidi and Hafed Rifaai came
back, just the two of them, to the porter's lodge.
Nourredine was covered in soot and dried blood, he must
have got into a fight. When we told him the managers
had all left he pushed us, my colleague and myself,
and grabbed the daybook and set fire to it, issuing
threats like: 'I'm going to burn the whole place
down.' I clearly remember thinking at the time that
this character was unhinged and a pyromaniac. Hafed
Rifaai tried to calm him down without success. The two
of them left and headed for the cafeteria, it must
have been around 19.30. More workers reappeared with
Hafed Rifaai at around 21.00 to review the question
of overnight security with us. Nourredine Hamidi was
not among them and things became much calmer. Then, at
21.43 precisely, the fire alarm went off...

Q. Who raised the alarm?

A. A man who came running out of the stockroom but
I was unable to identify him. We came out of the
porter's lodge and saw the smoke, so we rushed to call
the fire brigade. They arrived twelve minutes later.

Q. Do you think that Nourredine Hamidi set the Daewoo
factory on fire?

A. It wouldn't surprise me. Although I have no proof,
of course.

Q. Do you know Karim Bouziane?

A. Yes, he's been at Daewoo from the beginning. Our
colleagues told us about a barbecue behind the factory
on the day of the disturbances.

Q. Could he have set fire to the factory deliberately?

A. We know Karim Bouziane well, and have known him
for a long time. He's a wheeler-dealer, but he's not
a hothead and he's not dangerous. We don't think he
can be the arsonist. But someone else could have used
the embers from the barbecue if there were any left
smouldering.

Q. What names have you heard the workers mention in
connection with this act of arson?
A. The only name that's been going around since the
beginning, since the night of the fire, when everyone
was on the roundabout watching the factory burn, is
that of Nourredine Hamidi. What's more, as far as we
know he is the only person to have made public threats
against the factory.

The superintendent puts Lieutenant Michel's transcription of the statement down on the desk.

'This time, we've got him. You and Lambert have done an excellent job. The suspect is clearly identified. We won't question him straight away, but we'll build up a precise timetable of his movements between 20.00 hours, when he left the porter's lodge with Hafed Rifaai heading for the cafeteria, and 21.43 hours when the fire alert was given. According to Amrouche, a whole lot went on. We'll concentrate on the cafeteria, and on that time slot of less than two hours. According to the lists drawn up by your colleagues, Rolande Lepetit spent the whole afternoon and evening there. Question her before moving on to trickier witnesses like Hafed Rifaai or the suspect himself. But watch out, she seems to be a prickly character.'

Montoya saunters casually up to the Hôtel Lutétia. He's meeting Eugénie Flachat at seven o'clock in the bar and he's early. Tomorrow he leaves for Lorraine, for the valley of Pondange, where he lived for ten years as a child and which left him with only painful memories. The idea of returning after thirty-five years, for a trivial case that stinks of shit, makes him feel uncomfortable. He thought he was impervious to the ghosts of the past. Well he wasn't. Had he given in to Valentin's blackmail? Not necessarily. He didn't really believe his story. So what was it then? To revisit the place where he spent his childhood? Unlikely. To escape from the excruciating boredom of routine insurance investigations? Valentin's offer is hardly more exciting. *Don't try and fathom it. I took it on because it came along and because Valentin intrigues me.* Montoya hangs around in the lobby to kill time. Displayed conspicuously on the wall by the door is a framed, handwritten certificate that states:

> Hôtel Lutétia has been named the official hotel
> of the 50th Anniversary Committee for D-day –
> the Battle of Normandy and the Liberation of Europe

The 50th Anniversary Committee for D-day in this hotel, requisitioned by the German army during the Occupation and used to house its officers, subsequently a repatriation centre for returning deportees after the war, was no doubt symbolic, but of what? Without knowing why, he feels a growing sense of unease. A bitter taste in his mouth. Increasingly frequent these days. *Now, I really need a drink, a brandy.* He strides across the main lounge where a few journalists are talking in low voices, a photographer clicks madly at two faces, celebrities no doubt, no clue who they are, and American tourists are having pre-dinner drinks. At the far end is a dark, narrow bar under a low ceiling, done out in wood panelling and carpeting like a snug retreat. Barely six or seven tables, only one still free at this hour of the evening, the first on the right by the door. He sinks into an ample, low armchair and orders a vintage brandy. There's blues playing in the background, but the music can hardly be heard above the din of conversation and the clinking of the shakers and glasses. He cups the brandy balloon in his hands, without moving at first, until he gets a first whiff of the aroma, then warms it with tiny movements. The liquid is amber, almost dense, he inhales it, eyes closed, what a pleasure. *Tonight, I'm meeting a beautiful, young, intelligent woman with whom I'll never have sex. Tomorrow, I'm leaving this city which I love. And in a few days, I'll be fifty.* Bitterness and frustration swirl around with the complex, sublime smell of the brandy.

When he opens his eyes, Eugénie Flachat is sitting opposite him. Mid-length hair the colour of... brandy, exactly, tumbling over her shoulders, fine features, a clear expression, nothing too remarkable except those grey-green eyes, a mountain lake in a storm, frozen waters. He raises his glass towards her and takes a long, warm sip. She orders with a contrite smile as if to apologise: a *Murmure* – champagne, blackcurrant liqueur and amaretto. She always has a *Murmure* at the Lutétia. Nobody's perfect.

Eugénie Flachat is a loss adjustor in the accident division of a big insurance firm and often when she has a dubious case to deal with she calls on the services of Charles Montoya, turned private investigator after more than twenty years in the police force, mostly in the drug squad. They are an efficient team, she deals with officialdom and he pokes around in dustbins.

She leans towards him, speaking clearly, in a low voice, creating a bubble of intimacy around them in the crowded bar.

'You're right, Daewoo's insured with us. Or rather, was insured. I'll come back to that.' Hesitation in her green eyes. 'I'll try and summarise the case for you, from the beginning. The factory has been operational for two years. It's never made any money. In fact, it has always lost astronomical amounts.' A pause. 'There are two reasons why.' Montoya, with a little smile, sinks deeper into his armchair. The green eyes have become two blocks of ice, the sharp intellectual mind swings into gear, a real delight. 'First of all, the factory, which is supposed to manufacture cathode ray tubes, was designed to produce five hundred thousand tubes a year whereas it's internationally accepted that the profitability threshold is a million units. That could be possibly put down to managerial incompetence, you see it all the time. The second matter is more awkward. The factory almost exclusively buys from and sells to Daewoo subsidiaries in Eastern Europe, Poland in particular. Seventy per cent of its business is transacted with its Warsaw subsidiary. It is a textbook blueprint for tax evasion or money laundering. On the one hand you just need to raise the prices of the parts you purchase, and on the other to sell the finished products at a loss, and the money disappears into accounting black holes.'

'And what keeps the factory going?'

'Subsidies. EU mainly. It's in a region that comes under the European Development Plan, where the tap is full on. National, regional and local subsidies are also pouring in, unmonitored, the spectre of the iron and steelworks industry haunts everyone.'

'Could it be a system for diverting EU subsidies towards the former Eastern bloc countries?'

Eugénie leans back in her armchair, sips her cocktail, an absent look in her eyes. Then leans towards him again.

'I find that difficult to answer because I don't know how what I'm going to tell you can be of use, Charles. But I trust you, after six years of working together... Whatever happens, my company and I will be kept out of the frame?'

'Of course.'

'Siphoning off subsidies is the most likely scenario, but there's another, more sinister theory. We could possibly be dealing with a major embezzlement operation. The manager of Daewoo Warsaw is a curious character. In Korea, he had a few problems with the law for having bribed a senior government official with a rather large sum of Daewoo's money, and then blackmailing him with the threat of disclosure so as to recover the money for himself.'

'Clever.'

'Instead of firing him, Daewoo appointed him CEO in Poland.'

'That opens up new avenues.'

'I think it does. My glass is empty, Charles, and I have more to tell you.'

They wait in silence while the barman serves them another brandy and another *Murmure*, before Eugénie continues.

'The most surprising thing is the fire insurance policy. First of all, it was hugely inflated in relation to the value of the building.'

'Extensions might have been planned but never built.'

'Probably. A month before the fire, the contract was cancelled. Too expensive.' Montoya whistles between his teeth.

'The factory wasn't insured against fire?'

'No. Not any more.'

'At least that eliminates the run-of-the-mill insurance fiddle.'

'Sure, but it also eliminates investigations by insurance company loss adjustors, and we both know how awkward they can sometimes be for management. Especially if the loss adjustors start nosing around in the company's accounts. Lastly, immediately after the fire, the Korean managers were recalled to Seoul. And the factory, or what's left of it, is being run by a French acting manager about whom we have no information.'

Montoya leans back in his armchair and savours his second brandy appreciatively. The second is always better than the first, the senses of smell and taste are heightened. Valentin's words come back to him: 'evidence fabricated or not, I don't mind either way'... *It would be funny if... At least now I know what I'm getting myself into, and it looks as though it might be more fun than I thought.*

'Eugénie, tell me. In your view, is there a chance that the bosses set fire to the factory?' The green gaze becomes vague.

'In my view... I just don't know. The timing seems

inappropriate, bang in the middle of the Thomson Multimedia takeover. They won the bid, by the way, have you heard? We didn't think they had a hope in hell. And then the factory was occupied by the workers, that obviously puts it at risk. I expect the police will be taking a close interest in them first. But actually, if a thorough investigation were to point a finger at the management, I wouldn't be altogether surprised.'

21 October

It is drizzling, early on a gloomy morning in the lay-by of the southbound carriageway of the A31 motorway, some thirty kilometres from Pondange. It is a particularly Spartan lay-by with a few sodden grassy areas fringed by dark pines and a concrete toilet block. Karim drives around it twice to make sure there's nobody there and parks his red Clio about twenty metres from the toilets. Engine switched off, his head against the headrest, he closes his eyes and waits. Ten minutes. A black BMW crawls into the lay-by and drives past the Clio. Eyes half-closed, Karim doesn't move. It pulls up a little way ahead. Belgian licence plates, two men inside, dark suits, it's them. He sits up, gets out of the car, in a red anorak, same colour as the car, goes into the toilets. The two men also head for the toilets, stretching and chatting. One of them is carrying a black canvas briefcase. They come out after a few minutes, still carrying the briefcase, get back into the BMW and drive off. Powerful acceleration, a fine piece of engineering. Two minutes later, Karim emerges. He's wearing a black nylon rucksack which he flings into the Clio, then he drives off slowly, heading south and whistling.

Moments later, two men leap out of the pine trees ringing the toilets and meet at the door. They are wearing identical black leather jackets, black jeans and work boots. One of them has a barely visible white silk scarf knotted around his neck.

'Fucking resin. I hope it hasn't messed up my jacket. Anyway, it's in the can.'

'The light wasn't good and we didn't get the handover.'

'Only to be expected. These shots will be adequate for our purposes. Come on, we're out of here.'

They head into the trees, turning their backs on the motorway. On reaching the fencing they pick up a ladder lying in the grass, clamber over the wire netting, jump down on to a path that runs across the fields, then get into a car parked a hundred metres away and drive off towards Nancy.

Lieutenant Lambert sits facing Rolande Lepetit, feeling slightly awkward, eyes firmly on his computer screen. A beautiful woman sitting calmly staring at him. He wasn't expecting that.

```
Rolande Lepetit, born on 23 June 1956 in Pondange,
single,residing at 9 Cité des Jonquilles, Pondange,
machine operator at Daewoo for two years.
Q. Were you on the premises when disturbances broke
out in the Daewoo factory on 14 October?
```

'What do you call "disturbances"?'
Lambert stops taking notes.
'I was there when Émilienne Machaut's accident occurred, yes. In my view, a worker electrocuted at her workstation is a disturbance.'
Lambert smiles at her.
'I meant, were you in the factory when your colleagues downed tools?'
'That's more precise.'

```
A. No, I wasn't there any more, I'd been fired.
Q. Did you return to the factory at any time on 14
October?
A. Yes.
Q. When, exactly?
```

Rolande leans towards Lambert, smiling at her memories.
'I was at the supermarket when I heard the news: the lorries that came to move the stocks out hadn't been able to get into the factory. The whole town was talking about it. I wanted to go and congratulate my friends, and I went back to the factory.'

```
A. It must have been some time around 15.00.
Q. Then what did you do?
```

```
A. Everyone expected it to be a long day and a long
night. I went to the cafeteria to cook for those
involved in the occupation, and I stayed there until
the fire broke out.
Q. So you were there when Nourredine Hamidi came back
with Hafed Rifaai, at around 20.00?
A. Yes.
Q. Were there many people in the cafeteria at that
point?
A. Around thirty.
Q. What were you doing?
A. I was finishing making and serving the omelettes. I
was busy in the kitchen.
Q. And what were the others doing?
A. They were playing cards, chatting, eating.
Q. Were you present at the meeting when Nourredine
Hamidi proposed pouring chemicals into the river?
A. Yes, I was present.
```

'But you shouldn't overstress the importance of Nourredine's proposal. The managers had just left the factory. We felt less powerful. There were several proposals, including Nourredine's, which was overwhelmingly rejected, so we moved on to other issues.'

```
Q. Did you witness the attack carried out by
Nourredine Hamidi on Ali Amrouche?
```

'It wasn't an attack. Ali was opposed to Nourredine's proposal, which was rejected, and Nourredine felt hurt and betrayed. Besides, he was exhausted and overwrought from the day's events.'

```
A. On his way out for some fresh air, Nourredine
bumped into Ali. That's all. Anyway, Ali Amrouche
didn't make a big fuss about it.
Q. Some witnesses have spoken of a very violent fight.
A. Well I'm talking about a minor tussle, nothing more.
Q. What did Nourredine Hamidi do after this fight?
```

A. He went outside with Hafed Rifaai, to walk, calm
down, I don't know, I didn't ask him.
Q. Which door did they exit from?
A. The one that leads to the car park.
Q. Did he come back into the cafeteria?
A. Yes.
Q. At what time?
A. I have no idea. He wasn't outside for long, maybe
half an hour.
Q. Still with Hafed?
A. Yes.
Q. Then what did they do?
A. Hafed and some of the others went off to the
security control centre and Nourredine settled down to
sleep on a table in a corner of the cafeteria.
Q. Was he alone there?
A. No. There were five or six of them trying to get
some sleep in the darkest corner.
Q. Did you see Nourredine Hamidi leave the cafeteria
again?
A. No. He remained asleep until the fire alert.
Q. Are you positive?
A. Yes.
Q. Even though you were on the other side of the
cafeteria - busy in the kitchen, according to your
account - and there were several people lying down in
the dark corner? You might be mistaken.
A. If he'd gone out, I'd have noticed.

'Nobody else left the cafeteria after Hafed and his team.'

Q. But you had no particular reason to keep a constant
check on Nourredine Hamidi's movements while you were
busy in the kitchen?
A. No of course not, I had no particular reason.

She falters now, her face tense.

'I don't understand what you're trying to get me to say, or why
you've got it in for Nourredine. It's not the workers who set fire

to the damned factory. And Nourredine would be the last person to do a thing like that.'

'I'm not trying to get you to say anything, I'm taking down your statement, that's all. I'm simply trying to obtain the facts. One last question.'

Q. Among your colleagues, is there one particular
name, or names, that keep cropping up in connection
with who might have started the fire?
A. No, I've heard nothing like that.

Later that afternoon, the lawyer drives Karim off in his big four-wheel drive with tinted windows. 'We've got a business appointment, the two of us,' he tells him. When Karim sits down in the passenger seat, the lawyer caresses his face with his rough hand, following the hollows of his cheeks, brushing his lips until he touches his moist mouth. Surprised and worried, Karim doesn't recognise the man he took for a constipated Catholic, but he doesn't flinch. Then the lawyer pulls away sharply. He drives fast, along an almost straight secondary road across the plateau. Rounding sharp bends, the heavy car feels as if it's about to come off the road, and Karim instinctively checks his seat belt. What on earth's the guy on? Coke, speed? The lawyer smiles at him, his teeth prominent, ready to bite. (*Coke, most likely. He'd better not touch me, the arsehole*). Then without slowing down, he turns off on to a farm track and pulls up at the edge of a copse. He takes a packet of photos from his pocket and slides it across the dashboard to Karim who flicks through them. The Hakim brothers' most recent delivery, shot from every angle. Hot flush. *Don't bat an eyelid. Keep calm.* Playing for time, he looks at the whole set again. Faces, licence plates, very clear. Expensive equipment and the work of a pro. *What's he playing at, this arsehole? This isn't some sexual game. He's trying to trap me, but how? And who's behind it? Have to see.* Puts the photos down.

'So?'

'Your latest delivery. Aren't you surprised?'

'Delivery, that's what you say. The photos don't show any delivery. Guys going in and out of a toilet. In a court of law, a good lawyer will demolish that, right?'

'True.' *He's a real turn-on, falling into the trap, at my mercy, and he knows it. He's desperately trying to dig himself out, but he won't manage it.* The lawyer places a fax from Agence France Presse Lorraine in front of Karim. It'll hit the papers tomorrow.

MASSIVE CUSTOMS HAUL

In the course of a routine check at the Nancy toll booth on the A31 motorway, customs officers arrested two Belgian nationals of Moroccan origin, the Hakim brothers, who were driving south to the Riviera.

The customs officials found thirty kilos of pure heroin and 100,000 ecstasy tablets concealed under the back seat of their luxury BMW. This is the biggest drugs haul in Lorraine for several years.

At this stage the customs services and the Nancy departmental police are uncertain whether this is a one-off operation or a new drug-trafficking channel.

The lawyer continues.

'The Hakim brothers are in Metz prison. I am not their defence counsel. In all decency, I couldn't be. A left-wing human rights lawyer for ten years, then the lawyer for the local bigwigs since my marriage, I'll have to wait a while before taking on drug traffickers. But I've put a very good friend of mine on the case. How do you think the Hakim brothers would react if they found out that you were under police surveillance when they made their delivery to you and that you grassed on them to the cops? There is photographic evidence.' The lawyer caresses Karim's face again, almost affectionately. 'You're not saying anything?'

'I'm waiting for what you're going to say next.'

Smile. 'Concerning the Daewoo fire, the superintendent had you in his sights. Thanks to my father-in-law, he doesn't any more. Thank you? No... never mind. The investigators have identified the arsonist. Nourredine Hamidi. You know him...'

Karim nods. He pictures Nourredine, attentive, serious-minded, controlling comings and goings at the factory gates, then leaning over the boot of the Korean manager's car. *Uncompromising, holier-than-thou, pain in the ass, anything you like, but an arsonist...* Poor bastard, he's stuffed. The lawyer leans towards him, no further hint of a smile as he spells it out, articulating each word with deliberation.

'Tomorrow morning you are summoned to give a witness statement. You were in the cafeteria, before the fire. You saw the guy, he was trying to sleep on a bench in a dark corner. He couldn't get to sleep, he was too wound up. You saw him get up and leave by the door that leads to the factory just after nine p.m. The cops will help you get the facts right, you know what they're like. When it suits them, they feed you the answer in the question. Tell me you'll testify.'

'I'll do it.'

'Better than that.'

'I'll testify that I saw Nourredine leave the cafeteria after nine o'clock. I get it, OK?'

The lawyer grabs Karim's arm and indicates the back seat with a jerk of his head.

'Get your clothes off. I've got one hell of a hard-on.'

23 October

An autumn hunting scene on the Lorraine plateau. The beauty of the soft mist over the heavy, dark cornfields, eviscerated by the icy morning and the emerging sun which brings the countryside to life little by little. The beaters' shouts, the dogs' barks, the waiting, the tension, sudden shots. Three coveys of partridges flushed out, seven bagged. Of ten hares, five in the bag. The men are good shots.

The hunters in their brown jackets and heavy rubber waders make their way back from the hides and converge at the meeting point at the corner of the wood. Quignard and the superintendent walk side by side, their guns snapped in half under their arms, relaxed, content. Quignard walks along the edge of the field, he loves the feel of the slightly clinging soft clay underfoot. *This land is mine, I belong here.* He takes a glance around at the furrowed fields as far as the eye can see. *My land.* He can still hear the energetic flapping of wings as the covey of partridges rises, feels his own heart beating deafeningly, then the partridges are windborne and dive down towards his hide at nearly two hundred kilometres an hour. He follows their line of flight, shoots his first round – the dull thud of the bird falling – then he turns around, fires his second shot instinctively, a second bird hit. Almost in heaven.

His mind vaguely numbed. *Daewoo, sorted. Everything back to normal. Park's stupidity made up for, poor bastard. Now sole master on board. Efficient. Return to order. No waves in the national press. A glorious future ahead. The world's my oyster.* His feet sink into the clay. *You can be proud of yourself.* Smile. *Pay attention, the superintendent's talking to you.*

'Your tip-off about the Hakim brothers, terrific. Did you see, we teamed up with Customs. I shan't hide the fact that it's helped get me a transfer to Nancy, which is now on the cards. Nothing definite yet, but...

'Good. I told you about that business, which naturally I got wind of purely by chance in Brussels... especially because I hope we can protect the region from traffickers of that kind. But if you benefit from it, between you and me, I'm only too pleased.' Friendly thump. 'And I very much hope that after you've moved to Nancy, you'll still join us on the Grande Commune hunt, it's one of the best in the region.'

'I should hope so, if you carry on inviting me...'

Laughter. The two men are the last to reach the meeting point, around two big four-wheel drives. The gamekeeper composes the tableau, lining up the kill on the ground. The hunters admire and comment on each other's shots. The smell of blood and gun grease in the still air. Some thirty metres away the beaters, in white overalls, armed with big sticks, tuck into thick sandwiches and knock back the beer. Beside the vehicles are two small picnic tables covered with white tablecloths. On one are four hollowed-out loaves filled with canapés, and on the other, a selection of chilled red and white Loire valley wines and some glasses. Two drivers, seconded from the 3G company, pour the wine. The hunters jostle each other, laughing. The superintendent helps himself to a glass of red, raises it high, and booms:

'You're the first to hear the news. Tomorrow it'll be in the papers. The investigation into the Daewoo factory fire is over and the arsonist was arrested yesterday.'

Commotion. 'Bravo... Terrific... That was really fast... Congratulations.' The superintendent is beaming.

'Yes, I think we can say it was an exemplary investigation, speedy and efficient.'

A big-shot notary from Nancy goes over to Quignard.

'Congratulations. Tell me, Daewoo's hit the jackpot with the

Thomson privatisation. You've been keeping that close to your chest.'

'Business isn't bad, that's for sure.'

'Isn't this fire likely to damage you?'

'No, providing the investigation is closed quickly, as it has been. The arsonist is one of the factory workers who got over-excited. Nothing serious.'

An entrepreneur from the valley who prefers to hunt down EU subsidies, greatly indebted to Quignard, enquires after Park.

'I thought he'd be here today…'

'He's gone back to Korea to review things with the parent company.' Then with a broad smile: 'I bet the beaters are relieved, he's a lousy shot, a danger to the rest of us.' Quignard raises his voice. 'Come gentlemen, the break's over. Two more beats before lunch.'

The beaters have already left. The hunters move off towards another field, other hides. Quignard and Tomaso bring up the rear, side by side. Daniel Tomaso slows down to keep pace with Quignard. On this glorious day, his feet in the clay of the Lorraine plateau, on the Grande Commune hunt, he feels a growing sense of elation. A lot of ground covered in a very short time. A black sheep, the Foreign Legion, a mercenary, Lebanon, Croatia, one training's as good as another. Five years ago, sickened by the violence and penniless, he dropped everything to take over the garage in Nancy run by his father, until his recent death. A respectable business, nothing more. He expanded the garage, set up a limousine hire company with drivers and bodyguards, and then a security company. Next a nightclub, a brilliant idea of Kristina's, the mistress he'd brought back from Croatia, to grab all those bourgeois provincials by the short and curlies. His business is booming. He knows he owes his success mainly to Quignard, and he knows that his invitation to the hunt is the equivalent of a formal introduction into local society and a reward for the successful conclusion of the Daewoo Pondange factory occupation and fire. He leans towards Quignard.

'The case is closed, apparently.'

'Fingers crossed.'

'What about my security guards?'

'Fine in every respect. During the investigation they changed direction as obediently as on the parade ground.'

A few steps in silence. Quignard greets the chairman of the regional council with a smile. They go a long way back: having both been in the OAS in Algeria when young, with a shared past they have tacitly agreed to keep quiet about, they had created a staunch closeness and complicity neither had ever betrayed. The chairman is in hide number one. Not a good position. So much the better. A mediocre shot. Tomaso resumes.

'Do you really believe Park's gone back to Korea?'

Surprised. 'Yes. I asked for him and all the Korean managers to be recalled to the parent company. I felt they'd done enough harm as it was. Why?'

'Park is a man who's never suffered from scruples, if I'm not mistaken. He knows there's a lot of money to be made, and fast. He has inside information, and he's getting out?'

'And where do you think he might be?'

'Think, Maurice. Put yourself in his position. Where would you go to make your next move?' Quignard walks on in silence for a few moments. Not for long.

'Warsaw.'

'Just what I was thinking.'

'Now you've got me worried.' A silence, an exchange of pleasantries as they walk past a magistrate newly appointed to the Briey courts.

'Do you have any way of finding out if he's over there?'

'Perhaps. I have a car dealership network in Poland. Give me some photos, a description, I'll see what I can do.'

Then Tomaso stops at hide number three, an excellent position for an excellent marksman, and Quignard continues. He has number fifteen, at the very end of the line, a shitty number. Nothing ever happens that far out. Sigh.

At number six, a Luxembourg banker is sitting on a folding hunting stool, his eyes half shut. *Don't be taken in, he's quick off the mark, despite his corpulence. He's CEO of Daewoo Pondange's lead bank. The day after the fire, he agreed to defer all the firm's payment dates. On condition that Quignard was put in sole charge. On condition that you return the favour sometime, dear friend.* The two men exchange smiles.

At hide number ten, his son-in-law watches him arrive accompanied by Tomaso. *First time this fellow's invited to the Grande Commune hunt. I don't know how wise that is. He sticks out like a sore thumb with his past, his nightclub, the Oiseau Bleu, his loud mistress and all the rumours about him in town. I'll have to have a word with my father-in-law about it.* Quignard stops and taps his son-in-law on the shoulder.

'Bravo the lawyer. I don't know how you wangled it with Karim Bouziane, and I don't want to know. His testimony was decisive. The superintendent is delighted, and I owe you a big thank you.'

'You're most welcome. My pleasure.'

PART THREE

24 October

Quignard has maintained the habit of rising at dawn from his years of working in a factory. Breakfast is served on the ground floor, in the vast dining room which opens on to a terrace with a view over the entire valley. The Quignard residence is a small château, the former mansion of the owner of the ironworks, in the days when there were ironworks. He lives there alone with his wife since their only daughter got married and went to live in Nancy with her husband. He and his wife now live separate lives. She's asleep somewhere upstairs while he eats breakfast alone in the monumental room, and that suits him fine. Less time wasted.

A chauffeur-driven black Mercedes waits at the foot of the white stone steps. Car and driver come courtesy of 3G. Tomaso is not unappreciative. Impeccable, as always. On the fawn leather back seat, Quignard finds the national dailies, which the driver brings him from Nancy. He flicks through them. *Libération's* financial section is entirely taken up by a big article entitled: 'Thomson Multimedia turns down Korean marriage offer.' With a subheading: 'The Daewoo affair: emotions run high.' The opening lines read: 'The unions are fighting to stop their factory and its technology from being sold to the Korean group.' Half-smile. As long as there's nothing more serious... He turns the page and moves on to the sports section.

Montoya reaches Pondange via the plateau road, around mid-morning. He stops before heading down into the valley and gazes at the town spread out in front of him. Thirty-five years since he left. *Thirty-five years, a lifetime, my whole life, hold your breath, vertigo.* On the edge of the plateau, high up, the old town with its ramparts and ancient houses, nothing's changed. All around, descending down the valley, the workers' houses and housing estates. A little further away, high up on the flanks of the valley and surrounded by greenery are the residences of the ironworks owners, and on the plateau, outside the town, two social housing estates. It's all still there, but the street of factories along the river with its blast furnaces, the continuous fires hammering and puffing, the smoke and the smells, the men's activity, their all-consuming passions, the powerful, violent town, its heart beating day and night, has all been swallowed up, wiped out. He knew it, but to see it... He didn't want to come here. *Liar. You had to come back sooner or later. Valentin simply gave you an excuse. Now look what's become of Pondange, that monster you were so afraid of, amputated of its factory satellites, a little provincial town that's had a facelift, repainted, neat and tidy, dozing deep in its green valley.*

Unhesitatingly, he finds his way to the police station: it sits behind the local school where his father had been head teacher. He parks his car. A quick glance at the playground. To the left, the head teacher's house, his own bedroom window. A flood of painful memories. A motherless childhood. He'd never known whether she'd died or simply run off and abandoned him. A strict, tyrannical father who showed no affection, whose image superimposed itself, in his memory, on that of the blast furnaces gobbling up men. He'd run away from Pondange at the age of fourteen and his father had never tried to find him, accepting his disappearance as he had his mother's. They had never seen each other again. *What must he look like now, my father, since apparently he's still alive? A broken old man of tidy appearance? Is it his shadow that I've come to track down here, in this sleepy town?* He falters for a moment in the muffled mid-morning silence, his equilibrium perturbed, then walks into the police station.

'The superintendent's expecting you. First floor on the right.'

In the vast office, the superintendent rises to greet him. Good-looking, athletic, very elegant, he invites Montoya to take a seat in an armchair and sits down facing him.

'Let me introduce myself. Charles Montoya. I work for the Thomson group's security department...'

'I know. I got your entire pedigree from Sébastiani, the Nancy police chief, who obtained it from a deputy director of the judicial police, no less.' Smile. 'That is sufficient for me to consider you as a man who can be trusted.'

Efficient, Valentin's network. Rayssac, superintendent at Pondange. What can he hope for in this dump? Promotion to the rank of chief at Nancy. Who can help him to achieve that? Sébastiani in Nancy and Renaud at the judicial police department. All Valentin had to do was pick up the phone. Montoya is conscious of the gulf between a former top security services cop, and a poor bastard from the drug squad who left under a cloud. *My pedigree. If only you knew...* He too smiles.

'I'll put my cards on the table. I'm here to investigate Daewoo, on behalf of my employers. I glean what I can here and there, to help Thomson in the negotiations that are about to begin with the group's future buyer. Of course, I'm also seeking further information on last week's fire. My employer is a real stickler for security.'

'I'll do everything I can to assist you, especially as the investigation is now closed. We've just experienced a very unfortunate series of events, the questionable sacking of a woman worker, then one thing led to another and it all got out of hand, culminating in the fire. Fortunately we did a good job fast and effectively. A textbook investigation.' He enunciates every syllable. 'Textbook...'

Textbook, that brought back memories. Made-to-measure witnesses, hand-sewn, prefabricated evidence that comes in a kit. Textbook. A frightening word.

'...I've had a press file compiled for you on Daewoo and on our town, which you'll find in room 23, on the third floor. You can use the office for two hours, no one will disturb you. No point looking for a photocopier, there isn't one in the office or upstairs. Another thing, I request that you do not contact Karim Bouziane, the key prosecution witness, and that you inform me of anything you find out that may be useful to the investigation.'

'Naturally, and I'm grateful for your help. You will understand that I have to be very discreet. It is not desirable for Daewoo to know the precise nature of my visit. I plan to introduce myself as an Agence France Press journalist and if possible, without taking advantage of your kindness, I'd like to have a look around the factory, just to get an idea of what we're talking about.'

'I'll arrange that for you straight away.'

Room 23. As he expected, Montoya finds the 'forgotten' case file on the table, next to the press cuttings file. First of all he flicks rapidly through the newspaper cuttings, to get himself in the mood. In the local papers, there are pages on the fire, and the headlines are filled with praise for Quignard, the man who takes the company's future in hand after the disaster. A local man, formerly in the iron and steel industry where he'd started out as a technician and ended up as a factory manager. On the demise of the industry, he successfully retrained and became boss of a design office specialising in industrial reconversions, president of the commercial court, advisor on the European Development Plan, and in that capacity, the munificent dispenser of EU subsidy manna to the entire valley. Apparently, he's cherished Daewoo since it was set up, two years ago, and now he's taking over the helm, in the midst of the crisis (who crowned him king?), whereas all the Korean managers have gone back to Seoul. (Why? Not a word, the question isn't even asked.) Something widely regarded as evidence of a tremendous sense of responsibility and an admirable spirit of sacrifice. The regional press is proud of their local boy. Why does this exemplary track record immediately arouse Montoya's suspicions?

He comes across a neatly cut out little article from a local paper on the arrest of the Hakim brothers, known drug traffickers. Hakim... and now the Tangier case resurfaces in his memory, twice in such a short time. Coincidence? With men like the Hakims, always hanging out with the cops, and a man like Valentin, anything can happen. Or, quite simply, the Pondange superintendent had a hand in their arrest and wants to blow his own trumpet to someone with my connections. He reads carefully. Customs officers, routine check, looks familiar. Apparently the Hakim brothers are still involved in the drugs racket and are now based in Antwerp. It would be funny for them to have fallen victim to a war between Belgian and French customs officers. *But what part did the Pondange cops play? No mention in the article. The Hakim brothers: make a mental note. I'll put it to one side until I find out more, but the two men and their dealings remain in the frame.*

Now he skims through the file on the investigation, which seems to get off to a good start. List of those present during the strike, timetable of their movements, cross-checking of statements. The job is unfinished, and the names mean nothing to Montoya who moves on to the witness statements. He quickly draws the obvious conclusion: a trumped-up investigation. First of all a minor delinquent is targeted and then he becomes the prosecution witness. Classic. Once in the cops' hands he does his job rather cleverly. The factory security guards: clearly following orders. The first version is to incriminate the future witness, the second to discredit the suspect, they're 'yes' men. Which immediately raises a question about the exact nature of the company that employs them, 3G, in Nancy. Note that the minor delinquent, probably a grass, is a dope dealer. In Tangier, the Hakims also trafficked dope, as well as coke. Coincidence? Then there are the two proles. Amrouche, who makes vehement accusations. A management mole? But his hatred sounds genuine, which proves nothing, of course. And Rolande Lepetit, who offers only a limp defence. Is it limp or honest? She's the one who was 'unfairly' sacked, as the superintendent said. Her sacking sparked off the strike, so she was well liked. Amrouche also liked her, and Quignard's reinstated her. In exchange for what? I'll bet Quignard isn't the sort to give something for nothing. An exemplary worker? For a moment Montoya's mind wanders. He recalls the milieus he frequented as a youth. They all sought to emulate Stakhanov, the model worker of the Soviet Union's heyday. Was there still such a thing as a model worker? Rolande Lepetit Stakhanova. He pictured a tall, sturdy, fair-haired woman with clear blue eyes, a straight, rather thick waist, slightly stiff. Whoever this woman is, History has spoken: beware of Stakhanova. A final glance through the preliminary part of the investigation to check the movements of key witnesses: the security guards, Amrouche, Rolande Lepetit, Karim Bouziane. He's through in less than two hours.

In the early afternoon, Montoya parks his car in front of the remains of the Daewoo factory. The situation is simple: the hangar that housed the stocks is completely gutted, the production plant is intact, and all the machines are there. The offices too are intact and have been thoroughly cleared out. Not a single piece of paper, not a single computer. There are no police on the premises any more and the security guards are carrying out their routine duties. In fact it was the security firm itself that handled the clearing out of the offices the day after the fire, without it occurring to the police for a moment to stop them.

Seated at the wheel of his car, he telephones Valentin using the secure mobile connected directly to Valentin's private number. He keys in his personal code.

'The investigation's a sham, there's absolutely no doubt about it. My hunch is that the cops aren't aware of it, otherwise the superintendent wouldn't have been so willing to let me go through his files, even though he's desperate to make a good impression on yours truly. So he's either being leaned on or used. Not very illuminating.'

Valentin merely groans.

'For the time being, that's all I've got. But I have a request: Can you find out about the security firm 3G in Nancy?'

'Say that again.'

'Security firm, 3G, Nancy.'

'You'll have that information right away.'

Hôtel Vauban on the main square in Pondange, a former parade ground in the days when the fortress was in use. The square is vast, windswept and deserted with a seventeenth-century church on the far side, built in the severe style of the Jesuits. A Jesuit style for a military congregation. An elegant, neo-classical mansion is home to the town hall. Once upon a time the two façades were so black with grime that he had never noticed the beauty of the architecture and the stone. After eating a ham baguette washed down with a beer, Montoya has a shower and changes his clothes. He stretches out flat on the bed, a pillow under his knees to ease his back which sometimes aches, the result of a nasty fall during a chase through the streets of Istanbul. *Worn out, about to turn fifty. A whole past of half-successes and total cock-ups. Booted out of the police. Tactfully and with a farewell party, a cover-up, but still thrown out.* His back slowly relaxes, the base of the spine first, and then the shoulders. *Insurance investigator, some profession, always up hill and down dale, dosh, routine, boredom, and the iron grip of the lovely Eugénie with green eyes. You make enough dosh to blow on luxuries, and to make you want to earn even more. Yet never enough to be truly rich and not to give a damn. So it's a spiral: always more shit cases and an increasingly bitter taste in the mouth. Stop, take a breather. Get a grip, a bit of stability, an office in Paris, friends, a cosy relationship, that'd be nice. A job like Valentin's. Less important. I don't have the stature, or the con-tacts. A less strategic operation. Dreams of a quiet old age at last, so the whole journey does not seem simply absurd.* The feeling of well-being radiates to the back of his neck... *and now, where do I go from here? Stir the pot and see what comes to the surface. First point, various drugs are circulating, everyone seems to be aware of it and nobody's attaching any importance to it. A minor dope dealer at the centre of the investigation, the Hakims in the area, could there be a connection between the two? Premise: there's no such thing as chance.* His body now entirely relaxed, his thoughts, woolly, begin to fray...

He must have fallen asleep.

He is abruptly woken by shouting beneath his window. 'So-li-da-rity...' 'Free Nourredine...' 'Our bonuses...'

He rushes over to the window. More a gaggle than a demonstration. Thirty to forty people marching in a ragged procession without too much conviction. No banners, a few trade union flags, outbursts of shouting, the odd slogan taken up by the rest. The group appears to be breaking up, disappointed by the low turnout and a tangible general indifference. No one's taking any notice of the demonstration, and the few pedestrians they do meet hurry away. An Arab, an arsonist... the group walks past the houses and stays in the shade of the trees lining the square, probably intimidated by the empty expanse in the centre. Montoya spots a tall woman with short, bleach-blonde hair cut in a bob, who holds herself upright and seems tougher than the others. A hunch, a bet: Stakhanova? There's no harm in trying. The group speeds up, as if in a hurry to get the demonstration over with. Montoya slips on a leather coat and hurries after them. He catches them up in front of the town hall, where they are silently putting away the flags and starting to disperse, not even waiting for the return of the delegation that has gone inside to meet one of the mayor's deputies. From behind he approaches the blonde woman, a tall silhouette in a fitted black wool coat and black boots. She's smoking a cigarette with a calm elegance and talking to a man who is shorter than her, aged around fifty, heavy-set and solid.

'Thank you, Mr Maréchal.'

A slightly husky voice reminiscent of a 1930s cabaret singer. Montoya shivers; the man leaves.

'Ms Lepetit?'

She turns around, bright blue eyes, good bone structure, calm, regular features, a scar to the left of her upper lip. Definitely Stakhanova. Montoya's surprised: beautiful, a very beautiful woman, a strong presence. *I like that in a woman.*

'That's me. What do you want?'

'To buy you a drink. Is that possible?'

She finds herself looking at a slim, dark-haired man. *He's rather attractive, just my type, and a stranger around here. Not dragged down by the general misery. Whoever you are, for a fleeting moment, you'll be a breath of fresh air.* Smile.

'It's even welcome.'

There aren't many cafes in Pondange, and most of the remaining few have been redecorated, sterilised, like the whole town. Rolande leads Montoya towards the lower town and walks into a cafe that still has a big zinc counter at the far end of a dark room with mirrors on the walls, solid timber tables and chairs, and a wide variety of beers chalked up on a slate. There are only two or three regulars at this hour. She sits down at a table by the window, unbuttons her coat, sighs and smiles. Stunning.

'Tea with milk for me please, Simon.'

Montoya glances at the slate.

'Sudden Death is just the drink for me.'

She rests her forearms on the table, leans on them and talks as if they were old friends.

'The demo was very disappointing. A week ago, in the factory, there were two, three hundred of us, all standing together. Today in the square there were thirty of us, in disarray. It's over. Luckily there are a few good people like Maréchal.'

The drinks arrive. Sudden Death is a lovely warm colour, a head that's almost solid, cool droplets run down the glass. Rolande pours her tea, a drop of milk, warms her hands around the cup, her mind elsewhere. He resumes the conversation at random.

'In the old days, the steelworkers had bigger demos.'

She jumps, her expression hard.

'Not you too. I don't like fairy tales. When I was sixteen, I worked for a small textiles factory ten kilometres from here, and it wasn't unionised. We all went on strike over pay and conditions, and a delegation of us went to the local union in Pondange to ask if we could join. All the officials were steelworkers and they threw us out. They didn't want to know a bunch of women, judging by what they had to say. Ever since that day...'

'Don't hold it against me, I'm not from around here.'

'That's what I thought. And that's what I like about you. Now tell me why you invited me for this drink.'

'I'm a journalist. I'm writing a special report on Daewoo, its various factories in France. I'm interested in the strike and the fire, but also all the issues to do with working conditions and safety in the factory.'

'Which paper do you work for?'

'Not a paper, for Agence France Presse. Our reports are sold to the newspapers. At the moment, with Daewoo taking over Thomson, there's a lot of interest.'

'Who gave you my name?'

'A staff rep, Ali Amrouche.'

'He's a good man too, and a friend.' Bitterly: 'He wasn't at the demo.' Montoya refrains from asking: *Are you surprised?* She pours another cup of tea. 'You've come to the right person. I can tell you about working conditions at Daewoo.'

She launches into the story of Émilienne's accident. Montoya listens attentively, his gaze riveted by Rolande's square hands, her slightly swollen fingers, the skin worn and marked, her nails cut short. They appear to feel every sentence, emphasising and punctuating her words. After Émilienne, the clash with Maréchal. He's taken aback: the same Maréchal who was at the demonstration and who you said was a 'good' man? Mocking smile, yes, yes, the same Maréchal. She moves on to the account of her dismissal...

'I heard it caused some controversy...'

Rolande sits up straight with a slight smile, her hands are folded on the table.

'In any case Quignard, the new boss, reinstated me. It was worth it.'

'A new boss? Isn't it an odd time to change bosses?'

'All the Koreans left after the fire, very quickly within forty-eight hours. Quignard took things in hand and in my opinion is doing a good job.'

Amrouche, Maréchal, Quignard, all good guys, yet she still has that Stakhanova manner. Be careful. Why is she standing up for Nourredine? Doesn't she get it? She stops talking and slowly drinks her tea. A powerful memory from the day of the strike comes back to her. Aisha, her arms folded across her chest, her face white, describing the headless body, the emotion they all felt.

'I'm not a very good talker. I'll have to introduce you to my young neighbour, Aisha.' Her fingers drum on the table. 'It won't be easy. She hasn't set foot outside her flat since the strike.'

'Why not?'

The hands open, spread, hesitate. 'She's very young, her father is a strict man who tends to be violent, the mother's dead, the older brothers and sisters are married and have gone looking for work elsewhere. He's stayed here, alone with her, he gets a steelworker's pension, does nothing all day long. Like that for years, a man who's still able-bodied, he finds it hard to accept. He was furious with her for going on strike. And since then she's allowed herself to be shut up without protest. It's not like her.' She clasps her hands. 'I haven't seen her since. This would be a good opportunity.'

A silence as she lays her hand on top of Montoya's, skin on skin, pressing down. Her hand is soft and rasping like her voice. Montoya shivers with an unexpected thrill. *Careful. Let Stakhanova come to you.*

Rolande says, 'I like the way you listen. Calmly, not in a hurry. You make it easier for me to talk.' He thinks dark thoughts... *Even in the drug squad, my grasses talked more than other people's, fat lot of good that did me...*

'Come, I'll take you to my flat, it's the only place where you'll be able to meet Aisha.'

As Rolande leaves the cafe, she bumps into a short young man who is going in. On seeing her, he shrinks back.

'Karim. You weren't at the demo either.'

He stammers: 'I couldn't make it, Rolande.'

Montoya steps aside to let him pass and stares at him. Not striking, the key prosecution witness. Before leaving, he turns around and meets Karim's eye in the mirror observing him, prying and anxious.

Cité des Jonquilles, staircase A, first floor. Rolande leaves Montoya outside on the landing for a few minutes. He hears a brief conversation on the other side of the door, Rolande and another female voice, sounds of washing-up, doors banging. Then she shows him into a pleasant and well-lit living room. She keeps it impeccably tidy, spick and span in fact. Two windows, creamy white walls, pale wood furniture. On the wall facing the windows, there's a panoramic view of Venice as it appears when you arrive by sea, suspended between sky and lagoon, painted in blue and pink hues, the light of certain September mornings. A break in the wall, a break in life. A souvenir? A dream? Rolande motions him to sit in one of the three chintz armchairs facing the television while she goes and telephones in the hall, with the door closed. On a coffee table in front of him there's a photo of a smiling teenage boy wearing a polo-necked jumper and some books that look as if they're from a library.

Rolande comes back: Aisha will be here in a minute. She lives upstairs on the fourth floor.

Aisha arrives and the two women embrace. Rolande keeps her arms around her for a moment. 'I'm so pleased to see you. We haven't seen each other since the strike. How long is it? Ten days? It feels ages. How are you, Aisha?'

Aisha dismisses the question with a wave of her hand. Wan-faced, she stares at the floor and perches gingerly on the edge of the armchair facing Montoya. Rolande introduces him: a journalist friend (no more friend than journalist, thinks Montoya with irritation) who's writing a series of articles about Daewoo, about our strike. 'I couldn't tell him much because I stayed in the cafeteria kitchen all the time.' She breaks off, smiles at Montoya: 'Onion and potato omelettes, Spanish-style. But you were all over the place, you can tell him about it.' Aisha leans forward, hugging her chest.

'It's still so painful. Do we really have to go back over it?'

'Yes, we have to talk about it. Something's eating you up, I don't know what. Take advantage of my friend's presence (she stresses the word again), he's not from around here, he'll be gone in a few days and will listen to what you have to say.'

Montoya hears moaning from inside the apartment. The two women are unruffled. Aisha turns slightly towards Montoya, her eyes still lowered.

'I've been working in the factory for six years. People who haven't worked on the production line, like Rolande and me, can't understand what happened to me. When our shift came out on strike we all started walking around the factory, freely, the bosses had disappeared. I thought I'd go mad with joy. I felt as though I existed. I thought it was easy, and that I was changing my life. I'd already heard people say that, on the radio, on TV: nothing will ever be the same again.' Still tense and huddled up, she turns towards Rolande. 'I decided there and then that I'd never return to my father's house. And then, I met Étienne.' Montoya glances at Rolande, she seems to know who he is so leave out the questions. He mustn't interrupt Aisha who's talking as if under hypnosis. 'We slept together in the packaging workshop.' Rolande puts her hand on Aisha's arm and the girl smiles at her. 'It wasn't amazing, but it wasn't terrible either. I felt as though I was breaking away from my father once and for all. You know what he's like. It was the worst thing I could do to him. In my own way, I was doing everything I could so my life would be different.'

Aisha sighs, leans back in the armchair, then looks up and grows animated as she describes the arrival of the lorries, her elation, the overturned car, the occupation of the offices, the women becoming increasingly marginalised, wandering around the deserted factory.

'I bumped into Étienne in the cafeteria and we went back to the packaging workshop.' A little smile. 'Much better than the first time. While we're putting our clothes back on, Étienne hears a noise coming from the direction of the waste ground. He goes out of the back door to see what's going on. I hear him yell: "What are you doing? Who are you? Stop! Stop!" and he comes back like a madman, grabs my arm and drags me to the cafeteria, running, and he keeps yelling, "Quick, quick, there's a fire. I saw the guys who started it".'

Rolande and Montoya look at each other. She's surprised, he's alert. He sits back, relaxed. *Don't forget, you're not a cop. Journalist. Fragile girl. Discretion. Don't ruin everything, this is the first link in the chain, and you've been here less than seven hours. Not bad going.* Aisha continues. 'Then we both ended up on the roundabout in front of the factory. Do you remember? A lot of people were crying. I was crying. I saw my dreams and my new-found freedom going up in smoke. Afterwards Ali Amrouche walked me back here. On the way, he gently talked to me about Étienne, without pressing the point. A married man with two kids and the worst skirt-chaser in the whole factory. I didn't care, one guy or another, but I didn't tell him that. Can you imagine how shocked Ali would have been? He came up to see my father, told him about the strike, the occupation, and why I hadn't come home at the usual time, without a word about Étienne. Very proper. The old man didn't say anything but I think he understood the whole thing. I left the two of them and went to bed. The next morning, the old man didn't beat me, but he said I wasn't to leave the flat until Daewoo went back to work. And I've been there until this evening.' Now, she's very relaxed, almost smiling.

'In a way, I felt protected, I was taking time to heal. When I'm ready, I'll leave this town and this life.'

Leave. The word fills the room as they listen respectfully. From another room in the flat, the groaning has given way to snoring. Montoya turns to Rolande.

'This Étienne speaks of several arsonists, strangers by the sound of it. Can't he testify to clear your friend who's in prison?'

'No. He's dead.'

Montoya feels a shudder run up his spine. The violent smell of blood like in the old days. A host of forgotten, repressed sensations suddenly come flooding back. *I wouldn't have believed it was still possible.*

'How did he die?'

'An accident. The day after the fire, he was walking through the woods from his place, on the housing estate on the plateau, to Pondange. He probably took the wrong path and fell down a rocky slope. He broke his neck.'

'Was he alone when this accident happened?'

'Yes. Alone. His wife had taken the car as usual. She works in a supermarket in Briey.'

Hold on a minute. A young man catches arsonists in the act one evening, and has a fatal fall while walking alone in the woods the next morning. Nothing more natural? Aren't Stakhanova and her friend acting just a bit too naive? Montoya turns back to Aisha, who seems very calm in her armchair.

'Did you know about this?'

'Yes.' She sounds almost indifferent. 'Ali phoned to tell me before the funeral.'

'Were you the only person who heard him say: "I saw the guys who started the fire"?'

'No. Why?' She seems surprised by the question. 'When we were all on the roundabout during the fire, he was telling everyone. He went on and on about it but nobody took any notice.'

'It's true now you come to mention it. I remember hearing him, but it didn't sink in at the time.'

Astounding, this Stakhanova, thinks Montoya.

'We were all in shock. And completely spellbound by the fire… Besides, Étienne was off his head and nobody was taking any notice of what he was saying.'

'Off his head. In what way?'

Aisha darts Rolande an embarrassed look.

'When I met him in the cafeteria, in the late afternoon, he'd come back from the offices, which he'd occupied with the others. He was telling everyone that while playing on one of the managers' computers, he'd come across bank statements from banks in Luxembourg…' Another glance at Rolande, who still doesn't move a muscle. 'Accounts in the names of Nourredine, Amrouche and Maréchal. And you too, Rolande. Accounts into which Daewoo paid huge sums of money.'

Rolande jumps and the colour drains from her cheeks.

'I've never been paid a cent more than my wages. What on earth are you talking about?'

'What he was saying was all very muddled. He was talking about millions, it wasn't clear if he was talking about old francs, new francs or some other currency, he didn't seem to know himself…'

'And how did people react?'

'Nobody believed him, and because he kept on and on saying the same thing, everyone thought he was off his head.' Aisha stops, a smile on her face, the memory of the magic desk, the spliff in the dark. 'He often smoked dope, everyone knew, so naturally they didn't take any notice. But he really did see the guys who started the fire.'

'We'll have to get to the bottom of this bank account business. I can't have rumours like that going around.'

Montoya's no longer listening to the two women. He's picturing the managers' offices emptied of all their computer equipment, their files, moved out in a hurry. One thing he's certain of: *This is the second link in the chain.*

'Was there anyone with Étienne in the manager's office when he was playing on the computer?'

'I have no idea. There were at least twenty people involved in the occupation but I didn't stay. I don't know what went on.'

Montoya remembers security guard Schnerb's statement: the alarm was raised at 21.43 hours with no mention of who raised it or how.

'Did Étienne raise the alarm throughout the factory?'

'Yes, straight away. We went back to the cafeteria together, and he ran to the porter's lodge to tell the security guards to call the fire brigade.'

The true importance of security guard Schnerb's statement is beginning to emerge. It is vital to find out more about this company, 3G.

Late afternoon and darkness has already fallen over the valley when Quignard leaves the empty offices. He smokes the one cigar he allows himself during the day. In the big Mercedes, cigar in mouth, he skims the international press. Very favourable reactions to the privatisation of Thomson, praise for Lagardère and Kim, the Daewoo bosses, modern-day heroes. When this business is completely sewn up, he too will be one of the big boys. He'll see his own name in large print in the financial press. He daydreams. His driver's mobile phone rings.

'For you, Mr Quignard. It's Mr Tomaso. Will you take it?' Quignard nods and takes the phone.

'Yes?'

'I don't know whether this is good news or bad news, but we've found your man Park in Warsaw.' A silence. Quignard does not react. 'My men photographed him – you'll have the prints tomorrow morning – but as far as I'm concerned, there's no room for doubt, it's him.'

'So we need to prepare for war?'

'Looks like it.'

'Don't lose him, Daniel. We must be able to act under all circumstances.'

'Understood. You know my rates.'

Montoya gets into his car, drives for some ten kilometres and parks in the middle of the countryside with the lights switched off. A few moments without moving, in the dark, to gather his thoughts. The seat tilts back, he makes himself breathe slowly, deeply. Oxygenate the brain. *I'm making progress. Exciting, even in Pondange, even a minor case. To sum up: during the strike, the bosses try to remove some of the computers and fail. While the offices are occupied and the computers are in the hands of the strikers, a fire breaks out. This means immediate evacuation and the next day, or even that same night, the computers are taken away and hidden by 3G. Conclusion: those computers contain evidence that there's something dodgy going on at Daewoo. That's too vague a conclusion to be much use to me. More specifically: Étienne*

Neveu had time to play on one of the computers and came across a list of names of employees who hold bank accounts in Luxembourg. Am I certain that these accounts exist? For the time being, I've only got one source and an indirect report. Neveu could have invented the story about the arsonists and the Luxembourg accounts. But he didn't invent his broken neck. That confirms all the rest. So, I'll work on the hypothesis that these Luxembourg accounts exist. What for? No idea. They are in various names. Apparently Neveu mentioned Nourredine, Amrouche, Rolande Lepetit, Maréchal. There are probably others. Could they be willing front men? Rolande claims not to know anything about it. If we believe her, why use names of company employees? It makes no sense. Further probing needed. Find out whether Neveu was the only one to have seen the lists, and if I can find any trace of them.

Another lead, the dope. I already had the Hakims, the traffickers, and Bouziane, the dealer. Now I've got Bouziane the dealer, witness for the prosecution, and Neveu the consumer, the witness who's both a nuisance and the victim. There's every likelihood they knew each other well. I'll keep anything to do with drugs to myself for the time being in case Valentin's manipulating the Hakim brothers. Can't be too careful. Montoya brings his seat back to the upright position. Now it's time to call Valentin.

Over the telephone Valentin sounds relaxed. Montoya takes advantage of this to be a little more forthcoming.

'Things are moving fast here. You thought it would be quieter than in Tangier. That's not so sure. A young worker who saw the arsonists was murdered the following morning.'

'What do the police say?'

'Accidental death, apparently. No post-mortem. A mixture of incompetence, compromise and autosuggestion. The accident hypothesis seems to suit everyone.'

'The joys of provincial France. What about you, what do you say?'

'We already have a deliberate fire and a murder. I've also found signs of false accounting. Only signs, no evidence yet. But there's absolutely no doubt that Daewoo is a real mess. First of all, we have to find out what sort of mess before fabricating one of our own from start to finish.'

'That sounds reasonable. May I simply remind you that we have barely three weeks at the most. And I need evidence, of course.'

'I'm very optimistic.'

'Meanwhile I've got some interesting news too. 3G is registered at 2 Avenue des Érables in Nancy and the company is owned by Daniel Tomaso, ex-Foreign Legion, former mercenary, whose last playground was Croatia, in 1991. Officially 3G provides security guards for factories, and its clients include nearly all the factory owners in the valley of Pondange. It also handles security for political meetings, with customers ranging from the regional council to the various local political parties, mainly but not exclusively right-wing, and it has a garage specialising in limo hire whose drivers also double as bodyguards. Its biggest customers in this area are the European Commission and EU circles in Brussels. The firm's thriving but it also has less official sources of income. Its biggest profits come from the trafficking of stolen cars to Poland and Russia. And probably also from drug trafficking.' Montoya's mind goes into overdrive. 'But my informers can't be sure of that as yet.' A lull. 'You're very quiet?' Montoya groans. 'Even more interesting, 3G recruits local staff but it also acts as a haven for hardcore French and German mercenaries at a loose end between contracts.'

'Pheeew...An army of potential arsonists and hitmen if need be.'

'Precisely. And lastly, Tomaso's official mistress is a Croat he brought back with him. She runs a brothel in Nancy, more or less disguised as a swingers' club, the Oiseau Bleu. It's frequented by all the local bigwigs and some of their wives, cheap thrills guaranteed. In short, the whole works.' A silence. 'Coming across a character like this Tomaso in the environs of Daewoo Pondange doesn't make it the centre of the universe, nor does it make your investigation central to my case, but I take back what I said about your mission being a rest cure.' Another silence. 'I'm aware that you know your job, Montoya, but watch out with customers like this. Suicides happen so easily.'

'Don't worry. Good night.'

Back to the nocturnal quiet. *The key thing is to find the man in charge of the dodgy operations at Daewoo. The one in contact with Tomaso. My money's on Quignard, because I don't trust his type, but I don't have a shred of evidence, and I can't afford to make any mistakes on that score. It's beginning to get cold in this car, time to move. And it just so happens that the road ahead of me leads to Nancy.*

Jean-Louis Robin cruises slowly down the barely lit Avenue des Acacias where vague shapes in the bushes of the Bois de Boulogne beckon him. He can't help but blush, so looks away. He turns off down a pitch dark, narrow twisting road, opens his window and stops about a hundred metres from the junction without turning the engine off. He's been in the habit of meeting Alicia here for months. A tall figure in a fur coat and high heels leans in, elbows resting on the door, face heavily made-up, wide mouth with well-defined lips. She caresses the nape of his neck.

'Hi there, handsome blond, Alicia's not here. Rounded up by the police.' He reaches for the gear stick ready to drive off, but she restrains him with a hand on his arm. 'Don't panic, things are quiet now, and Alicia asked me to take care of you this evening.'

She straightens up, steps back a couple of paces and opens her coat. She's naked. He groans. A magnificent slender body with clean hard lines and smooth bronzed skin. Long slim legs, narrow hips, broad shoulders, a pair of generous silicon-enhanced breasts whose erect nipples he can almost feel cupped in his hands, and a man's cock. Balls and cock displayed invitingly, hairless, in the hollow of her thighs. She walks towards the car without bending, all he can see is the flat stomach, the cock. His hand moves, brushes the cock, the round balls whose skin tautens.

'Open up, handsome blond.'

The voice is authoritative. He groans again. She walks round the car, gets in and sits beside him, holding her coat open.

'You can touch a little, to get you in the mood.' She takes his hand and places it on her hot, throbbing cock, makes him caress it. 'But I don't fuck in cars. Especially not tonight with the cops on heat. I've got a studio flat near here, Rue du Docteur Blanche.' She leans towards his ear, and licks it as she murmurs: 'The lift goes directly up from the underground car park, discretion guaranteed.' Nibbles his ear. 'Alicia told me you like it up the arse from behind, dressed as a woman. Can you feel my cock swelling?' Bites his earlobe. 'You won't forget me, I'm stricter than Alicia.'

Hard to miss the Oiseau Bleu on the Nancy ring road, it stands out for miles around. It occupies a small three-storey building and the façade is painted with frescos depicting a tropical forest filled with multicoloured birds and lit up by flashing blue neon lights. No naked girls on display, notes Montoya. No bouncers on the door either. He enters the building. A vast lobby done out in red velvet and dark wood where two gorgeous young women in simple, figure-hugging long black dresses greet and seat the clients. On the ground floor are the bar, with its ambiance of an English private club, and the restaurant specialising in French cuisine. The hostesses hand guests the menu. In the basement is the nightclub with a striptease show, frequented by a clientele that's into swinging, the hostesses warn. This is reflected in the admission charge, especially for a man on his own. And upstairs? The private lounges are only available on reservation. Montoya realises that he's starving, but chooses the nightclub where there's probably more action.

He goes down a big, brightly-lit, white stone spiral staircase to a cloakroom with a heavy, perfectly soundproof padded door. It closes behind him, and he is immediately plunged into a world of deafening, monotonous techno music, flashing golden strobes and a warm darkness filled with cloying smells. A few moments to adjust before he's able to make out a large rectangular room with pillars supporting the ceiling. In the centre, a dance floor. On two sides, alcoves with cushions, some with curtains drawn. And on the other two sides, a bar, tables where guests can sit, relax and have a drink before re-entering the fray.

To keep things hot there are four pole-dancers in thongs on a podium in the middle of the tables. Nancy, US-style. Montoya takes refuge at the bar and orders a brandy. Sniffs it. Not bad. Warms it. Good even. Whatever happens, his evening won't be completely wasted. His eyes begin to adjust to the dark. There are a lot of people already on the dance floor, with at least fifty, skimpily-dressed women, not all hookers. Not far from him, seated at a table on the edge of the dance floor is a group of five young – or youngish – men. They're all tall and well-built, with close-cropped hair, tight-fitting T-shirts and tattoos. They're joking and drinking among themselves like a sports team playing away. The mercenaries. It was a good idea to come here.

While there could be wives in the room, the girls hanging around the bar are all hookers hanging out for punters. Another brandy. Montoya leans towards the barman and says loudly enough to make himself heard above the techno beat: 'Do you know if Mr Quignard is here tonight? I'm looking for him and I can't see him.' The barman glances distractedly around the room.

'I can't see him either, sir.'

'He told me he'd be here. I was hoping to meet him...'

The barman lets the conversation die. Montoya turns back to face the room. A buxom blonde in pastel pink and blue, skirt slit to the waist and a tight top with a plunging neckline, comes over to him and lays a hand on his arm.

'I'm Deborah. Anyone who's a friend of my friend Quignard is a friend of mine. He's not here tonight. If he were, I'd know. But you can take his place.'

'I can try.'

'He usually starts with a bottle of champagne.'

Montoya signals to the barman, picks up the bottle in an ice bucket and two glasses, and they go and sit at a vacant table on the edge of the dance floor. The barman gazes after them. A few metres away one of the mercenaries is dancing with a couple. He's removed his T-shirt and is showing off his scars, a star-shaped hole in his left shoulder and a long, straight, clean line on his chest, near the heart. The evidence of his mistakes, of his professional errors, thinks Montoya. The woman dancer, a somewhat insipid dark-haired woman in her forties, runs her finger over them, as if tracing a new map of Love. The handsome mercenary is wearing a very long white silk scarf around his neck which he uses to lasso the woman, moving her between the husband and himself.

'Pour a drink my friend, and don't forget about me.'

Montoya slides a hand inside her top, pops out a nipple and bites it playfully.

'How could I forget you, madam?'

She laughs. 'Quignard isn't so imaginative.' She loosens Montoya's tie and unbuttons his shirt. 'Let's go and dance.'

A chore. Montoya moves as little as possible and in the darkness concentrates on trying not to lose contact with Quignard's friend who goes wild to the beat of the music, both breasts now bouncing free. Montoya has to raise his voice loudly to make himself heard.

'Quignard told me he's very friendly with the owner of the Oiseau Bleu.'

A wink. 'That's true.'

'Have they known each other long?'

'I've been here for six months and I always see them together.'

A man has slipped between the girl and him, Montoya is yanked violently back and tripped up. He falls on to some cushions to find the man with the white scarf leaning over him. He looks more intimidating from this angle. The Incredible Hulk personified grabs his shirt collar with one hand and plants him back on his feet with no apparent effort. Another mercenary draws the curtains around the alcove, frisks him, finds his ID, reads it and tells the Hulk, with a grimace: 'Journalist.' Montoya tries to keep both men in his field of vision. The ringleader shakes him.

'Why are you asking about Quignard? What do you want of Quignard, eh?'

Think fast. A suicide can happen so easily. Maximum concentration.

'I don't want anything. Just to have a bit of fun with a girl, like everyone else here, right?' The second man has come to stand beside his chief, blocking the entrance to the alcove. *My back's clear, now's my chance. Fuck you.*

The chief swings back his arm and delivers a blow fit to stun an ox. Montoya ducks it by rotating his body slightly around the hand gripping his collar, then follows through his attacker's movement with both arms, knocking him off balance. As he topples forward Montoya lunges and knees him in the groin. A howl. Then an explosion. Pitch darkness. The world quakes. Montoya is lifted in the air as his opponent seems to have disintegrated, and lands flat on his back under a hail of rubble. His chest crushed, he pants in shallow breaths, the thick air feels like burning dust in his lungs. A bloody face, sticky at the corners of his mouth, under his hand. Total blackout. Blind? A plane engine roars in his head. Deaf? A reflex: get away. Crawl. A wall. Stands up. Stays upright. Feels like laughing, one thought: *Get out of here. Follow the wall.* Stumbles. *Obstacles. Go round them, push them away. Soft moving masses, bodies? Step over.* Legs feeling stronger and stronger. Taste of blood in his mouth. The staircase. Still in the dark. Several people trying to get out. A crush. At last, the street, fresh air, breathe, breathe, hiccup, spit, choke. No, he's not blind, he can make out, behind a haze, the illuminated street, the façade of the Oiseau Bleu with its tropical forest intact. He makes a rapid inventory of his wounds. He can walk, he can breathe, blood on his face, running down his neck, superficial wounds to his head. Vaguely hears the sirens of the fire engines getting closer. *Not deaf either. For now, don't try and understand, grab your chance and get the hell out.* Things were turning nasty down there.

25 October

Quignard finds the usual pile of national dailies on the back seat of his waiting Mercedes. They are folded over twice, and inside them is a set of clearly contrasted black-and-white photos. Without the least shade of doubt they show Park walking into the head office of Daewoo Poland; Park emerging and walking down the street; Park seated at a table in a cafe opposite a stranger; then Park coming out of a residential apartment block. There's even a photo of him in pyjamas, standing at a bedroom window, opening the shutters. You can see the unmade bed. A calm man, always alone, going freely about his business, not in any way trying to hide. Worrying or reassuring? That remains to be seen: no choice. Tomaso the indispensable. The man of the moment.

He glances quickly at the headlines. One on page six of *Libération* catches his eye: "The law hits Lagardère in the wallet." He skims the article: "The holding company's payment system... a shareholder filed a complaint four years ago... legal proceedings have just concluded with Jean-Luc Lagardère being charged with the misuse of company money."

Quignard settles back in his seat, torn between relief and anxiety. Lagardère's tough enough to weather this kind of attack. Proceedings that dragged on for four years now reaching their climax... the competition is pulling out all the stops. When will it be our turn? With a loose cannon like Park roaming around just to make things worse... Yes, definitely, Tomaso is indispensable.

Mid-morning Quignard's driver comes into his office.

'Mr Tomaso's just called me. He asked me to inform you that there was an explosion at the Oiseau Bleu last night.' Quignard freezes. 'As yet nobody knows what type of explosion or how it occurred. The boss is at the scene this morning, with the police.'

Which means he mustn't try and get hold of him. *Explosion, some kind of a racket? Dodgy customers. Will it affect me? Not sure. No connection between me and Tomaso for the moment. Invitation to the hunt, maybe not a good idea, won't repeat it. Be very careful.*

'Was anybody hurt?'

'A few people were slightly wounded. No one killed.'

So it'll be all right. Daniel will sort it out. We've all got our problems. Just then, his secretary rings through.

'Mr Maréchal is asking to see you.'

A pause. Tomaso's shadow behind the driver. *Maréchal, Tomaso, two worlds that must not meet. Awkward.* To the driver: 'Wait here, would you, while I get rid of my visitor?'

Quignard closes the door of his office behind him and walks over to Maréchal with a smile. A warm handshake before he leads him over to the coffee machine, an affable moment in an increasingly oppressive atmosphere. There follows a brief silence. Maréchal is tense and gets straight to the point.

'I've come to find out what's happening to my workers? When they ask me how long they're going to be laid off, what do I reply? When is the factory scheduled to reopen? After all, the machines were unscathed.'

Quignard looks at Maréchal, offers him a cup of coffee. *Hardly the moment to tell him that my main worry is the Thomson takeover. He'd be up for punching me in the face. Better not rub him up the wrong way, a valuable man.*

'I'm not sitting here twiddling my thumbs you know. I'm having to negotiate with the banks to review the company's financial situation. It's not brilliant. I'm trying to obtain deferments and extensions. Daewoo wasn't insured against fire…' Astonishment from Maréchal who spills coffee on his sleeve. 'So I'm having the losses assessed, to get an overview. I'm applying for subsidies to rebuild and start up again, and I'm talking to the local council to find out how they see our future. All that takes time. We should have a clearer picture within a couple of weeks.'

Maréchal chews his plastic cup.

'That's a long time when you haven't got a cent to live on.'

'Amrouche has been asked to look at the workers' records and put together proposals for retraining courses in the event that…'

'Oh right. Who could ask for more?'

'You know that there's a departmental manager's job waiting for you at Thomson, when we're the bosses, in a month or two.'

The tension increases palpably.

'I'm not talking to you about myself right now, Maurice. I'm talking to you about my people, the ones in my sector, more than a hundred workers. What are you doing for them? You're the boss of this factory now, aren't you?'

The door opens. Rolande Lepetit is standing on the threshold, spectacular in her black overcoat buttoned up to the chin, a hard, set expression. She has come on foot from the Cité des Jonquilles, going over and over two or three phrases in her mind, to the point of exasperation. *A bank account in Luxembourg. Me. Me, who supports my mother and my son. Never asked anyone for anything. Always earned every cent I spend. A bank account in Luxembourg. Their world, not mine. No respect. That's what it is, they lack respect. We have to talk. You're not afraid of him. Talk. Have to. Leave Aisha out of it, whatever happens.* She takes a step forward, closes the door and thrusts her hands deeper in her pockets.

'Mr Quignard, I've come to talk to you about something...'

She casts around for the right word, can't find it, and clenches her hands deep in her pockets. Maréchal makes as if to leave the room.

'Stay, Mr Maréchal. Just wait, this matter concerns you too.' The two men exchange a glance. 'Daewoo's accounts list a bank account in Luxembourg in my name with a very large sum of money in it.' The two men stand stock still. She leans forward, tense. 'Obviously I don't have a bank account in Luxembourg, and I want an explanation.'

She presents a solid wall of hostility and persistence.

'Ms Lepetit, please...'

She turns to Maréchal, punctuating each phrase with a jerk of her head and shoulders.

'And you too, Mr Maréchal, you're on the list, in case you weren't aware of it. One of these famous accounts is in your name.'

Maréchal's reaction is dramatic. His face turns ashen, he opens his mouth and closes it again with a gulp, but not a sound comes out. Quignard is finding the situation increasingly awkward, he needs to act fast. He walks over to Rolande, takes her by the arm and sits her down in an armchair. He sits down beside her and talks to her in a confidential tone.

'Ms Lepetit, I know nothing about any of this, I've just taken over the reins of Daewoo. Tell me first of all where you got your information.'

'During the occupation of the offices Étienne Neveu was playing around on one of the computers.' Rolande hears Maréchal exhale suddenly behind her, as if he'd just received a punch in the stomach. 'On it he found a list of bank accounts in Luxembourg. One is in my name and there are more in the names of Maréchal, Amrouche and Nourredine, and probably others too, but those names are for definite.'

'When did he tell you this?'

'He didn't. But he told a lot of people on the night of the occupation and the rumour found its way back to me yesterday. I find it completely unacceptable, and I want an explanation.'

'Ms Lepetit, I'm not taking this matter lightly. But please understand, the company's entire accounts were removed from the premises on the day after the fire. We couldn't leave them in a gutted factory. It will probably take several weeks before we get ourselves sorted out.' He gets to his feet, helps Rolande up and sees her to the door. 'I give you my word that I'll do everything I can to clarify this matter.' He opens the door for her and pushes her into the corridor. 'And you'll be informed the minute we find out anything.'

She's in the corridor as he closes the door again. Quignard leans against the wall for a moment, eyes closed as he blots his upper lip and the roots of his hair with a handkerchief.

'She's a pain in the arse, your protégée,' he says to Maréchal.

'I disagree.' Frostily: 'And don't forget you can't tell me you know nothing of all this. Are you sure this isn't to do with your friend Park's system of bogus invoices?'

'Yes, it probably is.'

'Park was embezzling company money, that's his business and yours. But I won't stand for him mixing up our names in it all. Your dumping ground for the unemployed can burn down for all I care, but for you to fail to lift a little finger to help the workers who were inside, that's a disgrace. What's more it wouldn't have bothered me in the least if Bouziane had taken the rap for the fire, with everything else he's got on his conscience. But finger

Nourredine, one of the few reliable workers out of the whole bunch, simply because he led the strike – no way will you get me to swallow that. And don't, whatever you do, tell me the tale of what happened to Étienne Neveu. You scare me. Your story's full of holes. I only ask one thing of you: make sure you leave me out of your master cock-up. Understood?'

The door slams.

When Quignard returns to his office, the driver is standing before the bay window contemplating the trees in the valley rippling in the wind.

Montoya had fallen asleep fully dressed on his bed. He awakens fairly late in the morning, body aching and mind numb. The first thing he does is to switch on the bedside radio and tune into a local station to try and find out what happened to him last night at the Oiseau Bleu. Schmaltzy music as he glances at his watch: the news will be on soon. *First of all, have a wash.* His reflection in the bathroom mirror is not a pretty sight. Jacket and shirt ripped. Flashback, the mercenary's burly frame above him as he lay on the floor, cornered in the alcove. Allowing himself to be caught out like that, black mark, lack of vigilance. *I knew what I was getting myself into. Won't happen again.* Then, the blow, dodging it, neat, nice move, nothing to say about that. Kneeing him in the balls: bullseye. Certainly effective. Smile. *I bet the Hulk's finding it hard to walk today.* And the explosion... *Full inventory: only minor damage.* Three nasty cuts to his scalp which he washes and disinfects, that'll do. Scratches on his face, hands, a wound in the neck, he applies an antiseptic cream. He steps under the shower. On the radio, the news. Metz football team is the main item. I don't give a shit. And then immediately afterwards:

Last night, around three a.m., a mysterious explosion caused major damage to the premises of the Oiseau Bleu, the well-known Nancy nightclub. Was it accidental or deliberate? The state prosecutor, who has opened an investigation, is keeping an open mind. Some fifty casualties were treated at Nancy hospital, around thirty people have been kept in, but nobody is in a critical condition and there were no deaths. The Oiseau Bleu remains closed for the time being.

He turns off the radio and meticulously puts on a beige silk and cotton mix shirt. He does the buttons up slowly, one by one. *Quignard is embroiled in this for sure. He had numerous opportunities to meet Tomaso in Brussels or in the valley. His car and driver? Check them out. No tie, no appointments that require one. What about Tomaso?* He remembers Valentin's words: *It's a case that requires intelligence, skill and imagination, lots of imagination.* Black trousers, checks the crease, impeccable, black leather belt with a polished steel buckle. *Give your imagination free rein. Tomaso is probably involved in the drug business, the secret services reckon, but it's not proven. So, it's recent, otherwise they'd know for sure. He has access to the ideal network of dealers through his drivers and bodyguards. They know the consumers who are loaded and have dealings with the concierges in the big hotels.* Woollen cardigan in a slightly darker beige than the shirt. *And the factory security guards in another sector of the market.* Black lace-up shoes, English leather. *If he wants to get involved in drugs, either he goes into business with those who are already there, or he ousts them and takes their place. Initially, he teams up with the Hakims. Then he takes advantage of his connection with Quignard and the local big shots to have them arrested. They take their revenge by blowing up the Oiseau Bleu. A moderate explosion: they're still in the negotiation phase. It all stacks up.* A final touch of the comb to disguise the gashes as best he can. *There's still Bouziane. He fits into this somehow, but I don't know how.* He looks at himself in the mirror. *That'll do. I'd better move fast. It won't take Tomaso and Quignard more than twenty-four hours to exchange notes and identify me. Keep on thinking. Bouziane isn't one of the security guard mafia. What emerges from the initial evidence against him is that he's been a small-time dealer for years, and everyone knows it. So Bouziane works with the Hakims. Tomaso and Quignard both used him, one to bring down the Hakims, the other to finger him as the arsonist. It still holds up.* Montoya slips on his black leather jacket. He feels on top form.

Montoya's having a couscous in a little restaurant in Pondange, sitting at the table next to Amrouche, with whom he's quickly struck up a conversation. A journalist looking for first-hand accounts of the Daewoo strike. Amrouche could have gone on for ever. Particularly on the subject of the occupation of the offices, in which he claims to have played a leading role. Sentimental, lost, hurt, with a profound hatred of Nourredine. Extraordinary how readily people talk. They need to tell someone about their traumatic experience, and not many people around here seem prepared to listen. But Montoya's a good listener. Chuffed, Amrouche invites him to drop into his new office to see him whenever he likes. The next conversation, scheduled later that afternoon, will probably be much more difficult.

Rossellini's singing loudly in the shower. His daily game of tennis, and he's never played better. He beat one of his usual partners hollow. Robin, who was not in good shape. So perhaps not so surprising. Dresses quickly. The game ahead is likely to be much harder. Pillbox, a little blue pill. Sure of himself. Barely a quarter of an hour left to grab a salad and a coffee at the clubhouse before going back to the office.

Robin's waiting for him at a table by the window. Rossellini looks him over. Tall, slim, fair-haired, a graduate of ENA, the prestigious École Nationale d'Administration, a state councillor getting on for fifty, and a member of the French stock exchange regulatory body: an excellent track record you could say. But he lacks ambition and is stagnating in the civil service. And he's a practising Catholic, married, father of six. Unlucky.

Rossellini sits down at the table and places on it an orange cardboard file which he slides towards Robin. A thrill of excitement, then he attacks the tomato and mozzarella salad in front of him. Robin half opens the file, a packet of large-format photos. The first one shows a close-up of his own face wearing a dark wig, his face caked with make-up, all smudged. His mouth is open, his eyes closed, in the throes of orgasm. Retches. How could he look so ugly? And standing over him, the drag queen from the night before, hands on his hips, fucking his arse. Closes the file, ashen. Pours himself a big glass of water, drinks it slowly, his eyes half closed. He looks up at Rossellini, who's almost finished his tomato and mozzarella salad.

'You astound me, Philippe, I thought I knew you...'

'Am I entitled to say the same to you?'

Weak smile. 'The ENA old boys' network isn't what people think. So what's this all about?'

'Today or tomorrow, courtesy of the Financial Securities

Committee, you'll be receiving at your office around ten anonymous letters drawing your attention to the fluctuations of Matra share prices at the time its takeover of Thomson was announced.'

'These fluctuations have not escaped the Financial Securities Committee's attention. But we can't see Lagardère becoming involved in this type of operation for the time being.'

'Lagardère, no. But his partner in the operation, Kim, the Daewoo boss? What was to stop him speculating on Matra shares? Do you know who Kim is?'

Robin finishes eating his warm goat's cheese on a bed of dandelion leaves. He chews meticulously, down to the last crumb, his gaze darting back and forth from his plate to the hardbound file. Then he puts down his knife and fork, wipes his mouth and gives a long sigh.

'Very well. I expect the prints and the negatives as soon as the investigation starts.'

'Of course.'

He rises. 'I'm in a bit of a hurry today. No time for coffee. Sorry I played so badly, I was a bit tired. Rough night, work, worries...'

And he smiles, picks up the orange file as though it were the most natural thing in the world, and walks out, leaving Rossellini to pick up the bill. Classy, you've got to hand it to him. And the wild sex, who'd have believed it? Rossellini feels a pang of jealousy. Flashback: *Valentin, we'll cross-check my contacts and yours. You'll see, you'll be surprised. This is probably only the beginning.* He's about to get an insight into Kim's crooked system. He'll have to probe deep and rummage around. *Life is assuming unexpected colours.* A ray of sunshine on his back as he extends his legs, *let the pressure relax, savour the moment.* Blackmail: a new sport that gives him a thrill and a great deal of pleasure.

The door half opens.

'Mrs Neveu?'

'Mm...'

A wall of suspicion. Montoya puts his shoulder to the door and shoves, flashing his press pass.

'I'm a journalist and I'm writing an article on Daewoo.' He steps inside. I wasn't able to get to the cemetery. Please accept my condolences.' Now he's standing in the cramped hallway. 'May I talk to you?'

She shrugs.

'Seeing as you're already inside, come into the kitchen. The girls are in the front room watching TV.'

American cartoons, probably. Tinny voices and outbursts of children's laughter. The kitchen isn't big. He sits down, she walks round in circles before sitting down too.

'Mrs Neveu, before his accident, did your husband talk to you about the Daewoo strike?' She's still very tense.

'No. He came home very late and I was asleep. Next morning when the alarm went off, he just told me that the factory had burned down and that I should let him sleep. I got the girls ready and we left together. Then I dropped them off at school on my way to work as usual. I never saw him again.'

'Did you know that your husband smoked a bit of dope from time to time at the factory?'

Smile. She's beginning to relax. 'I don't know what you want, but that's not news. He wasn't the only one.'

'Do you know his dealer?'

'Are you joking? Do you think I've got time to think about all that? With my job, my two girls, and a husband to look after? I'll show you my schedule if you like.'

'How did you find out that he'd had an accident and that he was dead?'

'The police told me. The first night, he didn't come home. Well, I wasn't too worried. He was a womaniser, my husband. A womaniser and he lived life in the fast lane. I went to bed and slept. The next morning, he still wasn't back and he didn't often spend the whole night away. When he didn't come home the next night either, I started to get worried and called the police. They found his body the day after. They told me that when I reported him missing they took a look in the woods below our estate, and that's where they found him. An accidental fall which broke his neck.'

'Have you seen the forensic report?' She immediately becomes suspicious again.

'No.'

'Didn't you ask to see it?'

She gets up, walks over to the window, and stands gazing out over the plateau stretching as far as the horizon. Apart from a few clumps of trees and silhouettes of gigantic silos to break it up, the prospect is endlessly flat under the bleak late afternoon light of a day without sunshine. After what seems like an age, she comes back over to him, a look of profound exhaustion on her face.

'I'm from the countryside. My parents have a farm on the plateau. When I met Étienne, I was sixteen, I dreamed of the city, of going out and having fun, seeing shows, meeting people. I got a job as a cashier in a supermarket thirty kilometres from here. I see people all right, that's for sure. A husband who's always chasing women, never at home, two kids to look after, to bring up almost alone on a housing estate that's miles from everywhere. And this view. It's unbelievable how beautiful the plateau can look when you see it from the windows of our farm, and how desolate and sinister it seems from the third floor of a council flat. So, when Mr Quignard came to tell me that he would ensure that the funeral expenses would be borne by Daewoo, and that the company will pay me compensation for my husband's death, I didn't ask any questions, I said fine. Straight away. I'm going back to the farm with my two girls, and that'll be the end of it. It'll be cheaper for me and I'll always be able to find a job. And what Daewoo gives me, even if it doesn't amount to much, will help me and my girls with the move. Now, go away and leave me alone.'

She turns her back on him and fumbles in a cupboard to occupy her hands. Montoya gets up and leaves, slamming the front door. On the landing, he leans against the door jamb, listening. He hears the TV and the girls' voices, their mother bustling about. *She must be wishing she hadn't talked to me. But she had to unburden herself, one way or another, in her solitude. She's wondering what she can get out of it.* He waits. And then the click as she picks up the telephone, which he'd noticed on the wall in the hall. She dials a number with nervous concentration.

'Mr Quignard?... I had a visit from a journalist... No, I don't know who he is. He asked me questions about Étienne's death... If he was in the habit of walking down that path, if I'd read the forensic report... Of course... Like we said... but I wanted to let you know that I'm prepared to move right away, this week. Only it'll cost me...'

At least she's got her head screwed on. Montoya escapes noiselessly down the stairs before the end of the phone call.

Quignard replaces the handset very gently, trying to control his movement. *Be calm, calm. Today could turn into a nightmare if*

I'm not careful. Pours a double brandy, turns on Radio Classique and sinks into his armchair. *Let's take stock. This morning, I find out from that half-crazy Lepetit woman that Park's fraudulent accounts were seen by Étienne Neveu. Perhaps. She wouldn't be capable of making up something like that. Who does Neveu tell about these lists? She answers: everyone. That I don't believe. It happened more than ten days ago. And Maréchal wasn't aware of it? I wouldn't have heard anything from Amrouche? Impossible. Neveu was with someone when he saw the lists. Someone who, for one reason or another, didn't say anything until yesterday. Lepetit couldn't keep it to herself for more than twenty-four hours. Now, think. At the same time, a journalist tries to talk to Neveu's widow and asks her questions that prove he thinks Étienne Neveu's death was no accident. A brilliant accident, well orchestrated, everyone was convinced.* Quignard pictures the blaze, its unexpected fierceness, the roar, familiar in a strange way, the showers of sparks, the iridescent flashes, a lavish display that had everybody mesmerised, and Étienne's diminutive physique, rushing from one group to another, nobody taking any notice or listening to him. Not a single witness mentioned him to the police. *Even Maréchal, standing next to me, his eyes riveted, a fire in his valley, had forgotten about him, until the arrival of that pain-in-the-arse this morning. Question: how had this shit-stirrer got on the trail of Neveu's widow? Someone talked yesterday, to Lepetit and to the shit-stirrer. Someone who was in the factory with Neveu. Who saw the lists with Neveu. And who'd kept quiet about it until yesterday. Why? Because he and Neveu must have been up to something together. Who can know? I can't count on Maréchal any more, he's put himself out of the running. Amrouche. Of course, Amrouche.* Glance at his watch. *Not quite six o'clock. He's probably still there, he always works very late.* Smug little smile. *Smart move, taking him on. I knew he'd be useful to me sooner or later.* He turns off the radio, sends the secretary home, then heads for Amrouche's office near the staff lounge and the coffee machine. He hammers on the door and pushes it open. Amrouche, hunched over his work in the light of his desk lamp, is handwriting a note about a Daewoo worker he'd spoken to that afternoon to find out if he was willing to take on a job elsewhere.

'Ali, come and have a coffee with me. We're the only ones still here, and you and I need to discuss a delicate matter.'

Amrouche leaps up. Quignard is already at the machine, he hands him a cup of coffee, picks up his own, and the two men sit down.

'I'm finishing off the paperwork for Étienne Neveu's compensation.' A pause. 'Well, for his widow and his two girls. Do you know about it?'

Amrouche nods. Bosses like Quignard are rare.

'I have a problem. Someone came to see me this afternoon,' he hesitates, 'he asked me not to divulge his visit.' Hesitates again. 'He's not a Daewoo employee. In short, he claims that Neveu was involved in drug trafficking in Pondange, and that he was hanging around in the woods to do a deal on the day he died. That would be awkward.'

'I don't think it's true.'

'If the police arrest any dealers over the next few months who implicate Neveu, it'll make things difficult for me.'

'In my view, there's no danger. Étienne smoked a bit, like a lot of kids in the factory. But I've never heard of him being involved in any dealing.'

'My contact claims Neveu took advantage of the strike to deal on the actual factory premises.'

Big smile. 'He was much too busy for that.'

'What do you mean?'

Amrouche falters, blots out the insistent image of Karim and Étienne slumped in front of the computer and closes his eyes for a moment to try and shut out the arses jiggling mechanically on the screen. Then: 'He spent most of the day with a girl.'

'Do you know her? Can you send her to see me so I can complete the paperwork?'

'I know her, yes, but I can't send her to you. She's a very well brought-up girl, and very reserved. She allowed herself to be sweet-talked by Neveu, who was an incorrigible skirt-chaser, because she was devastated by Émilienne's accident that morning and thrown off balance by everything that happened that day. But she couldn't bear anyone to know about her fling, or me to have told you about it. Or her father. She hasn't set foot outside her home since the strike. No, don't count on me for that.'

'Fine. I'll just have to take your word for it, Ali. Which I will, because you know Daewoo's employees better than anyone, and I trust you completely. Thank you for your help.'

Quignard returns to his office. Computer. Daewoo personnel file. If the girl was devastated by this Émilienne's accident, she must have been on the same production line, the same shift. So she saw the electrocution. An accident is only devastating if you witness it directly. Otherwise the factories would all be empty, it would be impossible to find anyone to work in them. He ends up with a list of eight girls. Eliminate Émilienne, and Rolande Lepetit, since I know where she was during the strike. I'm looking for a young girl – the allusion to her father suggests she was probably unmarried. The records list two unmarried girls on Rolande Lepetit's shift: Jeanne Beauvallon and Aisha Saidani. *Or her father.* I'll take Aisha Saidani first. He reads the employee record carefully. It's her. She lives at the same address as Rolande Lepetit. The shit-stirrer comes and questions Rolande. That makes sense, her dismissal sparked off the strike, and he meets Aisha into the bargain. Cosy little chat, all three of them. Aisha, who's kept quiet so far to protect her reputation as a shy virgin, probably opens up and confides in the shit-stirrer – the power of the media – and tells him about her experience of the strike like a porn film, and mentions the lists. And the arsonists? Lepetit turns up in my office, the journalist at the widow's. *It all fits. And I'm up shit creek.*

What to do? No rush. First of all, think. Quignard pours himself a third brandy, switches off the lights and sits in the dark looking out over the valley, his feet on the bay windowsill. To recap the sequence of events: Aisha looks at the lists with Neveu. Talks to Rolande Lepetit about it and yesterday, also to the journalist. Nothing to suggest she saw the arsonists too, since nobody's mentioned it. They could have parted company at the end of the day. The journalist goes to see Neveu's widow. So he's made a connection between the lists and Neveu's death, he can do that by simple logical deduction. He gets nothing out of Neveu's widow. *For the time being he has no proof and I'm in the clear. Two good points. As for Aisha, it's unlikely she'll talk to the police. She'd have to face her father, public opprobrium, and the Neveu family. That's a lot. Anyway, what would be the point? The police won't go looking for her. If she did decide to testify they'd undermine her testimony to salvage their investigation. Take a worst-case scenario and all that will take time, longer than I need. As a last resort, we pin it all on Park. As for Maréchal... Old solidarity between steelworkers. Worn out. As Head of Department he can always say he doesn't give a damn. I don't believe him. He'll keep it shut.* He takes a large swig of brandy, there's a feeling of well-being, ripples of pleasure. *The smartest way is to use Amrouche to keep an eye on the father and the daughter, do nothing and see what happens.*

Quignard puts down his empty glass, gets up, stretches, then walks down through the empty, ill-lit building to the exit where his driver's waiting for him.

'Mr Tomaso asks if you can have dinner with him this evening at the Oiseau Bleu.' Quignard looks at his watch.

'This late?'

'Mr Tomaso seems very insistent.'

To talk about the explosion in his nightclub, no doubt. He climbs into the Mercedes. After all why not? A slap-up meal, the girls, Deborah, much better than eating a solitary dinner at home staring at the valley while listening to Beethoven's *Fifth Symphony.*

'Fine. Head for Nancy.'

As soon as he leaves the Neveu apartment, Montoya phones Valentin.

'Call me back in five minutes.'

He checks his watch. Five minutes to kill, hanging around the car park where kids are playing football. He walks to the edge of the woods, spots the start of the path Étienne Neveu must have taken the day he died. It can be seen clearly from the windows of the apartment block. Was Neveu alone when he set off down this path? Did the cops make any effort to get statements? Doesn't know. *And you won't get to know either. Poor guy. A little wad of dosh and the deal is done.*

The football flies in his direction. Montoya dives forward, blocks it with his chest, swerves away from two kids charging towards him, aims a long, plunging ball from his instep which sails between the two heaps of clothes marking the goal. Then he saunters off, feeling light. *I've got my man. Quignard. I haven't felt so good for… a very long time.* The five minutes are up.

It's Valentin on the other end of the phone again. Montoya opens fire.

'I've identified the kingpin in our case, the man who's pulling the strings at Daewoo and who's in business with Tomaso. One Quignard, boss of a design consultancy and a local bigwig;

so far, run-of-the-mill for a little provincial town. But he's also very well connected in Brussels, the strongman of the European Development Plan, the man who rubber-stamps all the region's subsidy grants. He's been a non-executive director of Daewoo for some time, and since the fire he's taken over the reins.'

'Do you have proof?'

'No. But I have convictions.'

'What happens next?'

'Quignard and Tomaso are hyperactive, they don't have the experience or the mettle to wait and let things calm down. If I push a bit harder they'll make a move. And make mistakes, which will give me ammunition against them.'

'I'll think about it. Is that all you have to tell me?'

'For the time being.'

Valentin is silent. Then:

'A bomb went off at the Oiseau Bleu last night. Had you heard about it?'

'Yes.' *Bite the bullet. You've got no choice.* 'I was there.'

'Why didn't you tell me?'

'Because I think the Hakims are involved. They've resurfaced as drug traffickers in Antwerp during the last few days. Knowing their tendency to work with the cops I'm not sure whether they're closely in touch with you or not.'

'We're not yet used to working together, Montoya. I've just got one thing to say: I never play against my own side. Was the explosion connected to our business?'

'Yes, without a doubt, but I don't yet know how. Indirectly, I'd say.'

'Let's get back to your Mr Quignard. Here, in Paris, our affairs are going well, smoothly. There in Pondange it sounds like the Wild West. And this Quignard character changes everything. We're no longer talking about provincial wheeling and dealing. The sums handled by the bureaucrats in Brussels put this in a different league of corruption altogether, and that's what interests us. We're going to take drastic action.' Montoya tenses. *He's giving me the boot.* 'Does Quignard have offices in Pondange?'

'Yes.'

'That'll make our job easier. Tomorrow evening I'm sending you an expert in phone-tapping and bugging. Find a way of getting him into Quignard's office tomorrow night. He and I will take care of the rest. Call me back tomorrow afternoon so I can fix up a meeting.' Montoya exhales, *I'm still in.* Valentin hesitates for a moment. 'In the meantime, your instructions stay the same: watch out.'

'Goodbye, chief.'

In the meantime, I'm off to fuck Stakhanova.

Montoya has a date with Rolande. Dinner in Brussels. They could have gone somewhere closer, but it was her idea, and she seemed keen on it. 'If you want a good night out, you can't go to Metz or Nancy, only Brussels will do,' she said. 'It's more cheerful, more lively, a capital city.' She's standing waiting for him on the pavement in front of the Cité des Jonquilles estate. She's a tall figure in a severe, well-cut grey wool suit, the black overcoat flung around her shoulders in a casual fashion, carefully contrived. As she stands immobile beneath a lamp post, smoking, her light helmet of bleached hair cut in a bob is eyecatching. Hard to say what it is that makes her a beauty. Men's eyes are drawn to Rolande in the way that the spotlight loves some actresses. When he pulls up, she throws away her cigarette, slides inside the car, and slams the door.

'Let's get out of here quickly, you never know. If they catch up with us…'

When the car moves into the fast lane she sighs, loosens her overcoat, stretches out her legs in her beautiful black leather boots, and turns to Montoya.

'So you've got your article on the strike, thanks to my friend's story.'

Montoya concentrates on the road so as not to miss the Brussels turn-off.

'More or less. I'm still looking for more information about this and that.'

'I'm always amazed when she finally opens her mouth. I don't know where she gets her strength from. It's as though her words come from her gut and have the texture of flesh.'

She fiddles with the radio and soon finds a Belgian station that plays popular, all-purpose disco music which she seems to like. She hums along. Montoya returns to the subject.

'Did you notice that Aisha mentioned several arsonists, most likely people unknown to Étienne Neveu?'

'Of course.' Pointing: 'Turn right. There, now it's straight ahead to Brussels.' Silence for a while. 'I'd never have thought of asking her to talk about her experience of the strike if you hadn't been there. I don't know, perhaps I assumed it had been the same for all of us so there was no point talking about it. I was very taken aback.'

Montoya stares into the rear-view mirror.

'What she says clears your friend, this Nourredine who's in prison. But will she agree to testify, to tell the police, the judges, the whole of Pondange, what she told us yesterday?'

'Announce to her father and to the whole town: I slept with Étienne Neveu during the strike? I wouldn't bet on it. Though I already talked to her about it today and I think she'll come round. She needs a little time. The day when she does that, she'll be free. She knows it, and wants it.'

He feels like telling her: If your friend agrees to testify, she won't be free, she'll be in danger of being killed. Étienne Neveu was murdered because he saw the men who started the fire. He looks at her. Relaxed and happy. Brussels is a long way away. *If you explode this bombshell in her face, you've blown it. You won't get any more out of her. He decides not to.*

'What kind of man was Étienne Neveu?'

'I don't really know. A skirt-chaser, for sure, but you know, men and women hardly mixed at the factory.'

'Did he have any friends?'

'No idea.'

'Did he know Karim Bouziane?'

'I really don't know.' She thinks. 'They're quite similar, the pair of them. Why are you asking me that question?'

He avoids answering. 'If Nourredine didn't start the fire, then who did, in your opinion?' She suddenly looks pensive.

'It was a strange outfit, Daewoo. I say "was" because I don't believe it'll ever re-open. Amrouche is already trying to find alternative employment for as many people as possible. An odd outfit.' Her hands caress the dashboard, wipe away an imaginary speck of dust. 'The atmosphere was weird. Not easy to put into words. There were huge numbers of Korean managers, too many for that kind of operation, and you never knew where they were or what they were doing. At first, it used to make Maréchal furious, then he calmed down. The workers turned up when and if they felt like it and the production lines carried on, even if the shift was short-staffed. Safety levels were a disaster, with the highest accident rate in the region. Even though we were handling hazardous chemicals, nobody gave a damn. The same went for the quality of the products. No real quality control. In my opinion, what we produced was pretty much worthless.' Her hands flutter and hesitate, in front of the windscreen swallowing up the road. 'The workers were all very young. For a lot of them, it was their first job, it all seemed normal to them. But I... it's as though the whole factory was a stage set, and we were acting in a play without understanding what it was about...'

Montoya sees another woman, poised over her *Murmure* in the bar at the Lutétia. She belongs in another world and comes from a different perspective but, while speaking a different language in different tones, she says more or less the same thing: the factory was a front for money laundering and embezzlement. The weight of two overlapping views. The weight of Rolande's hand on his arm.

'...It's almost as though the director had had enough and set fire to the theatre. I like that idea. Besides, the Korean managers vanished into thin air like extras after the show.' She smiles. 'Or you could also imagine that the audience burned the whole place down, enraged at the sight of the actors' rebellion.' She rubs her hands together. 'You can imagine anything.' She dreams for a moment, leaning against the door, looking out at the road, absently listening to the disco songs which keep on thumping out. 'It's funny, I almost said: you can hope for anything.'

'Rolande, may I ask you a question?'

'Of course.'

'Aren't you intrigued by those lists of bank accounts in Luxembourg that Neveu was talking about and on which your name appears?'

'Of course I am.' Silence. Her hands smooth her trouser pleats. 'I went and asked Quignard for an explanation this morning.' Montoya's hands clench the steering wheel. He concentrates on overtaking an articulated lorry. 'Maréchal was there, he also...'

She allows a silence to set in.

'Maréchal, the foreman?'

'Yes.' A hand flutters, seeking a word. 'A brute. I slapped him after Émilienne's accident.' Her hand pauses on the armrest, caressing it. 'But he's also a man who respects the worker, and a man I respect in return.'

He respects the worker. A covert glance at Rolande's profile. No trace of irony. The last witness of a vanished world, Atlantis, or not far off. She continues: 'Well, I did have respect for him until today.'

'Do he and Quignard know each other?'

'Very well. They used to work in the same steelworks. That creates a bond and they've remained very close. Quignard listens to what Maréchal tells him. They may not be friends, because now Quignard's a boss and Maréchal's still a foreman, just a glorified worker, but they're very close.' She turns to him, looks at him, hesitates, makes up her mind. 'I'm convinced Maréchal and Quignard knew about the lists of bank accounts. They merely asked who'd told me. And then Quignard threw me out, like a little girl who's slightly simple. If Maréchal's in on it, he's also…'

'Did you mention Aisha to them?'

'No.' Montoya's relieved, a few days' respite. 'I have a very funny feeling. The factory isn't a factory, it's a stage set. Quignard isn't a concerned boss, he's a crook. And you, you're no journalist, but I won't ask who you are for the time being. As for me, I'm no longer a factory worker.'

Montoya reclines against the seat and sighs. It feels as if relations with Rolande are suddenly becoming very simple. She isn't, or has ceased being, Stakhanova. And he doesn't have to act the journalist any more, but that doesn't stop him from continuing to brood. *If Maréchal knows about those damn lists, how to tackle him without Quignard finding out about it straight away?* A glance at Rolande's profile. Interconnected networks, utterly impenetrable as far as he's concerned, vaguely exotic, no further away than the next street. *You can live your whole life without setting foot inside a factory.* At last, the outskirts of Brussels. Rolande smiles at him.

Once in Brussels and with the car parked, she places her hand on his shoulder as they enter Léon's: 'Enough. We're not going to talk about the factory any more.'

He follows her through a maze of staircases and dining rooms, amid the smell of mussels and chips and the waiters bustling about. In a cosy low-ceilinged dining room on the first floor, painted a cheerful orange and yellow, they sit at a window table overlooking a narrow street swarming with people. Mussels and chips for both of them, and a Sudden Death for him, Perrier for her. She attacks her mussels with impressive gusto.

'What about that big photo of Venice, in the living room? Have you ever been to Venice?' The question delights Rolande.

'No, I haven't, unfortunately. I've never been anywhere. I was born in Pondange, like my mother and my grandmother. My mother's dependent on me, and dependent is the word. Yesterday evening you pretended not to hear the groans and the snoring from the next room, because you're well brought up. I'd double-locked my mother in the end room, because she was drunk out of her skull, to stop her making a scene. I was already picking her up off the kitchen floor when I was ten. I can never leave her alone in the evenings or at night. This evening Aisha's going to drop by to put her to bed. I'm not going to make a big deal of it, she's my mother. I look after her, it's only natural, but it's hard work.' She licks her fingers. 'I'm going to have another plate of chips, with mayonnaise. And I've got a son. I've sent him to a boarding school run by Jesuits in Metz. I had no other option. He works hard, takes his baccalaureate in two years' time. But I miss him a lot. In the evenings, when I come home from work, I'd like to hug him, cook special meals for him. And the boarding school's costing me more and more.' She stops, suddenly serious. 'That's why being reinstated mattered so much to me. I get back my entitlements, my allowances, time to look for another job...'

'We said we wouldn't talk about the factory any more.'

'We did.' She rests her chin on her two fists, her eyes wide, and smiles at him. 'My travels are my lovers, as you see. Always casual affairs. Can't take the risk of anyone wanting to tie me down. With my mother and my son, I've got enough on my plate.'

He returns her smile.

'From what I understand, I belong to the category of those who wouldn't tie you down, so I'm in with a chance. I'm very pleased. But what about Venice?'

'I've already talked a lot. Now it's your turn. Journalist or whatever, you must travel a lot. Tell me about a city that'll give me something to dream about.'

Dream, nightmare, city, Tangier, a recurring memory these days. He looks at Rolande, a woman who quietly gets on with life without making a fuss. *You're not going to start crying?* And he tells her about the old city clinging to the rocks, white, the intense light burning your eyes, the sumptuous villas from another era, a little dilapidated and their gardens tumbling down to the sea, or the ocean shores where, you never know, people can take refuge at night, in the cool air, to smoke kif under the bougainvillaea. And that morning when the sea washed dozens of plastic sachets filled with cocaine on to the rocks. The whole city went fishing and went crazy with music, singing, dancing, one long party that lasted for twenty-four hours until the US secret services turned up at dawn to take charge of things, as the Moroccan police lacked motivation and were already well stoned. They gathered up what was left and burned it in the boiler of a freighter in the port. It gave off a suffocating black smoke, in front of hundreds of children gathered on the quayside, silently weeping.

She's enjoying this, he's brilliant. In his memory, Tangier changes colour.

'What about Venice? I'm not going to let you avoid my question.'

'The photo was a goodbye present from an Italian, a Venetian. I was very young. I thought he was very handsome. He's the father of my son. Thanks to him, I broke the curse on my family: single mothers, from mother to daughter, for generations. But I had a boy, the chain of misery is broken. For me, Venice is the pearl in life's ocean.'

The desserts arrive: copious, plumed mountains of cream studded with garish colours. Montoya orders a brandy to wash it down.

The bill. He helps her on with her coat.

'Let's walk to the Grand'Place.'

He takes her arm, she leans against him. She's almost as tall as he is. They walk hip to hip, their rhythmic steps in sync. A prelude to love, muses Montoya, his eyes half closed, attentive to every gesture, every tremor, to the mounting tension of desire. He stops in front of the entrance to a discreet luxury hotel, a few metres from the Grand'Place.

'Shall we go in?'

She enters first, he follows. A vast room done out entirely in greys and whites, a huge copper bedstead, white duvet, drawn grey velvet curtains. The bathroom is in grey and white marble. Rolande removes her coat, takes off her shoes and, barefoot, turns on the bath taps, pours in some foam, then continues to undress without inhibition, scattering her clothes haphazardly on a chair, the edge of the bed, the floor. Propped against the washbasin, Montoya watches her. A long streamlined body, long legs, long thighs, narrow hips, not much of a waist, high, round breasts, lovely shoulders, a solid body, full, not many curves, with delicate, pale skin. The triangle of dark curly hairs emphasises the artificiality of her blonde helmet. As if she wore a wig, as if she weren't completely naked. She comes towards him.

'You're not allowed to touch anything while you've still got your clothes on.'

And she steps into the bathtub, lies down and disappears under the foam. He undresses in the bedroom, carefully folding his clothes, then joins her. The warmth of the water, groping contact between two smooth bodies, barely glimpsed, slithering, eluding, seeking each other, passionately embracing, legs extended, intertwined, feet colliding, he kisses her in the foam, under water, breathless, eyes swimming, head spinning, weightless. Her hands seek his cock, find it, he's inside her before he even realises it, a great shudder runs through him from the nape of his neck to the small of his back, specks of iridescent foam fly as far as the bedroom. He grasps her shoulders and, half drowning amid gales of laughter, climaxes, long shudders racking his entire body, and she seems to do likewise.

No sooner does she regain her breath than she gets out of the bath, gazes at him for a moment, streaming water. 'Not a bad start,' she says, slipping into a grey bathrobe embroidered with the hotel's crest. She dries her hair and runs a comb through it. 'Shall we continue in bed?' And she goes into the bedroom. He hears her light a cigarette.

He relaxes in the water, no hurry. Savour this blissful feeling of blessed well-being. An athletic woman who takes the initiative in a luxury hotel. *I'm reliving the flavour of my youth, other women in other luxury hotels, my early years of freedom. I was very young, fourteen, fifteen, they were older. I was a bit of a gigolo in those days, they were in charge, it was delicious and I had a good time.*

The entrance to the Oiseau Bleu is concealed behind plywood boards, and a cop is pacing up and down the pavement. Quignard enters through the back door and goes up to the third floor, entirely taken up by Tomaso's private apartment. The latter already awaits him, and leads him into a small office done out in mahogany like a yacht. Quignard half lies on a chaise longue with wooden slats. Tomaso opens a casket with copper corners, containing six glasses and six crystal decanters filled with peaty malt whiskies of different strengths. 'Medium,' says Quignard, his mind on other things. Tomaso serves him then pours himself a glass that gives off a strong peaty whiff, takes a sip, goes over to a chair and straddles it, his arms on the back, a mocking expression on his face. At that precise moment, Quignard knows he's sitting opposite the war dog of the old days.

'So, Maurice, there's something fishy going on in Pondange, and you haven't said a word to me about it?' Quignard looks stunned. Tomaso continues: 'Who were the man and woman who came to see you in your office this morning?'

A punch in the stomach probably has a similar effect: your body snaps in half, winded, your mind's in a haze. Mustn't bat an eyelid. The driver in the office. Fuck. It's too late to improvise and too dangerous.

Quignard rapidly explains the situation as he sees it, carefully leaving out the journalist and his visit to Neveu's widow. There's no point in making things worse. He concludes:

'In my view, there's no immediate danger, which is why I decided not to say anything to you.'

'That's not what I think. First of all, a journalist came sniffing round the Oiseau Bleu last night, asking questions about you and your connection to me...'

A second blow to the stomach. Hard. How does he always manage to be one step ahead? The journalist, the same one who went to see the Neveu widow, for certain. How did he trace things back to me? And how did he discover the link between Tomaso and me? Quignard feels himself going into a tailspin.

'...my man had just got hold of him when the explosion went off, and they couldn't find him afterwards. I infer that there are people poking around who know a lot more than you imagine. So we can't allow an eyewitness to what happened in the factory to be left hanging around. That's the golden rule in my profession. No eyewitnesses.' He rises. Standing, his legs slightly apart, his hands still resting on the back of the chair. 'This girl's name.'

It isn't a question, it's an order. Quignard blurts out in anguish, with a mixture of fear and pleasure:

'Aisha Saidani.'

'Where do we find her?'

'Cité des Jonquilles, staircase A.'

'I'm holding on to you, Maurice, you'll have dinner with us. An intimate dinner among friends, here at the club, there'll only be about ten of us. It's seabass *en croûte*, and Deborah's waiting for you. She was thrilled to hear you'll be joining us. Trust me. In any case you have no option.'

26 October

When he hears the Mercedes pull up in front of the steps, at first Quignard retches. Last night, he was too smashed to realise he was being driven home. He'd been so drunk that he could almost claim he didn't remember having told Tomaso: *Aisha Saidani, Cité des Jonquilles*. But this morning, sobered up and on an empty stomach, the idea of seeing his spy driver depresses him. *Send him away? Delicate. That would be to sever relations with Tomaso. Could he? The blaze, Neveu, Park in Warsaw. Of course not.* Does he want to? The tall, hard form leaning over him yesterday evening, the pent-up violence, the shudder of pleasure he experienced at that moment, which he remembers very clearly, and the uneasy feeling of abandon that followed. *Of course not.* He gulped down his coffee and cut breakfast short. Back to his daily routine: the morning papers, anxious to know. He hurries.

The Mercedes is there as usual. The driver is someone new. Tomaso had the bright idea of substituting him. He greets him with a groan, slumps on the back seat and spreads out the front pages of the three national dailies. Identical headlines: Thomson Multimedia employees organise national strike and demonstrate against Daewoo taking over their company. Relief. *No point reading the articles. What effect can a strike have on the great machinations of international finance? None, it's almost laughable. These people will never understand.* He folds up the newspapers. Then anxiety resurfaces. *Daewoo is the press's main target, for the second time. Not being shielded by Matra makes that dangerous, with the shit-stirrer in the area who's already traced things back to Tomaso. According to the superintendent, he's straight. But it's so easy to get it wrong. I'm going to have another chat to him about it.* He leans back in his seat and admires the last patches of forest shrouded in fog, fragmenting as they near the city. The trees are turning russet, the leaves will soon fall, and they'll be able to go hunting in the woods. *I must take a tour of the Grande Commune with the gamekeeper to see where the pheasants are. Time's going on. We've only got to hold out for a few more weeks, three or four at the most, get the Privatisation Commission's approval, Brussels' approval, and it's all in the bag. We've held out so far. And yet…* His stomach is in knots, it's hard to breathe. Spiral. Park's tricks first of all, right under his nose, without him noticing a thing, and he'd thought he was totally in control, the devastating blaze when he'd been expecting a dustbin fire. With that question nagging him since last night: *Supposing Tomaso had deliberately overstepped the mark?* With Neveu the infernal machine is set in motion, the discovery of Park's fraudulent accounting system, Maréchal who drops him, the unstoppable Tomaso who takes charge. *Admit it: I've lost control.* The driver's broad, impassive back and neck. They're all the same, I'm free but under close surveillance. Random images of last night's blondes, Deborah and the other one whose name he doesn't even know, abundant flesh, pink and white, moist, wet, and that feeling of being cocooned. A phrase goes round and round in his head: *an old man's pleasures.* He fears the days to come.

Quignard realises that the car has stopped outside his office, it's probably been there for a while. He leans towards his driver.

'Take me to the Grande Commune. I'm unavailable for the rest of the day. Unless Tomaso calls, of course.'

Montoya drops Rolande at the Cité des Jonquilles around mid-morning (*no, let's not arrange to meet, Pondange is a very small town, you know, you'll find me easily*), a smile, and the door slams. Then he stops at a cafe and drinks a coffee and brandy standing at the bar. Alone and glad to be on his own. A break before getting back to work. Time to plan the bugging of Quignard's office.

The offices of Quignard's design consultancy specialising in industrial reconversions are in Pondange, in the Grands Bureaux building, formerly the head office of the Pondange Steelworks Company. In other words, the nerve centre of the entire valley. Montoya has a very clear, physical, almost painful memory of it. A massive cube of blackish stone, standing at the frontier between the world of the city and that of the blast furnaces, with the roar of the steelworks always in the background. The main façade opened on to the town. There were two doors, side by side. One, the monumental doorway, white stone steps, colonnade supporting a balcony, solid carved wooden double door, was opened just once a month for board meetings, both doors flung wide open for the occasion. Only the directors in their dark suits and Homburgs were entitled to cross the threshold, watched by the local press photographers. The other, very ordinary, door was used by the staff going in to work each day. The young Montoya used to imagine the hundreds of employees shut up in there all day long, labouring like the workers you could glimpse through the factory gates, and he would never go near it, for fear that these barracks might gobble him up. The idea of returning under cover thirty-five years later, breaking in and installing an illegal phone tap puts him in a mood of slight elation mingled with the physical tiredness of the night, his muscles stiff, the image of straight wisps of damp hair plastered against Rolande's cheeks, gales of laughter, the memory of the faint taste of soap bubbles in the corner of his mouth, stimulating a sense of fulfilment.

Carry out a recce. Hard to recognise the Grands Bureaux of his childhood. The building, of beautiful Lorraine limestone, has been cleaned up and glows golden yellow in the sun. The staff and the guest entrances are both neglected. The two trees either side of the colonnade are no longer pruned, and their branches reach down to the ground encroaching on to the terrace where the big French doors of the boardroom are protected by wooden shutters. An easy way in, sheltered from view. *We'll enter through here.* He walks round to the building's rear façade which used to overlook the yard of the great ironworks, and comes to carefully manicured lawns running down to the river where poplars, trees that grow quickly, have been planted. A new entrance, all in glass, has been added, facing the verdant valley. In the sun-drenched lobby, a charming receptionist behind a counter smiles at him. The names of all the companies with offices in the building are on a huge board. Employment and training on every floor. The parasites that thrive on the social management of unemployment have all found refuge here, thanks to the hospitality of the municipality, which bought the Grands Bureaux. *You did the right thing in getting out, kid.*

'Mr Amrouche of the COFEP design consultancy, please?'

'First floor, door 110.'

He climbs the stairs, follows the long corridor which goes all round the building and on to which all the offices open. He is totally alone. He takes the time to study the walls and ceilings carefully. No indication of any surveillance cameras or alarms. Quite logical really. Guarantee the security of what? Employment? He walks all the way round to the wing where the grand entrance is. A huge monumental staircase flanked by early twentieth-century stained-glass windows celebrating the men of iron and fire in blues and yellows made vivid by the sunlight. The factories have been razed, but the windows have been preserved. Opposite are the padded double doors of the boardroom. Still no one in sight. He hunches over the lock, holding a bunch of master keys, it's child's play, and soon finds himself in the large dark room with a pervasively musty smell. He gropes his way forward to the French door, which he opens a crack. Free entry tonight. He turns round. Rows of tables and chairs, baize, ashtrays, crystal chandeliers. At the far end is the chairman's armchair. Ghosts. The smell grows stronger, haunting, he finds it suffocating, got to get out. Another long corridor, still no living soul, and at last, door 110 which leads to COFEP's offices.

An internal area furnished as a waiting room or small lounge, containing three armchairs, a water fountain, a coffee machine, and five doors. Quignard's name is on the door at the end and Amrouche's is on the door to his left. No visible security system. He knocks and enters.

'I hope I'm not disturbing you? If possible I'd like to continue the enjoyable conversation we began yesterday.'

Without hesitation, Amrouche closes the file spread open in front of him and stands up.

'It will be a pleasure. Come, we'll be more comfortable by the coffee machine.'

There's a danger of bumping into Quignard. Too bad, impossible to refuse, have to be quick. Behind a door, phones ringing and a woman's voice. His secretary most likely. Amrouche fills two cups with coffee and comes and sits beside Montoya, stretches his leg and back muscles and smiles.

'What did you want to talk about?'

'The occupation of the offices. You were the ringleader. Were there many of you occupying?'

'At first, yes. More than fifty. One or two hours later, I walked around and there were only twenty or so of us at most.'

'I know that Bouziane and Neveu were there. Did you see them?'

Amrouche fidgets in his armchair, looks away, suddenly assailed by images of arses jerking up and down, clears his throat, hesitates, then answers.

'Yes, they were playing video games on a computer. Why?'

Montoya takes his time, sips his coffee, not bad by the way. Bouziane, the trail's getting warm. At last.

'I'm interested in the drug dealing at Daewoo.'

Relieved, Amrouche laughs.

'You're not the only one. And you are utterly mistaken. Bouziane was a small-time dealer and Neveu liked the odd spliff. That's it and honestly nothing to write an article about.'

A place known as the Haute Chapelle, on the Paris-Nancy road. On the edge of the village, Montoya pulls up in an improvised car park cluttered with a few articulated lorries. Between the car park and the road, stands an isolated, one-storey house, its shutters closed. On the front a sign in big black lettering reads "*Au rendez-vous des voyageurs*" beside a round blue and red Relais des Routiers plaque. The place is poorly lit, and looks deserted and sinister. Montoya pushes open the door and finds himself in the bar where he is immediately hit by heat, noise and smoke. The room is packed with young and not-so-young men, beer drinkers, jostling and yelling at each other. The owner and his wife are busy behind the bar, and in a corner, at two Formica tables, a small group is eating pork and cabbage hotpot from soup bowls. On the telephone, Valentin had said: 'Don't stop at the bar, go into the restaurant.' At the back to the left, there's a door masked by a bead curtain, and above it an enamel plaque: Dining room. In the low-ceilinged, dimly-lit room, twenty or so tables with check tablecloths and bunches of plastic flowers. A strapping

waitress greets Montoya, who chooses an isolated table in a corner and sits facing the door. Ten or so lone men are eating in silence, probably in need of some peace and quiet before driving through most of the night. *So do I,* thinks Montoya, *I need peace and quiet. Valentin pays amazing attention to detail.*

A rare steak, chips, and a carafe of water. It comes quickly – here everyone knows their job – and Montoya starts eating.

The bead curtain rustles, a burst of conversation from the bar, a man comes in. Montoya lifts his head and looks at him. Tall, thin, a khaki parka down to his knees, close-cropped hair, his face furrowed with wrinkles and a pasty complexion. His dull, faded eyes darting everywhere meet Montoya's gaze. The man comes towards him.

'Christophe.'

'Sébastien.'

'Our mutual friend sent me.'

A subdued, croaking, broken voice, a tormented voice. *He's probably had his trachea crushed, his vocal chords damaged. Fight, accident or punishment? A battered life. Valentin's probably got him by the balls.*

'Sit down. Pleased to meet you.'

The man orders steak and chips and begins to eat slowly, without saying a word, his eyes always on the lookout.

'You know what we have to do tonight?'

'More or less. Bug an office.'

'I'm in charge of getting in and getting out. You're in charge of the work inside. And our friend takes care of the rest.' The man nods while chewing. 'I've carried out a recce, the operation shouldn't be difficult.'

A wan smile. 'If you say so...'

The restaurant empties, no point hanging around. Coffee. The man toys with the spoon, long, elegant, bony fingers, never still. Relentless training? The bill. He thrusts his nervous hands into the vast pockets of his parka. Coins deep in the corners of his pockets, notes, an amber rosary? Montoya reckons he's done a spell in detox, and that it was rough. Maybe in jail. Familiar world. He's come across hundreds of men of his ilk. Without knowing why, he has a hunch that he's an excellent professional. As long as someone's there to lead the way.

In the car park, the two men part company, each gets into his own car, rendezvous in Pondange at eleven-thirty in the main square.

Rubber gloves, cotton balaclavas pulled over their eyes, the two men prepare in the shelter of a tree. Then a rope slipped over a branch, a jump up on to the balcony, a few rapid steps, bent double under the cover of the balustrade, an open French door, groping their way through the boardroom, empty corridor, the two men walk quickly, without running, barely breathing. Door 110, master key in the lock, on into the waiting room, yet another door, at last Quignard's office. Montoya gets his breath back while the expert unwraps his toolkit carefully stowed in a wide canvas belt hidden under the voluminous parka, and sets to work. Speed, the precision of his long bony fingers. The man knows what he has to do. Montoya glances at the desk piled high with files. Banks, Department of Labour, chartered accountants... Valentin doesn't want Montoya to search his papers: don't arouse Quignard's suspicions for nothing, a responsible boss doesn't leave compromising documents lying around in his office. You never know... but orders are orders. He moves away, walks over to the big bay window looking out over the valley. In the moonlight, a rural landscape in grey and ice-blue, poplars, meadows, river, the foothills of the plateau, the dark mass of the forest. No variations in the light, not the least nuance, no breath of air, not a creature stirring. And no sound penetrates the double glazing. Death valley. The expert brushes his shoulder, he's done.

Return by the same route, Montoya ensuring he shuts all the doors behind him.

At the foot of the tree, the two men remove their gloves, the balaclavas, touch hands, palm to palm.

'I've known worse,' breathes the expert. And they go their separate ways. The entire operation took seventeen minutes.

PART FOUR

27 October

Quignard has an early business breakfast appointment in Brussels today, and leaves Pondange in the small hours, before the national press reaches the region. He feels a mounting anxiety during the journey, and by the time he reaches the suburbs of Brussels, he's having difficulty breathing.

In the lobby of the Silken Berlaymont Brussels, he rushes over to the newspaper stand and flicks rapidly through the papers: no headlines. He begins to breathe more easily. That's a good sign, the worst of the attacks is probably over. He heads for the dining room leafing through the papers in search of the financial section. He finds the *Figaro*'s. It reads:

THOMSON PRIVATISATION

COB LAUNCHES INVESTIGATION INTO INSIDER DEALING

The financial editor hasn't had time to write an article and merely reproduces the AFP despatch:

Following several anonymous tip-offs, an initial examination of Matra share fluctuations suggests the possibility of insider dealing, with funds being channelled into private accounts in Luxembourg. COB, the stock market regulator, has decided to launch a full investigation.

Quignard suddenly feels faint. His heart turns to ice, sweat streams down his face, he is unable to move and can no longer follow what the people around him are saying. The maître d'hôtel and a waiter race over, sit him in an armchair, loosen his tie and shirt collar and remove his jacket. He gradually recovers his wits, and his first instinct is to run away, as far away as possible. To Mongolia, his favourite fantasy, to ride the stocky little horses with short legs and large heads and track snow tigers with their thick white fur striped with black, *ad infinitum*. But he doesn't run away. Several anxious faces ask him if he's feeling better. Much better. In fact he feels fine. A dizzy spell due to exhaustion, travelling on an empty stomach, it's nothing. He hears himself grinding his teeth. A COB investigation takes several months. By that time… By that time he only knows that he's no longer certain of anything, and that he's afraid.

A few minutes later, having washed his face and hands, he's at the table of three EU officials, calmly and competently discussing the reorganisation of the railway system in the European Development Plan zone, while tucking into toast and marmalade.

It's nearly nine a.m. and dead quiet in the Cité des Jonquilles. Two men cross the lawn in bomber jackets, jeans and work boots. They go up staircase A and stop on the first-floor landing. The one wearing a white silk scarf around his neck takes a short crowbar out of his jacket, and attacks Rolande Lepetit's door which gives way with a sharp snap at the first blow. The two men enter and shut the door behind them. An elderly woman in a blue towelling dressing gown is sitting at the kitchen table facing three cans of beer. Her long white hair is in a plait, from which a few stray tousled strands escape. Her mouth drops open, her eyes staring, as she attempts to rise. One man is already upon her, stuffs a rubber gag in her mouth, folds the dressing gown behind her to pin her arms, grabs her plait, yanks her head back and knees her in the small of the back. The man with the white scarf strolls round the apartment.

'Nobody home. We can get on with it.'

He contemplates the elderly woman in a long blue floral-print cotton nightdress immobilised before him. She chokes convulsively. He pulls out his knife, and slits the fabric from the neck to the hem in a single movement. The elderly woman struggles, wriggles, helpless, is naked, breasts swinging, her flesh badly mottled, with purplish fatty lumps in places. He laughs, biting his lips, traces the folds of her stomach with the tip of the knife barely applying any pressure, the skin splits, a long gash from one hip to the other, scarcely a trail of blood. He shoves the elderly woman against the table and pushes her over on to her back. She chokes, her legs flailing.

'Hold her down, I won't be long. Just want to see if the equipment's still working.'

He puts his knife down on the table, unzips his flies, grabs her hips with both hands, penetrates her, a few violent up-and-down movements, he climaxes, releases her, zips up his flies. Winks at his associate.

'Best way to show them who's boss.'

He leans over the elderly woman who remains spreadeagled on the table, her body jerking convulsively, the gash has begun to bleed more seriously, her eyes show their whites, she's no longer breathing.

'Get her up.'

He gives her two hard slaps and the elderly woman opens her eyes. He presses the tip of the knife to her throat.'

'Listen, slag. I'm going to take off your gag.' Presses the knife harder, cuts. 'You keep it shut, otherwise I'll slit your throat. And you know I mean it.'

He removes the gag. The elderly woman, mouth gaping, gasps frenziedly, a low, hoarse groan, not a scream.

'Perfect.'

He signals to his associate. They drag the elderly woman over to the telephone in the hall.

'I'm going to dial Aisha's number, and you're going to ask her to come here, you need her to come now, you're ill. When she's here, my friend here and I will ask her some questions quite politely, and then we'll leave the pair of you alone. Understood?'

The elderly woman nods, her eyes closed. He presses the tip of the knife to her throat again.

'This time, I want to hear your voice. Find out whether you can still talk. Say: "Yes, sir".'

'Yes, sir.'

The man with the white scarf takes a walkie-talkie from his belt, presses the button.

'Here we go.'

Lying on the roof of the Cité des Jonquilles, next to the fanlight above stairwell A, two men receive the walkie-talkie message.

'Over to us.'

They open the fanlight, jump down on to the fourth-floor landing and hide on the staircase. Barely two minutes' wait before Aisha comes out of her apartment wearing blue jeans and a red polo-necked sweater. As she turns round to lock her door, a man grabs her round the waist and forces a rubber gag into her mouth. She arches her body, her legs buckle as she grabs for the support of the wall. The other man comes to help and gives her an injection in the waist, through her sweater. Her body immediately goes limp. While one carries the unconscious Aisha, the other takes her keys, enters the apartment and comes out with a kitchen stool, locks the door and puts the key back in the pocket of Aisha's jeans. He positions the stool under the fanlight. As the first guy climbs on to it, passes a rope through the handle of the fanlight then a slipknot around Aisha's neck, the other retrieves the rubber gag while keeping hold of her body, and slips it into his jacket pocket. Between them, they haul up the body and let go. Aisha's body revolves slowly. One man kicks over the stool, the other encircles her hips and swings himself from her body. A snap. The two men give a final glance to check: girl dead, body hanged, stool kicked over, fanlight closed, gag in pocket. They both then calmly walk down the four flights of stairs.

On the first-floor landing, the door to Rolande Lepetit's apartment is still open. They don't look inside.

Rendezvous in the main square, the teams meet up, divide themselves between three cars and drive off in the direction of Nancy.

Montoya parks his car in the car park opposite the police station without hurrying. The superintendent asked him to drop in: to review the progress of his investigation, he said. Have a chat. By the entrance to the car park, a big black Mercedes is waiting, engine running. A man is sitting alone at the wheel, very close-cropped hair, bomber jacket, square shoulders. Montoya has no difficulty in recognising one of the two mercenaries who cornered him in the alcove at the Oiseau Bleu less than forty-eight hours ago. The man calmly stares at him and smiles. We know who you are, we know who you're going to see. Pure intimidation. *When they stop showing themselves, then it'll be time to worry.* He's not entirely convinced by his own argument.

In the superintendent's office, a polite exchange of greetings. To avoid touching on other subjects, Montoya talks drugs. At Daewoo, hash was definitely being smoked, perhaps regularly? Dealing on the factory premises, worrying in terms of security. No, the superintendent doesn't find the situation a matter of concern. Grossly exaggerated, the amount of hash circulating at Daewoo. In a small town like Pondange, it doesn't take much for people to get upset. Montoya starts fishing: trafficking linked to the arrest of the Hakim brothers, maybe? The superintendent ducks the question and the conversation continues to flag, when the door suddenly bursts open and a podgy young police officer wearing glasses rushes in theatrically, then stands rooted to the spot, gawping. The superintendent rises, tense.

'Dumont, don't tell me…'

'Yes, superintendent. Two bodies at the Cité des Jonquilles.'

Montoya suddenly feels drained. *Aisha and Rolande.* Drained and chilled. He knew the danger, said nothing, did nothing, and so those two women, friends, so full of life. *Criminal. Think about it later. For the moment, get over there, hurry up, don't think about anything.* The police drive off, sirens wailing. Montoya follows in his own car. The black Mercedes is no longer waiting by the car park entrance.

In front of the entrance to staircase A, two uniformed police officers are holding back a small crowd of neighbours and onlookers. People are talking about Aisha and Rolande's mother. Montoya, his throat dry, his mind in turmoil, doesn't ask any questions. And waits. A police car pulls up and Rolande stumbles out. A police officer escorts her through the crowd, which abruptly falls silent, and they disappear up staircase A.

The door to the apartment is wide open. Rolande freezes on the threshold, head lowered. On the floor in the middle of the hall lies a shapeless form beneath a white sheet, a few scraps of blue towelling dressing gown peeping out, and the tip of the white-haired plait bound with a very ordinary red elastic band. Her gaze rests on the elastic band. Then she looks up. All the apartment doors are open, she sees overturned furniture, things on the floor. She thinks: *a battle scene.* And again: *stage scenery. None of this is real.*

The superintendent stands close to her, one of his two men raises the sheet. Face butchered, the right temple and cheekbone smashed in, mouth open, twisted, dentures broken, body naked, terrifying. Poor, poor woman, what a wretched life. Immense pity but not a tear. The superintendent points to a long gash across her stomach.

'Prowlers obviously. They must have tortured her to find out where the money was, then knocked her out with the crowbar they used to force open the front door. The weapon was found by the telephone.'

He covers up the body. Again that overwhelming feeling of strangeness.

'I don't believe it. We've never had a bean and everyone knows it,' says Rolande in a very low, very hoarse voice.

Montoya's still milling among the small crowd of onlookers. His mind starts working again. He broods over his silence and his mistakes, his doubts too. *You thought you had time, and she's dead. How did Quignard trace things back to her so quickly?* He feels sluggish, heavy, out of his depth. He decides to leave. Phone Valentin. The reflex of a subordinate, deferring to his boss, like in the old days in the police. Sometimes it's useful. His gaze falls on Karim Bouziane, at the back of the crowd, standing slightly apart, ashen, dishevelled. Electric shock. Suddenly he feels a tingling in his fingers, takes a deep breath, mind in overdrive. *Bouziane-Amrouche. Amrouche, of course. Amrouche who put you on Bouziane's track and tipped off Quignard about Aisha. Why do you think he put him in an office next to his? Quignard alerted perhaps by the Neveu widow's phone call… Time for regrets later, must never let an opportunity slip.* Bouziane roams from one knot of people to another, tries to catch a phrase here and there, his eyes on the lookout. Flashback: *eyes meeting in the cafe. He's seen me before. Careful.* Karim takes out a packet of cigarettes, three attempts before he manages to light one, throws it away after two drags. *I know that bitter taste at the back of the throat when you can't swallow anything, not even cigarette smoke. This guy's in a very bad way. He senses he's in danger, isn't used to it, and doesn't know why. Don't lose sight of him. He saw the lists at the same time as Neveu. For the time being, Quignard doesn't know that, but at the rate he's going, Karim may not have long left. He's got to talk.*

Karim walks away from the crowd, his steps faltering, reaches the car park, gets into an old red Clio and sits there for several minutes, his head resting on the steering wheel. He's got to find a way out, he's going round in circles, can't find one. Montoya slides behind the wheel of his car, waits. Karim starts up his engine, manoeuvres and drives slowly out of the car park. He appears to be heading towards the plateau. The motorway to Paris? Montoya allows him to get ahead, and then catches up with him. Tailing him is easy as long as he stays on the plateau with its straight, sloping roads. Karim leaves the main road, so he's not heading for Paris and turns on to a secondary road, driving slowly, his mind elsewhere. He probably still hasn't decided where he's going. It's lunchtime, not much traffic, lonely road. Risky but doable. Montoya hangs back, rummages in the glove compartment, leaves the revolver but takes the plastic handcuffs which he flings on to the back seat. Goes over the controlled-crash training course he'd been on in the old days. He'd never used the technique until now. Recites the advice and recommendations. *Above all, don't injure Karim. As they say in the movies, I want him alive.* Action. Puts his foot down on the accelerator. The red Clio reappears. No one in front, no one behind. Overtakes, brakes, cuts in front of the Clio's wing, which he hits with his bumper. Karim, thrown off course, his expression terrified behind the windscreen, tries to straighten up, jerks the wheel and swerves into the ditch where the Clio lands, bonnet first. Montoya stops on the verge, roars into reverse, pulls up level with the Clio, jumps out, opens the driver's door where a dazed Karim is trying to unfasten his seat belt. Montoya grabs him by the shoulder, extricates him from the car, leans him against the bonnet, and with his right hand straight, fingers taut, gives him a blow to the plexus. Karim crumples to the ground. Montoya picks him up, throws him on to the back seat of his car, handcuffs him tightly, *that'll loosen his tongue*, attaches the handcuffs to the seat belt anchor, gets behind the wheel and drives off at speed.

Karim slowly comes to his senses. Feels like throwing up. Utterly lost. His last memory: *Aisha's dead.* He groans. He got into the Clio. *Was going where? Can't remember.* He's half lying down. Glimpses foliage and blinks, the trees are very close and aren't moving. Rubs his cheek against a familiar fabric, blinks, grey fabric, he's lying on a seat in a stationary car. A surge of panic. Sits up, sharp pain in his chest, a man is sitting on the front seat, watching him without moving, hazy face, the lawyer? Tries to get up. Impossible, arm hurts, pinned behind his back. The nightmare comes back, tied up in the four-wheel drive, the lawyer. He howls, pulls frantically on his arms, kicks the back of the seat with both feet, a spasm, vomits on his shoes.

'Finished blubbering like a woman? I'm not going to rape you, for fuck's sake.'

Down to earth with a bump. Recognises the guy who was in the cafe with Rolande. Still doesn't understand what's happened to him. Shuts up. Wipes his mouth on his right shoulder.

'That's better. Are you capable of understanding what I say to you?'

Nods. 'Who are you?'

'The Hakim brothers, does that name ring a bell?'

Karim feels his bladder empty into his trousers. Dense trees all around, dusk outside, no way out. He closes his eyes, leans back and groans.

'My wrists and arms really hurt. Can't you loosen these handcuffs?'

'Let's try and make this quick. The brothers weren't very happy about you grassing on them.'

'I didn't grass.'

'But they seem to think you did.'

'When they came to pick up their last delivery, someone had tipped off the cops. They took photos.'

'Who snitched then, if you didn't?'

'I don't know.'

'And they forced you to testify against Nourredine.'

'You know about that too?'

'I know a lot about it. Except that it wasn't the cops that were behind it, it was Tomaso. The cops only saw the fire.' Karim opens his eyes and wriggles his back slightly.

'You know more than I do. I don't know any Tomaso.'

'A guy from Nancy who used you to grass on the Hakims and is taking over their business. I don't think they'll let him walk all over them. There was an explosion in Tomaso's nightclub two days ago, and the battle has only just begun. And you're right in the middle of it. Not a good place to be.'

'Why me? I'm small fry, I don't count.'

Here we come to the epistemological disassociation, as my intellectual student friends would have said. Concentrate and cross your fingers in the hope that the kid will be scared enough not to realise that you're changing the subject and that there's no logical link between the two.

Montoya leans over towards Karim and strokes his cheek. A nervous twitch from the corner of his mouth to the corner of his eye. The smell of vomit, urine, sour sweat.

'Poor kid. You saw the lists of names in the Daewoo accounts, when you were playing on the computer with Neveu, and everyone's interested in those lists. Neveu was murdered because he'd seen them.' The cheek twitches again. 'Aisha was murdered because she was with Neveu during the strike. You haven't been murdered yet because I'm the only person who knows that you were messing around on the computer with Neveu.' Karim pictures himself sitting next to Étienne, shoulder to shoulder, the porn pop-ups against a background of accounting information which he didn't even glance at. He hears Amrouche coming in and going out, slamming the door. Amrouche... 'So you see, you may not have too long to live.'

Karim's arms have gone numb. Now, all the pain is concentrated between his shoulders and up into the back of his neck. *How long before Amrouche grasses on me, to Quignard, Tomaso, whoever?* Despair. He shouts, 'But I never saw those accounts. We were watching the porn. Étienne copied it on to a disk for me. We wanted to duplicate it and sell it. I took it with me and went home, that's all, I never saw anything else. I haven't even had time to do anything with it yet. I don't know anything about disks and computers. Étienne was going to do the editing, and I was just going to sell it.'

Montoya turned back to face the windscreen. *This kid's telling the truth. I got close, but missed it. Wait. Pursue this idea to the end.*

'Give me the disk.'

'Whenever you like. Right away, if you want. It's in the Clio's glove box.' Montoya starts up the engine.

'Fine, we'll go there. Then, I'll let you go and I advise you to disappear for a month or two, until things calm down. You're out of your depth.'

Montoya pulls up at a junction between a farm track and a secondary road. A sweeping glance over the plateau's clear horizon to check that he's not being followed. The majestic swell of ploughed fields, as far as the eye can see. He hears Neveu's widow: 'It's unbelievable how beautiful the plateau can look when you see it from the windows of our farm.' He takes out his 'special Valentin' phone and calls him.

A groan. Montoya smiles.

'I've got the list of Luxembourg accounts.'

'Well... What does it look like?'

'It looks like provincial wheeling and dealing. That's what you called it, isn't it?'

'Something like that. Fill me in on the detail.'

'Ten names of Daewoo workers, payments every month for just over a year which all come from another Luxembourg bank account. Sums ranging from fifty thousand to a hundred thousand francs.'

'Which amounts to around three million a year. It's a wealthy region.'

'But these aren't the sort of figures you're interested in, am I right?'

'Yes, but we can still make good use of them. Do you have the instructions?'

'Not yet. The files I have were copied by mistake. The person who made the disk thought he was copying the porn videos the accountant watched while performing his onerous duties, but he copied the bank statements instead. I have an idea of how to find an explanation for all this. I just need a little time – forty-eight hours.'

'That's much too long. Fax me that list and we'll work on it at our end too. I'll give you twenty-four hours.'

Laughs. 'I can't do exactly as I please here. You said yourself that Pondange was the Wild West. This morning, we had two more corpses.'

Silence. 'Clearly, you're not joking.'

'Clearly.'

'Have the corpses got anything to do with our affair?'

'Of course. Elimination of a potential witness.'

'Fine. Forty-eight hours, if you insist. Things have been dead quiet at this end. Quignard hasn't set foot in his office. More worrying, our phone tap hasn't picked up any calls between Quignard and Tomaso.'

Silence. Montoya rubs the bridge of his nose. 'Is Quignard's driver employed by 3G?'

'Good question. We'll find out. I'll page you on this phone as soon as I have any news. Don't forget to check it. And be careful.'

'That goes without saying. Goodbye, chief.'

Montoya is patiently waiting for Rolande outside Pondange police station. He's parked across the street from the entrance and has been leaning against the car for more than an hour. Darkness is falling, he can feel the cold and damp in his bones. Behind him stands the local primary school, silent and empty. He hasn't glanced at it, the memories it stirred are fading. The dark shape of the police station looms before him. The neon-lit entrance can be seen through the open door, hinting at the activity going on inside and casting a band of light on the white stone steps and the neat lawn.

Rolande's tall, slim, upright silhouette in its black overcoat steps into the light as she descends the three steps, her hands in her pockets. He straightens up, takes a step towards her when she sees him. Her entire body freezes on the spot, hesitates. He thinks of her hands fluttering as she struggles for words, her eloquent body. A rush of affection. He walks swiftly towards her, offers his arm, which she takes without looking at him. The two bodies brush, touch, recognise each other, then move apart. Observation: between them, a silent, dead space. He leads her to the car and opens the door for her. She sits down. He sits behind the wheel.

'I'll drive you wherever you want to go. There's a room for you at the Hôtel Vauban if you like. And you can have something to eat there too, with or without me, as you wish.'

She nods and signals to him to get going.

A quick dinner in the Hôtel Vauban's empty, dimly-lit dining room. Not a word. She doesn't meet his eye, concentrates on eating a vegetable soup and cheese with slow movements, her head bowed. Then she sits upright.

'I spent hours in the apartment with the superintendent, drawing up an inventory. He wanted me to tell him what had been stolen. Of course nothing had been stolen.' She gives him a harsh stare. 'Don't you think it's time you told me who you are and what's going on? Don't you think I've paid dearly enough to find out?'

He takes her into the lobby. The security guard has left, the main door is locked and the curtains are drawn across the bay window overlooking the main square. The night lights give off a dim glow and the only light comes from a single bright lamp with a big shade standing on a coffee table. They sit side by side in two big chintz armchairs. Rolande sinks back in hers, her arms on the rests, her hands spread flat, tensing occasionally. Montoya tells her in a low, monotonous voice about Matra and Alcatel's rival bids for Thomson, how he came to be hired, his arrival in Pondange. *Note that I arrived after the fire and after Étienne's death. I have nothing to do with the start of the trouble.* He tells her about the bogus Daewoo accounts, what he knows about the collaboration between Quignard and Tomaso. He tells her that the fire was started deliberately and that Étienne was murdered, about Amrouche's statement fingering Nourredine – she closes her eyes, ashen – and about Karim Bouziane. He doesn't tell her about his meeting with Neveu's widow or her phone call to Quignard. At that particular point, he underestimated the enemy. At that particular point, he pushed Aisha towards her death. He'll never tell her that. Not because he doesn't want to lose her, he knows it's already too late for that. But because he doesn't want to admit responsibility and make it official.

Then he gives her a list of the Luxembourg bank accounts which has her name on it. 'It got into my hands sort of by mistake. The person who copied it from the computer thought he was copying porn videos, the pastime of the person who kept the accounts.' She becomes more animated, turns the sheets over and over, reads them several times, folds them, puts them in her coat pocket. Montoya reckons he's winning and is almost surprised. She's changing, fast.

'I'm telling you these things, Rolande, because I'm almost certain of them, and am acting accordingly. But I have no proof. So you must be very careful what you say, including to the cops. Especially to the cops. Because in this affair, anyone who knows anything is in danger of being murdered. I'm not exaggerating, that's really what happened.'

'So I gather.'

'One question: Aisha?'

'It was terrible. Hanged from the handle of the roof fanlight at the top of our staircase, in front of the door to her apartment.' Rolande buries her face in her hands for a long moment. Those hands, the memory of their touch, her caresses both gentle and rough at the same time, Montoya shivers. Then she continues in a calm voice: 'The cops are clueless and are beginning to talk about suicide. I don't believe it. Aisha had a strength that I haven't always had. Aisha was a force of nature. What do you think?'

'Murdered, like Étienne, because she was with Étienne during the strike. Quignard didn't know that at first. And then he must have found out from Amrouche, in an informal conversation.

Amrouche wasn't exactly cautious. In any case, he didn't see any reason to be wary.'

'What about my mother?'

'I don't know. Maybe they used her to lure Aisha out of her apartment? Possibly with a telephone call?' She nods. 'Where were you this morning?'

'In Amrouche's office. He called me to offer me a job. What a farce.'

'What about Aisha's father?'

'At the Social Security office. An appointment came in the post. It was a mistake.'

A long silence. Rolande has a vacant look, her hands mechanically caress the armrests.

'Rolande, I want to know who kept these accounts and what their purpose was. I need you. You told me Maréchal was in the know. He wouldn't tell me, but he'd talk to you.'

'Yes, he probably would. But I'd have to want to get involved. I don't give a shit about the competition between Alcatel and Matra.' Silence, then Rolande gets up. 'I'm going to bed. I'll think about it, I'm giving myself a bit of time, I'm going to bury my dead. We'll talk about it again tomorrow.'

'Is your son coming back?'

'No. He's staying in Metz. I phoned him. I told him his grandmother was dead. And I forbade him to leave the school. I don't want him mixed up in all this.'

'I hoped he'd be there to support you.' A pause. 'I've brought you some sleeping tablets.' He proffers a tube in its cardboard packaging. 'Use them sparingly.'

She smiles for the first time.

'I don't have suicidal tendencies. Any more than Aisha did.'

28 October

Impossible to work. Quignard's unable to read the file lying open on his desk. Plagued by his obsessive thoughts. Largardère's being investigated again for fraud, the making and use of forgeries, and misuse of company money. Lagardère is alleged to have falsified his company's results during his group's merger with Hachette, two years ago. Two years, in other words, an age. The list is frightening. Two investigations, a tax inspection and a COB investigation, in under a fortnight.

Plus a national strike and demonstration over Thomson Multimedia. He swivels his armchair, puts his feet up on the windowsill and stares out at the peaceful autumnal landscape of the valley, the deep green of the meadows, the varied shades of brown of the trees, the grey of the sky. A brief respite. He is physically conscious of the weight of the huge machine that's been set in motion, beyond his reach in Paris, pressing on his shoulder and back. For the first time, a little question worms its way into his mind: *Supposing ultimately we lose? Unthinkable. True, but no more unthinkable than what's happened here, the chain of disasters at Pondange. Time will pass and people will forget. No, no one will forget while Tomaso's there, he's got me. He won't let go. And I'll be under his heel.*

The phone rings, he jumps, spins around and picks it up.

'Mr Quignard, I have a certain Mr Chan on the line who's asking to speak to you. It's personal.'

'His name doesn't mean anything to me. Put him through.'

'My dear friend, I am so pleased to be talking to you…'

Quignard sits up, that refined tone, the slight accent that was so familiar… this is it, Tomaso was right, it had to happen. He settles back into his armchair with a faint smile: a flesh-and-blood adversary at last.

'To what do I owe the honour of this call?'

'I've just read the French press. Rather late, I admit. What can I do, being so far away… and I learn that an investigation is apparently under way into the insider dealing of Matra shares…' Silence. 'I want my percentage of the profits.' His tone changes, becoming harsh and vindictive. 'Consider it a redundancy payment…'

'You've got a nerve.'

'…a golden parachute if you like. We've seen worse, much more exorbitant than what I'm asking for. You took a big risk in firing me like a subordinate. You made an error of judgement.'

'You should know that I'm only in charge of the Daewoo plant in Lorraine. I know nothing of financial matters nor anything about the alleged insider dealing. These matters are handled at a more senior level, by the Daewoo group management, and the steering committee for the Thomson bid in Paris, of which I am not a member.'

'I should like you to pass on my request to them. And to let them know how vulnerable they are at the moment. The newspaper articles mention anonymous letters. If anonymous letters are sufficient to trigger a COB investigation, what would happen if documents relating to Daewoo's Polish scheme were to be sent anonymously to the press?'

'I don't know what you are talking about.'

'I think that you're unaware of a great number of things, Mr Quignard. You knew what was going on in France, but not in Poland. The ultimate target wasn't the company as you assumed, or as you purported to, but a matter of revenge. Did you believe that the Daewoo-Thomson takeover idea came from you, you pathetically pretentious little creep?' A hearty guffaw on the other end of the phone. *First time I've heard him laugh,* thinks Quignard, with a lump in his throat and no voice. Silence. 'Are you still there? Now listen to me carefully. Day in, day out, over the past two years, the major investors have paid for this special relationship with Matra with the money from your subsidies. I have the list of the bank account holders, and I'm sure that if you think a little, you'll recognise them. Can you picture the scandal? So I'm demanding my share of profits from the Matra share dealing. It's my due. On second thoughts, call it five million francs, and I'd consider that a fair return…' Silence. 'You're not saying anything, Mr Quignard, that's up to you. Just do what has to be done. I'll call you back in two days so that we can agree on the method of payment.'

The line goes dead.

The first stage of the investigation is over, say the police. You may go home. Rolande clears up the apartment, working furiously. Keep busy, don't stop. The murderers emptied all the cupboards and threw the contents on the floor. Sort out, throw out everything that's broken: crockery, a bedside lamp, an alarm clock, a standard lamp, her son's photo frame, not that much stuff in the end. She straightens up. In the kitchen are the enamel beer mugs which her mother used to drink from, the times when she bothered to use a glass rather than drink the beer straight from the bottle. They go straight into the dustbin. Clear out the bathroom and chuck away her toiletries: a brush matted with long white hair, an empty perfume bottle kept as a souvenir. Of what? She goes into her mother's room. Throw out the teddy bear won at a fairground, the doll in traditional Lorraine costume, odds and ends and mementos, the cushion in which she hid her treasures and the things she nicked. She'd ended up stealing her grandson's pocket money. All her clothes too, while she was at it, without stopping to sort them out. And bedlinen. A mattress airing in an empty room.

Rolande leaves the room, automatically locking the door behind her. Finished, over, that whole part of my life. A feeling of immense relief, an unfamiliar lightness. She still has to tidy up the rest of the apartment. *My life remains inside. Address: Cité des Jonquilles, Pondange.* Rolande feels a surge of cold rage. Pile up the crockery and clothes into the cupboards, quick. Any old how, without thinking. Then shut the cupboards. Now to wash away the blood. First the kitchen, then the living room. This is where the old woman liked to sit and drink, often playing patience. A few stains left on the table, on the tiled floor, this is where they found her. In the hall, much bigger stains on the floor and on the wall, by the phone. Montoya's voice: the telephone used to lure Aisha out of there. This is where they killed her. Pondange, not for much longer.

Summons to a small downstairs meeting room at the Reims Novotel, halfway between Paris and Pondange. Montoya arrives first. On the phone, Valentin simply arranged the meeting. *Make sure you're not followed, of course, and expect two solid hours' work. Nothing more.* Doesn't he trust his secure phone line? Or is he going for maximum effect? Perhaps by putting on the pressure? Standing in front of the French doors, carefully concealed by net curtains, he contemplates the empty garden and the pool covered with a blue tarpaulin. He sees Rolande's image reflected in the glass, her face buried in her hands as she absorbs the fact that her life has been turned upside down and she's now alone, as she always wished. A memory of their meeting last night, outside the police station, their two bodies briefly attuned, echoing their walk through Brussels. Whatever happens, that moment was real, nothing can destroy it. He wanders over to a buffet of cold meats and salads standing in a corner and realises he's starving. He makes himself a roast pork and mustard sandwich and washes it down with a glass of Beaujolais.

The door opens, he turns around. Two men he doesn't know, still young, energetic, clean-shaven and well groomed, in dark suits and ties, carrying briefcases. Predictable. They introduce themselves: Pierre Benoît-Rey (warm), Philippe Rossellini (uncommunicative). Handshakes. 'We'll wait for Valentin.' He says nothing.

Valentin arrives. Montoya is struck by his peasant appearance: stocky physique, thick socks, corduroy trousers, baggy at the knees, and grey wool sweater. He gives Montoya a vague but warm embrace and makes the appropriate introductions. 'Those in charge of the Alcatel working party for the Thomson bid.' 'Our very special agent in Pondange.' Inquisitive looks. 'I've been keeping them up-to-date on the findings of your mission as it progresses.' Maybe. *Be careful my friend, say as little as possible.*

They all gather around the buffet, salads and mineral water for the Alcatel men, cold meat and Beaujolais for Valentin and Montoya. Then the four of them sit down at the table to work. Valentin takes out a small tape recorder.

'I'm going to play you a conversation that took place at eight this morning between Quignard and an unidentified party, perhaps a Korean, calling from Warsaw. We're trying to pinpoint the precise location. I think this conversation is important, and I'd like your opinion.' He presses *play.*

The phone rings: 'Mr Quignard...' Then a secretary's voice, a voice Montoya doesn't know. Listening to the anonymous words and sentences, he relives an old, long-forgotten feeling, hunting snipe with Moroccan friends in the marshes near Rabat. The stunning landscape, a completely flat stretch of land covered in short grass floating on the water, your feet sinking in with every step; the water rose, sometimes covering the feet of your boots, sometimes up to your knees, sometimes up to your waist, and there was always the fear that you'd go right under with the next step. The land immediately closed over your footsteps, obliterating all traces of your passing. This conversation is like the marsh: no bearings, no support, shifting. *Everything is true, everything is false, nothing exists.* A glance at the two executives, they look very excited. Flashback: Rolande, *I don't give a shit about the competition between Alcatel and Matra.* Neither do I, sweetheart. And most probably nor do they. But we're at the gaming table, and we want to win. '...*in two days so that we can agree on the method of payment.*' The phone goes dead, the tape hisses gently. Rossellini jumps when Valentin stops the tape recorder. *The fat cop was right: weapons, strategy, industrial restructuring, all a stage set. This is where the decisions were made, in the bogus accounts of a second-rate business. I'll never forget this lesson.* Valentin turns to Montoya.

'Charles, tell me, who is it talking to Quignard?'

'In my opinion, it's Park, the CEO of Daewoo Pondange, who left town within forty-eight hours of the fire. He was Quignard's usual contact, and he recognised his voice immediately. But it could be someone else, I didn't meet any of the Korean managers. They'd all left by the time I arrived in Pondange.'

'He speaks like a CEO,' says Benoît-Rey.

'Let's suppose it's Park. Now, what do you make of this conversation?'

'We seem to be on the right track.'

'Strange that people aren't more guarded about speaking on the phone.'

'Haven't you ever done any confidential business over the phone?'

Laughter. 'Yes, but never again from now on, I swear it.'

'It's funny to be hearing about the insider dealing again.' Rossellini turns to Montoya. 'It's a set-up. I wrote the anonymous letters myself, and we forced the hand of the COB just a little, to get them to launch an investigation.'

'That doesn't prove that there was no insider dealing,' retorts Montoya. Rossellini freezes. Valentin smiles.

'What do you make of what Park calls the "Polish scheme"?'

Benoît-Rey embarks on a long explanation of how the losses and subsidies are orchestrated in Pondange and the profits in Warsaw, for the benefit of Montoya, who stops him with a gesture.

'I know all that. It was explained to me by an expert before I left for Pondange.' Benoît-Rey turns to Valentin.

'That is exactly the problem. The Polish scheme is fraudulent, but a large number if not all of the multinationals operate in a similar fashion, and declare as they please, whenever they please, that one or other of their subsidiaries has gone bankrupt. Clearly in this case Daewoo chose Warsaw, and Pondange was only set up in order to channel the subsidies into Warsaw. But I very much doubt that the disclosure of the "Polish scheme" will get things moving in Paris. Everyone knows that's how things are done. If the funding bodies are stupid enough to continue granting subsidies, that's their business.'

'We need the lists of personal accounts into which the payments were made through this scheme. Once we have those lists, we win by a knockout.'

'True. The financial arrangements remain obscure, and the journalists don't understand the first thing about it. But if we can say to them that so-and-so was caught with his hand in the till, we hit the jackpot.'

Montoya gets up, picks up a new bottle of Beaujolais and fills two glasses for Valentin and himself.

'There's no proof that these personal accounts exist, or that lists were drawn up, even that Park has them if they do exist. And Park is definitely behind this.'

Valentin takes a sip of wine and twirls his glass, watching the liquid shimmer.

'You're right, Charles, in theory. That conversation could be pure bluff, straight out of a game of poker. But we know the boss of Daewoo Poland. He's a swindler and a blackmailer appointed by the CEO of the entire group. Unless it's to set up an embezzlement scheme using the personal accounts Park mentions, why else would it exist? Let me tell you what I think: there is insider dealing going on, but we drop that aspect. There is embezzlement, and Park has the lists, we concentrate on that.'

'You're the chief.'

'Then I have two questions. The first one's for you, Charles: How is Quignard going to react?'

Montoya takes his time.

'It depends how much he knows. He doesn't necessarily know that Park is calling him from Warsaw.'

'If he's clever, he'll have a suspicion...'

'He's very clever.'

'...and I have some bad news. Tomaso controls a network that sells stolen cars in Warsaw.'

'That's very bad news indeed. To go by what I've seen in

Pondange, he'll react fast and violently. If he negotiates, it will only be to gain time.'

'Second question, for all three of you: How are we going to get hold of those lists?'

Benoît-Rey: 'Find out where Park is, talk to him, negotiate, pay him off.'

Rossellini: 'Tell him that there's no insider dealing, Valentin, since we're all in the bluffing business. Tell him that we set the whole thing up ourselves, and that Quignard hasn't got the wherewithal to pay.'

Montoya: 'Give him a scare, a big scare. Point the finger at him for embezzlement at Pondange and the factory fire. With as much concrete evidence as possible, which I'll have tomorrow. To soften him up, show him that we know all about it. But above all, frighten him by telling him what Quignard and Tomaso are capable of. He left Pondange straight after the fire. We have to tell him in great detail about all three murders. So that he understands that this is no small-time blackmail scenario, that he's risking his hide. Make him understand that only we can protect and hide him, and that he's going to need us. If he's really scared, he'll be more flexible, the deal will be easier, and the price lower.'

Valentin leans back in his chair, his arms behind his head, and flexes his back. Gives a broad smile.

'I remember what my father always used to say: "My son, you mustn't kill, because he who kills ends up stealing, and he who steals ends up lying, and lying is really very bad." This is a very bad business.'

The bodies of both Aisha and Rolande's mother have been deposited at the undertaker's and will be returned to their families late that afternoon. When she's finished tidying her apartment, Rolande goes up to the fourth floor, closes her eyes, hunches her shoulders as she crosses the landing and walks underneath the fanlight, to ring the Saidani family's doorbell. The father opens the door, he's expecting her. He's not alone; Amrouche is keeping him company. The three of them leave together, without exchanging a word. The old man holds himself erect, his face impassive, and does not walk beside her.

When they reach the undertaker's, Rolande and Aisha's father are received in separate rooms by the 'authorities', keen to inform them of the progress of the investigation. The watchwords are 'transparency' and 'concern for the victims' families'.

Rolande is greeted by two men – a doctor in a white coat and a plainclothes policeman – and a woman in a tailored grey suit with a sympathetic expression. She's a psychologist specialising in bereavement counselling. Rolande refuses to sit down, and remains standing, stiffly erect, her hands thrust in her coat pockets. The doctor speaks first.

'The cause of death is absolutely certain. Your mother received a very violent blow to the temple from the crowbar found beside her body. Death was instantaneous. I'm afraid I have to inform you (the psychologist moves closer to Rolande) that your mother was raped (the psychologist puts her arm around Rolande's shoulders) before she was killed.'

Rolande gently extricates herself.

'Please leave me alone, my grief is mine alone, and I'm keeping it to myself.' She turns towards the doctor: 'What time did my mother die?'

'Between nine and nine-thirty a.m., I can't be any more precise than that, the presence of vast amounts of alcohol…'

'I know. Did Aisha die at the same time?'

'Around the same time, yes.'

The cop steps in.

'We are pursuing every line of enquiry, every lead. Samples have been taken. We found fingerprints in the kitchen and in the hall of your apartment. We checked for the same fingerprints on the fourth floor. So far, we haven't found any. In fact, we didn't find any significant fingerprints on the fourth-floor landing. In your mother's case, we think the murder was probably committed by a prowler, a drug addict most likely. We're going through our records and we'll carry out all the necessary checks. We will find the murderer.'

'Did you check whether my mother made any phone calls in the hour before her death?' The cop stalls, slightly worried.

'I repeat that we are doing, and will do, everything in our power.'

In the lobby, Aisha's father is pacing up and down, yelling a string of unintelligible curses, wailing and banging the walls with

his fists and his head. Beside him, Amrouche is desperately trying to calm him down. Rolande comes out of the room. Aisha's
father throws himself upon her, grabs her by the coat collar and
shakes her, howling, then throws her to the ground and runs
off. The psychologist is there like a shot, helping her to her feet.
Amrouche also comes over.

'Ali, can you tell me what's going on?'

'Saidani repudiates his daughter and holds you responsible for
all his misfortunes.'

'But why?'

'The doctor told him that his daughter was pregnant.' Silence.
'And that she probably committed suicide because she didn't dare
tell him. The old man is blaming the factory, her girlfriends – you
included – for corrupting his daughter. He won't forgive her, and
he won't forgive you.'

Appalled, Rolande glances around the foyer. There is no one
there except Amrouche, the psychologist, and herself. She sees
a bench against a wall. Her legs give way, she collapses on to it,
breathless and trembling, her hands resting on her knees.

'I don't believe it. I just don't believe it. How can anyone have
said such terrible things to Aisha's father?'

'Rolande, calm down. Aisha could have been pregnant. During
the strike she did... you know... what people do to end up
pregnant.'

'That was two weeks ago. How would she have known? And
decided to commit suicide because of that?'

'Women know when they're pregnant, they know it straight
away, that's all.'

'What do you know about women, Ali, can you tell me? You
always side with management and the cops. You're a scab, Ali. Go
away, it would better for everyone if you cleared off.' She turns to
the psychologist. 'Where is she, the psychologist who told Aisha's
father all that filth? I want to give her a piece of my mind.'

The woman in the simple, elegant suit hesitates, clearly ill at
ease, before coming over and sitting on the bench beside Rolande.
Then she takes the plunge.

'There was no psychologist present during the interview with
Mr Saidani, only the forensic doctor and a police officer. As it is
a suicide, you understand, Mr Saidani isn't strictly speaking the
father of a victim...'

Rolande feels giddy, as if she's spiralling down into a bottom-less well.

'You don't believe these things, you don't believe them until they happen to you. The lives of the working class count for nothing. We can be raped, crushed or hanged, and nobody gives a shit.'

The two coffins sit side by side on trestles in the windowless room inside the morgue, which serves as the chapel of rest. Aisha's coffin is open: her ashen face is very beautiful with her eyes closed and her hair parted down the middle and looped back at the sides. On seeing her, Rolande cries. Rolande's mother's coffin is closed. A corpse not fit to be seen. Soft lighting, two big candles burning, and chairs around the coffins. Rolande has decided to spend the night keeping vigil over her two dead, a priest will come and bless them tomorrow morning. Later the coffins will be buried in Pondange's small cemetery.

The room gradually fills up. Women. Her workmates. Word has got around, they come with bunches of flowers picked from their gardens, sprays of autumnal leaves gathered in the forest. They need vases, the morgue's supplies are exhausted, and they rush off home to fetch some more. Soon the two coffins disappear beneath a sea of plants. Rolande smiles. Hands over hands, warm kisses on her cheeks, arms around her shoulders, it reminds her of the atmosphere in the factory, women together, understanding, supportive. The women settle down to spend the night there. One has brought a thermos of mulled wine, another a plum tart, still others cakes, chocolates. It's getting late. The women break up into small groups. The work shifts have more or less re-formed, they chat to keep themselves awake. Sitting on a chair, her elbows on her knees and her face in her hands, Rolande listens to the hubbub of conversation all around her. Aisha, her beauty, her way of speaking, intense, determined, naive too. Aisha, the virgin without a man, hardly surprising given the father she had, he'd beat her first, ask questions later. 'You know he left Pondange today?' 'Apparently he's gone to live with his son, not even attending his daughter's funeral, can you understand that?' 'Not a happy person, Aisha. Do you remember the Korean engineer's accident? Covered in blood, a nightmare, Aisha was so distraught I thought she'd never return to the factory.' But she did return.

'Brave woman.' And then, same thing again, Émilienne's accident. Unlucky. 'She never laughed, did she?' 'We should have rallied round her, then maybe she wouldn't have killed herself.'

Killed herself. Aisha. Rolande clamps her mouth shut with both hands to stop herself from screaming. *You didn't commit suicide, I know you didn't.* Flashback: Étienne's funeral, accidents happen so easily, she hears her own voice, the woods, the dead leaves at this time of year, the grounds slippery... the cops say accident. The cops say suicide. What would be the point of saying to the girls: Étienne and Aisha were murdered? They'd never admit it. Life's hard enough as it is. Order, justice, you've got to believe in something. Otherwise, what would they do from now on? *But you, you can't believe in them any more. You've seen it first-hand. It's a question of dignity.*

29 October

The men arrive in the morning. The room is beginning to feel stuffy and smell of wilted flowers. Amrouche is the first, touching with his clumsy kindness and concern. He sits down beside Rolande.

'If you don't want to go back to your apartment after all this, I'll lend you my house for as long as you need to get over it all. I can turn the top floor into a flat for you, it's not big but it's comfortable and quiet, you know, you'll be completely independent. And then there's the garden...'

Rolande cries for the second time that night, her face buried in her hands. Maréchal has appeared too. Rolande gets up and takes his arm.

'Come for a walk, I want to talk to you.'

They pace up and down the empty foyer, where Rolande hears Aisha's father's helpless rage echoing again. From her coat pocket she takes the list Montoya gave her. Maréchal gives it a cursory glance, then gives it back to her without a word.

'Naturally, you know about this Mr Maréchal, you've already seen this list, you know who produced it and why. You have to explain.'

'If you're asking me to...'

Maréchal tells her how he was in Quignard's office when Park telephoned him during the occupation; about the 'bonuses' paid to the Korean managers in guise of payment of phoney invoices; about Quignard, who finds out about the scam when it's too late to do anything about it. Then he pauses.

'You didn't let matters rest there, Mr Maréchal, I know you. I saw quite clearly that you were as upset as I was to see your name on that list. If I managed to get hold of it, then you...'

Maréchal puts his arm around Rolande's shoulders and they take a few steps in silence.

'Come and sit down.'

He steers Rolande towards the bench. They sit down side by side. He turns to face her while he speaks.

'Given where this list of bank accounts was found by Neveu, one of the company accountants was clearly involved. There are only two. I plumped for Germont. A sad character, married to a harridan who's pathologically jealous and keeps an eye on him the minute he sets foot outside the factory, but he can afford to bet heavily on the horses. So he's making money on the side. I went to see him and he spilled the beans. I shan't explain the entire scheme to you, because I didn't understand it completely. It was a complicated set-up that Daewoo negotiated directly with the Luxembourg bank. The main thing, Ms Lepetit, is how the accounts operate. We are supposed to have signed proxies for Germont and Park. With our names and code numbers, Germont can make transfers from one account to another on his own. But it needs both Germont and Park's signatures to withdraw money. Or the signature of one of the account holders, you or me for example, as long as they know the code. As this eventuality had never been envisaged, it hadn't been ruled out either. Is that what you wanted to know?'

'Weren't you tempted, Mr Maréchal?'

'I thought about it. It would mean going away. I can't leave this place. I belong to this land with every fibre of my body. I know it by heart. I was young here, and happy. I've worked hard here. I can't see myself living anywhere else.' A long silence. Maréchal has an absent look. 'In any case, I'm probably worn out. Too many memories.' Then: 'Germont lives in the Rue Saint-Louis, just above the bar-cum-tobacconists-cum-betting-shop.' A silence.

'Watch out for his wife.' Another silence. 'I have a lot of respect for you, Ms Lepetit. I wish you the best of luck.'

The room is packed when Montoya arrives at the funeral. Small groups are hanging around in the foyer, but Rolande isn't there. She's gone off to wash and get changed. 'We're waiting for her before we begin,' her friends tell him. She arrives, bareheaded, in a very simple, black woollen dress under her overcoat and high black leather boots. Her face is composed, no trace of the strain of the last forty-eight hours, a radiant presence in this gloomy place. Montoya is surprised. Rolande smiles at him, takes his arm and, side by side, they lead the procession which makes its way slowly uphill to the cemetery behind the two hearses. Halfway there, she leans towards him.

'A system of bogus invoices set up by Park to pay the Koreans' bonuses, directly negotiated with the bank. Quignard kept in the dark until the strike, a call from Park himself, panic-stricken, when the occupation of the offices began. Is that enough for you?'

'That's enough. You're a magnificent woman.'

Rolande clings to Montoya's arm until the two coffins are lowered into the ground. No condolences. They leave the cemetery together. On reaching the road, Rolande stops, looks intently at Montoya's face, one finger carefully traces the shape of his eyebrows, cheekbones, the bridge of his nose, as if to try and memorise them. She leans forward, places a chaste, affectionate kiss on his lips, and walks off quickly. Twenty metres away, a car is waiting, a man at the wheel, whose features Montoya can't make out. Rolande gets into the passenger seat, the car starts up and drives off. It takes the stunned Montoya a few moments to recover his wits. *Let her leave, that's understandable, but with another man, in front of my eyes... I'll think about it tomorrow.* Then he moves away from the stream of people leaving the cemetery to phone Valentin.

Two hours later, Rolande emerges from the Parillaud-Luxembourg bank on the arm of Germont, Daewoo's accountant. He's just transferred the contents of the ten accounts he was managing into one opened in the name of Rolande Lepetit, and she's just emptied it, using her signature and the secret code. A tidy sum, nearly a million francs, in crisp new notes. Now carefully stashed in a black plastic briefcase, which she holds at arm's length, flabbergasted that such a huge sum can fit into such a small space. They've agreed to go fifty-fifty, as soon as they're safely back in France.

Rolande pauses on the steps outside the bank. She blinks, dazzled by the sunshine, spots the taxi rank further down the street and turns to the accountant. He's a small, very ordinary man in a cheap suit, his hair plastered down, glasses, flabby features. She gives him a radiant smile, strokes his cheek, takes his arm and pulls him into the street. They take a few steps, leaning against each other, then Rolande stops in front of the first taxi in the line, closes in on the short accountant and kisses him on the mouth. He puts his arms around her, surprised at first, then delighted at his good luck. Just as he embraces her, a woman rushes across the street, screaming insults: his wife, the harridan Maréchal had mentioned, alerted that same morning by an anonymous phone call, a slightly husky woman's voice telling her the time and the place where her husband would be meeting his blonde mistress. A native of Luxembourg and a top executive at the Parillaud bank, the anonymous voice had explained. The harridan slaps Rolande, and clutches her man. Rolande doesn't hang around, she simply leans over to open the taxi door and climbs in hugging the black plastic briefcase to her chest.

'Go, quick. Straight ahead, anywhere.' The taxi starts up. 'I hate domestic fights. She wants her man, she can keep him. Did you see the guy? I'll get over it.'

Rolande does not look back. Behind her she leaves the accountant who's beside himself with fury, and his astounded wife. After a few minutes, the driver asks his customer: 'Where to, madam?'

First of all, pick up my son, then get out of here.

'How much will you charge to drive me to Metz?'

30 October

Montoya's off to scout around Warsaw. Comfortably installed in first class, he's put his seat into the reclining position and is lying back and dozing. Valentin had entered into brisk negotiations with Park. *You're going to find a little guy scared shitless, completely out of his depth in this game. Positive in one way, dangerous in another. Fear is not a wise counsel. We return the lists of Korean managers to him. We have a copy. We give him a payment in dollars. Comfortable, no more. Rossellini will have the money on him. We promise the Korean that we will ensure his extradition and his transfer elsewhere. We could do it that way, but I really don't see how. In any case, that side of things doesn't concern you. You're going to be operating on foreign soil with no preparation, no support, and without any real fallback position. And I'm saddling you with Rossellini, who will be of no help to you and might even embark on some ill-advised course of action, but you have to guarantee his safety, and that of the cash. That's life, my friend.* Montoya, half asleep. *That's life.*

Warsaw. Taxi to Daewoo's head office on the main avenue from the airport to the city centre. A four-storey glass and steel building with a plaza paved in white stone, set back from the avenue and surrounded by landscaped gardens, shrubs, trimmed hedges, lawns and clumps of trees. Here and there, other luxury office blocks. During working hours, the place is fairly deserted. Montoya hangs around in the vicinity, locates a possible way into the building through the unlocked dustbin room at the back.

A little scout around town. Montoya hides near the apartment block where Park lives and eventually spots his man, at around eight p.m., encased in a voluminous grey wool coat with a fur collar and a dark grey trilby, his moon face reduced by huge tortoiseshell spectacles. He's alone, stops for a drink at the local cafe and, still alone, enters his apartment block, followed by Montoya. Fourth floor, nothing to report. *A very brief recce, but I don't see what more I could have done.* Montoya heads back to the vicinity of the airport to sleep in an anonymous hotel.

31 October

Rossellini's sitting by the window gazing out at the shifting layer of luminous white cloud thousands of metres below, stretching as far as the eye can see. *We've reached the denouement.* An electric tingle. *Each day he handles tens of millions by simply clicking* his mouse, shifting huge sums around, transferring them across borders, hiding and making them reappear without the slightest emotion, sometimes even with a faint sense of boredom. Today he has a much smaller sum inside the lining of his jacket, but it's in cash, which he feels rub against his chest when he turns to look out of the window. He's got to physically transport it across the border, walking calmly, looking preoccupied and absent, right under the noses of the customs officers. Thrilling in a different way. He fishes a pillbox from his pocket, takes out a little blue tablet which he swallows, and continues gazing at the hypnotic clouds. The odd chuckle escapes him from time to time, like a schoolboy raiding a condom machine in a supermarket.

He clears customs without any difficulty. Montoya's waiting for him at the exit. Handshake. Rossellini swings between a sense of complicity with a fellow fighter, and aloof disdain.

A taxi drops them in the midst of the lawns and copses. The weather is fine and cool – 'Just perfect for a little stroll,' says Montoya with a half-smile – and he leads Rossellini through the gardens to the edge of the empty plaza in front of Daewoo's head office. Montoya telephones.

'Park hasn't arrived yet. He shouldn't be long. We'll wait for him under this pine tree. Once he's inside the building, we'll sneak in behind him.'

Rossellini feels an irrepressible urge to laugh again. He chuckles. Is this a game? He decides to be patient.

'You're a walking safe, and Park may not be the only person who knows it. We're dealing with a bunch of crooks about whom we know nothing, except that they're already involved in more than one murder. Valentin asked me to bring you back alive, if possible, so I'm trying to minimise the risks. This empty plaza surrounded by trees looks to me like the perfect place to practise shooting at a moving target. OK? You might find it amusing, but you'll do as I say, and don't lose control.'

Rossellini, shaken, takes his pillbox out of his pocket and swallows a small blue tablet.

'Don't overdo it,' snaps Montoya.

Just then, he catches sight of Park at the entrance to the plaza, muffled in his coat. He's alone, walking briskly, swinging a black leather briefcase at arm's length. Montoya grabs Rossellini by the shoulder.

'There he is. Don't move.'

The words are barely out of his mouth when two sharp shots ring out in quick succession. The figure stumbles, as if pushed from behind, spreads his arms, jerks and crumples to the ground, his arms outspread, without a sound. Indubitably dead. Montoya is still squeezing Rossellini's shoulder, which he can feel shaking, while keeping an eye all around them. The shots must have been fired from the other side of the avenue. He locates a clump of trees, the killer probably has a gun with a telescopic sight trained on the path across the plaza to the main door of the building. It must have a super-efficient firing mechanism. He just catches a glimpse of two men walking calmly away from the trees, across the gardens.

'We're not the target. The killers probably don't even know we're here.' He turns to Rossellini for a rapid check. He's pale, after all it's the first time he's witnessed a murder at close hand, but still calm. He's reliable and bearing up better than expected. 'Now you're going to leave the gardens without hurrying, and stay out of sight until you reach the avenue. Take a taxi or a bus, go back to the airport and wait for me there. See you at the cafe in departures. No pills before I get back. Go.'

Rossellini disappears without a word. As yet nobody on the plaza, or near the prone form. Montoya runs over to the body and turns it on to its back. *Mind the spreading pool of blood.* He searches Park's inside pockets and his jacket and coat pockets. Nothing. The briefcase is locked. Forces the lock: blank paper, two pens, a packet of Kleenex. He straightens up and runs to the entrance of the Daewoo building, calling for help and waving his arms around. In reception, a stunning young blonde is standing on tiptoe behind the desk, trying to see what's going on outside and discover the reason for this unusual commotion without leaving her post. Montoya talks very fast, in rapid, stilted English.

'A man shot, there, on the plaza, murder, two bullets in the back. A Korean, one of your employees, call the police, your manager. Mr Park's office?'

The receptionist, overwhelmed, has her hand on the telephone: 'Office 23, sixth floor.' Montoya rushes to the lift. But he's not there yet. The lift door closes. A helpless shrug then she gets busy raising the alarm throughout the building.

Montoya takes the lift up to the sixth floor where the executive offices are. By the time he steps out, news of the murder of 'one of us' on the plaza is beginning to spread and people are pouring out of the offices. He takes refuge in the toilets and emerges when he reckons the coast is clear. He finds door 23, picks the lock and goes inside. Luckily the office is small and uncluttered. Not exactly overworked in Warsaw, Park. Move fast. Go for the most obvious: two files on the desk, *not what I'm looking for.* Three drawers, not locked, magazines, an English novel, a bottle of Scotch. A metal filing cabinet, ten or so files that look more like stage props than work tools, like the empty briefcase earlier. *Still haven't found what I'm looking for. Perhaps I'd better stop and think instead of being quite so busy.* Montoya sits at the desk in Park's chair and breathes deeply. Calm. It all comes back to the same question: *Do the lists exist?* Doubt enters in: *It's too good to be true.* Apparently Quignard believed it, because he had Park killed. And he knows the outfit well. *Supposing they do exist. Valentin told us he'd realised the seriousness of his situation, he was scared and he really wanted to negotiate with us so he could disappear. He turned up for our appointment. So either he must have had the lists on him or else they're here. Second point: if he was really scared, to the point of agreeing to do business with us, it was because here he was working alone. Blackmailing Quignard was his own idea. He stole the lists. He knows the Koreans here are crooks and he's afraid of them, as afraid as he is of Quignard. He's afraid of everyone. So the lists have to be hidden. In an unusual place, on his person or here. I didn't search him thoroughly enough, but it's too late for that now. Either I find them at once or I tear the office apart.* Montoya stands up again, looks on and under the furniture, checks the backs of the drawers, inspects the desk top, still nothing. The white moulded plastic desk chair has a round, padded cushion with a brown cover. He picks up the cushion. Nothing. Feels it. The cover has a zip. Opens it. Inside the cover, a plastic sleeve as brown as the cushion cover, and inside that, twenty or so sheets of paper, which he flicks through very quickly. The first few are summaries, purchases, sales and delivery orders, Pondange-Warsaw, no time to read them, this must be the scheme mentioned in the phone conversation between Park and Quignard. On the next sheets, names of banks, account numbers and code numbers, a few dates and sums paid in. Finally, on the very last sheet, the names of the numbered account holders. A few names leap out – all senior French state figures. *This is dynamite.*

Montoya closes the file straight away. *If anyone asks me, I've never seen that piece of paper, I've not read anything.* Runs his fingertips over the brown sleeve. *In the eye of the storm. Real life.* And a hint of curiosity: How is Valentin going to get rid of a bombshell like this? What if it's too sensational to be of any use? *Not my problem.* He folds the sleeve lengthways, slips it into the innermost pocket of his coat, which he buttons up, suddenly calm, pleased and sure of himself. *I've won, this affair is over. Affair... Rolande. Free. Gone. All I have of her is the delightful memory of her smooth wet skin, her wacky vamp look, and the ambiguous gentleness of her fluttering hands. What bliss.* He puts the cushion back on the chair and leaves the office without hurrying. Corridor, lift, basement, find the back exit at the rear of the building, still no one around, this is easy.

Rossellini's waiting for him at the airport bar, where he's downing coffee after coffee, leafing through the English language newspapers. Montoya sits down at his table, stretches out his legs, and smiles.

'I've got the documents. Do you still have the money?'

Smile. 'Of course. What would I spend it on here?' He takes the plane tickets out of his pocket. 'Let's go. The next plane for Paris takes off in less than an hour. I was worried you'd miss it.'

1 November

All Saints' Day and a public holiday. Alcatel's head office is silent, empty. Just an occasional security guard doing the rounds. In Valentin's little office on the top floor the soundproofed door is carefully locked, there's quite a crush. Valentin has placed photocopies of the documents Montoya brought back the day before on the table. Fayolle, personal lawyer and right-hand man of the big boss of Alcatel, Rossellini and Benoît-Rey, all three casually dressed in fine wool sweaters and corduroy jackets, as if to emphasise the completely informal nature of the meeting, are reading the documents avidly, page by page. Suppressed sighs and sidelong glances. Valentin makes coffee, and Montoya remains on his feet to one side, leaning against the desk with a vacant air.

Rossellini and Benoît-Rey look up at the same time. Their sentiments are the same: it's a knockout victory. A job well done. But no one speaks, waiting to hear what Fayolle has to say. He takes his time, reading and rereading the last page before opening his mouth, his face a stiff mask.

'We have enough to bring down the government, which was not our original intention. Everyone would lose out massively.' He pushes the documents back to the centre of the table. 'This is so big, I don't see how we could use it.'

Valentin serves coffee. Fayolle drinks his standing in front of the window, absorbed in contemplation of the Eiffel Tower, the top of which is lost in the haze of an autumn mist. Benoît-Rey clenches his teeth in exasperation. What did the big boss expect, sending us off to rummage around in dustbins? So we could bring him a bunch of dead flowers? All that for nothing? As for this Fayolle, what credibility does he have? Rossellini, elbows on the table, clutching his head, repeats to himself: *Fayolle's going to back down. If he backs down, what happens to me? How do we force him to act? Anonymous phone call to the Prime Minister? No. Leaks to the press… Names are already coming to mind…* Fayolle puts down his empty cup and turns round.

'What do you think, Valentin?'

Valentin gathers up the files, makes a neat pile of them, then folds and rests his hands on the top.

'I share your point of view, dear sir. We can't make any public use whatsoever of this information. The situation would run out of control. But nor can we pretend this file doesn't exist and simply drop the matter. If Daewoo takes over Thomson Multimedia we now know for certain that with its management methods the company will go belly up, and probably very soon. How do you know that this list of backhanders won't surface again then? If we were able to dig it up, others can do the same. On the other hand, if Daewoo loses the bid, nobody will have the least interest in it any more and a scandal will have been averted.'

Montoya turns back to the coffee machine with a smile. Alcatel, the white knight, to the rescue of the Republic. Great cops and the Jesuits definitely have a number of things in common. He pours himself another cup.

Sitting down again, Benoît-Rey carefully weighs his words.

'Let's take things one at a time. The choice of Daewoo was the result of bribery, we have the documents to prove it. Although there's no point in us making this public, those who are implicated have a lot more to lose than we do.' Fayolle makes a gesture. 'Or at least, they'll think they do. We make it discreetly known that we have these papers, the decision is quashed. On that point, I share the view that Valentin has held from the start, it doesn't matter how. And all these documents we have here disappear.'

'The whole problem, Pierre, rests on the word "discreetly". It is out of question for us to go and see the senior politicians to tell them, and I don't see who'd agree to act as our spokesperson. These days, as in the past, they shoot the messenger.'

Valentin speaks up again.

'We shouldn't look for an individual, but rather an influential association or body that has moral authority, with contacts in each camp. Haven't you got someone suitable among your alumni networks? What else is the old school tie for?'

'Yes, we do. The École Polytechnique Engineers association which I belong to.'

Silence. Everyone thinking. Then Fayolle, slightly more relaxed:

'That sounds like an excellent idea, Pierre. In any case, I can't come up with anything better. Among the association's staff, Dubernard is very involved with Matra; Meynial with Alcatel, in the nuclear sector; and the chairman, Leroy, is on the Matra supervisory board. The Association's clout will probably shield them from any potential ill feeling. But will they agree to do it?'

'Shall I set up a meeting?'

Fayolle nods and ends up smiling.

'I feel as though I'm bungee jumping. And that's not something I usually do.'

'You get used to it,' mutters Rossellini. 'Worse still, you come to enjoy it.'

Montoya is left alone with Valentin, who collects up the dirty coffee cups.

'You led them exactly where you wanted them to go. Did you know about this Association?'

'Of course. In a slightly old company like ours, which has its own ways of working, if you want to be effective, you have to know where the real power networks are. The Association is one of them, and its members are at the helm of half the French economy. As the *esprit de corps* isn't as strong within their organisation as it is among us cops... Their Association won't be able to resist the pleasure of flexing its muscle, and people will listen, believe you me.'

'Bravo.'

'Compliments are always nice when they come from a connoisseur.' Valentin brings out a bottle of brandy. 'I believe you're a brandy drinker? Let's drink to our past and future collaboration.'

For Montoya, the brandy has the flavour of a journey's end.

All Saints' Day and a well-earned rest. Yesterday, the Warsaw contact telephoned. Mission accomplished. Tomaso dreams of acquiring holdings in Quignard's businesses, big international deals that are being struck at this very moment. *I don't see how he can say no. Even if I don't know exactly what they're about yet, I'm not going to be short of cash to invest if I can take over the Hakim brothers' business. Which shouldn't be too difficult. Quignard's major operations can launder the money and provide a seal of respectability. Respectability. Perhaps it'll be my turn to buy a hunt. That would be funny, ending up as a patriarch, a landowner. The builders start work on the Oiseau Bleu tomorrow. Make the place a bit less steamy while we're at it? Kristina won't agree. Talk to her about it, but not today. Today's a holiday.* He's taken the morning in bed with Kristina, his Croatian mistress, luxuriant flesh and feisty attitude, even in love. His hands and his mind wander. It's more than just physical attraction, a genuine affection for a woman who's lived on the edge. When he met her, she was wearing fatigues, the black beret of the Croatian militia, a Kalashnikov slung over her shoulder. To avenge her father killed by the Serbs, she said. He hadn't delved any further. Everyone has their own reasons for fighting. It seemed to him as if she enjoyed it. Just like him. *My wife. A desire to get married. A church wedding. After all, you're a Catholic, like me. In white.* She laughs. 'Our customers wouldn't like it.' *Fuck the lot of them.*

Plans for the day: a makeshift brunch, then a long slow walk to Place Stanislas, arms entwined. 'This evening I'll take you to eat frogs' legs in the country.'

Around eight p.m., the two of them get into the magnificent shiny black Mercedes that a driver had left in front of the Oiseau Bleu that morning, Tomaso at the wheel. He switches on the ignition, starts up the engine, and the car explodes. Demolished, twisted like an iron straw. Tomaso's body is ripped apart, his head blown off, and his passenger is rushed to hospital by ambulance. She's badly wounded but may perhaps survive.

All Saints' Day and the hunting was superb. Quignard, on excellent form, shot like a god. All the guests except the superintendent have left after the evening meal. The two men are in the small lounge of the hunting lodge, reclining in vast leather armchairs before a log fire, nursing glasses of brandy. A day spent walking in the countryside in the cold, their boots heavy with mud. There's the thrill as they approach their prey, gun in hand or on their shoulder, the shots, the smell of powder, of blood. A copious dinner, the alcohol, the tiredness, the warmth of the fire, moments of bliss.

The superintendent speaks first.

'My transfer to Nancy is going through. It'll be official in a week. You're the first to know.' Quignard raises his glass to his guest.

'Congratulations. I'm delighted for you.' A pause. 'You're going to have a big case as soon as you arrive. Do you remember Tomaso? You met him here, on the hunt a couple of weeks ago. My son-in-law, the lawyer Lavaudant, phoned me during dinner to tell me that Tomaso was killed when his car blew up today, outside his joint in Nancy.'

'He had a nightclub in Nancy, the Oiseau Bleu, didn't he?' Quignard nods. 'A club with a dubious reputation, from what my colleagues say. And where one explosion already took place a few days ago.'

'True. I met Tomaso in Brussels, where he had some big car hire contracts with the European Commission. I had his security company working in quite a few of the factories down the valley. I found him rather a pleasant man. But my son-in-law gave me a warning when he met Tomaso here, at the Grande Commune hunt. According to him, Tomaso was a rather disreputable character, a former mercenary in the pay of Croatia. His legitimate business was allegedly a front for trafficking stolen cars to Eastern Europe. His death must have been a gangland killing.'

'Perhaps. The chosen method of operation could lead one to suppose something of that nature. The investigation will establish that.'

'By the way. I must introduce you to my son-in-law. He has a big legal practice in Nancy. He's just taken on the defence of the Hakim brothers. And do you know what? About a decade ago, the Hakims were working with the French police in Tangier. According to my son-in-law, they wouldn't be averse to doing so again.'

'Interesting. But I'm the new boy in Nancy. I don't know the ropes, the way I do here. I'm going to start by seeing how things work.'

'Of course. Well, you know of my son-in-law's existence, and that he can always act as a go-between if need be.'

'Thank you. I'll bear that in mind.'

Two days later

Robert Leroy, an elderly man with white hair, very erect, with a great deal of style and dressed in indoor wear, velvet trousers and a silk and wool jacket, pours drinks for his two guests, Dubernard and Meynial. They are in his cosy little smoking room whose wide picture window overlooks the treetops of the Bois de Boulogne and the Auteuil racecourse, invisible in the dark at this hour and time of year.

'Yesterday, Benoît-Rey called me for a meeting, it sounded urgent, and he suggested that you should also be present. He'll be coming alone.'

'We're here on behalf of the École Polytechnique Alumni Association.'

'Absolutely. Myself as chairman, you two as members of the board. Benoît-Rey is a graduate of course, and a member of the Association.'

'Of course.'

'We were at school at the same time. He graduated in '71 and I in '70.'

'What does he want to discuss?'

'He hasn't breathed a word to me.'

DOMINIQUE MANOTTI

'Certainly not the Thomson privatisation. He's head of the Alcatel steering group for the bid.' The three men look at each other.

'That's likely to be tricky. You're at Alcatel, and Robert and I are with Matra...'

'Should the Association allow itself to get involved in this business?'

'Benoît-Rey is no joker, and he doesn't take risks for nothing. If he's referring a matter to the Association, then I'm sure he has excellent reasons for doing so.'

'That's what worries me.'

'Let's wait and see what Benoît-Rey has to say before we discuss it.'

The three men drink in silence. The doorbell rings. A few moments later, Benoît-Rey is shown into the smoking room. The three men rise and Leroy makes the introductions. Complicit smiles all round, everyone knows each other.

'What would you like to drink?'

A glance at the drinks trolley laden with a variety of bottles.

'A Suze for a change, thank you.'

They sit down, all eyes on Leroy, who nods his impeccably brushed white head towards Benoît-Rey with an encouraging smile.

'You asked for a meeting with the board of the Association, and most of us are here. Over to you.'

Benoît-Rey takes out twenty or so sheets of paper folded in half, puts them on the coffee table in front of him, leans forward, elbows on knees and hands clasped, then looks from one to the other.

'I received these documents in my office at Alcatel from a more or less anonymous source. I've carried out a whole battery of checks, as discreetly as possible, which reveal: one, that the Daewoo factory in Lorraine, opened two years ago in a European priority development area, has benefited from a large number of subsidies; two, that it has transferred these subsidies to Daewoo Poland, with which it does eighty per cent of its business, by simply falsifying the purchase and sales ledgers; and three, that the super-profits thus earned were paid into personal accounts (he taps the documents sitting on the table in front of him) on arrival in Poland. Here you have their numbers and code names and the amounts and payment dates.' Silence. They are paying close attention. 'There's one more sheet, which bears the names of the account holders. I've decided not to show this sheet to anyone.' A pause. 'For the time being. Not even to my chairman or my colleagues. We have discussed this case in the Alcatel working party which I head up, and we think that the European Development funding misappropriated for the past two years by Daewoo has been used as bribes to garner support for their Thomson Multimedia bid. Not just any old support. That of the key decision-makers. At the top of the political ladder.'

A break to allow the idea to sink in. The chairman speaks up:

'Why come and tell the Association about this?'

'We want the Matra-Daewoo takeover of Thomson to be halted, which will save us having to publish the information we have. The world of politics and the business community have a lot to gain from complying, no need to go into detail. You're well aware of the disastrous consequences such a scandal would have. For this to be achieved without doing any damage, this information must be placed in the hands of the proper people, through neutral, credible and reliable channels. Channels that everyone knows would not orchestrate the leaks themselves. We've thought long and hard, and we think the board of the Association is the best placed – perhaps even the only possible – option.'

Meynial sits up, shakes his head, taps the file with his fingertips.

'Difficult if we don't have all the information, especially that last page you mention.'

'I don't think so. The people whose names are on that document will never forgive those who have read it. On the other hand, if you tell them it exists, but that you haven't seen it, they will know who they are, and will be grateful to you for having preserved a degree of anonymity. The information simply has to reach the right people, those who were genuinely in a position to make a decision on this bid, and who are therefore likely to have received bribes. There's no point naming names. We all know who they are.'

A few moments' silence, then Leroy rises.

'I agree with your line of reasoning, which seems wise to me. Give us a few days to examine the documents, discuss the matter and arrange the rest.'

Praise for *Rough Trade*:

'The novel I like more this year . . . extraordinarily vivid' – Joan Smith, *Independent*

'Highly evocative' – *Time Out*

'Manotti has Ellroy's gift for complex plotting, but she has a grip on the economics, politics and social history of Paris which marks her as special . . . *le flair* in abundance' – *TLS*

'A splendid neo-realistic tale of everyday bleakness and transgression' – Maxim Jakubowski, *Guardian*

'It's difficult to believe that this gripping, politically sophisticated mystery is the author's first novel' – Marcel Berlins, *The Times*

'The complexity and uncompromising tone has drawn comparisons with American writers such as James Ellroy. But Manotti's ability to convey the unique rhythms of a French police investigation distinguishes *Rough Trade*' – *Daily Telegraph*

'This vivid portrait, with a clever twist, shows a side of Paris that a tourist will rarely see' – *Sunday Times*

'A memorable trip down the mean streets of the 10th arrondissement' – *Independent*

'Utterly-convincing realism' – *The Herald* (Glasgow)

'Stopped me in my tracks . . . I've been begging Arcadia to fast-track translations of everything she's written' – Anne Beech (Pluto Press), *Bookseller*

'Hard-hitting' – Bob Cornwall, *Tangled Web*

'Outstanding . . . the sexual exploitation of Thai children, the unspeakable sadism of zealots and the pornography of the rich are all themes that she uses with total command' – Colin Spencer, *Gay Times*

'First rate' – *Crime Time*